Catastrophic Brew:
The Cozy Purrch Café Mysteries
Book 2

Erica J Whelton

Publisher: Sunseri Design Publishing
ISBN: 978-1-956069-50-1

Printed in the United States of America

To my daughter for her love of cats and all things magical

Chapter One

"Lily," I whispered.

She crossed the café in seconds and pulled me into a hug so tightly I could barely breathe. She smelled like rain and herbs and home, and despite the fear coursing through me, despite the thousand questions screaming in my head, I hugged her back.

"I've been looking everywhere," she said into my shoulder. "For months. I followed rumors and whispers and hints of magic, and it finally led me here. To you."

My hands were shaking. I pulled back, trying to compose myself, trying to think past the rushing in my ears.

I glanced around the café. It was Tuesday, four in the afternoon. The lunch rush was long over, and only old Horace sat in the corner nursing his third cup of coffee while pretending to read the newspaper. Usually I'd stay open until six, but this was different.

"Can we talk?" Lily's smile was tentative, hopeful. "Somewhere private?"

"Yes," I said. "Just give me a minute."

I turned to Horace, forcing my voice to stay steady. "I'm so sorry, but I need to close early today. Family emergency."

He looked up, his weathered face creasing with concern. "Everything all right, Alexis?"

"It will be," I said, and hoped I wasn't lying.

Horace gathered his things without complaint, dropping a few bills on the counter that more than covered his coffee. "You take care now. See you tomorrow."

After he left, I locked the front door and flipped the sign to closed. The simple action felt surreal. I'd built this routine, this life, this careful safety over the past year. And now Lily was here, and everything I'd worked for felt fragile as spun sugar.

When I turned back, Lily was kneeling on the floor, and my breath caught.

The cats had emerged.

Poppy approached first, her calico fur bright in the afternoon light. She walked right up to Lily and bumped her head against Lily's outstretched hand, purring loud enough to hear across the room.

"This one's safe," Poppy told me. "She has good magic. Old friend magic."

Gus was more cautious, hanging back near the counter. His black and white bulk made him look intimidating, but I could feel his uncertainty. "Don't know her," he grumbled. "Why is she here?"

Rocky, my orange tabby troublemaker, had no such reservations. He bounded over and immediately flopped at Lily's feet, demanding belly rubs. Millie, my shy Siamese, peeked out from behind the potted fern, watching but not approaching. And Sage, my little gray and white rescue kitten, crept forward with wide-eyed curiosity.

"You can hear them," Lily said softly, not a question. She was scratching Rocky behind the ears, and the traitor was purring like a motor. "I can feel it. That connection. It's stronger than it used to be."

My throat tightened. "Lily, how did you find me?"

She looked up, and I saw the exhaustion in her eyes. The kind that came from months of searching, of hoping, of fearing you'd never find what you were looking for.

"Can we go somewhere more comfortable?" she asked. "I promise I'll explain everything. But I've been traveling for days, and I'm..." She laughed, the sound a little broken. "I'm tired, Alexis. So tired."

Guilt hit me like a fist. Here I was, standing frozen with fear and suspicion, and my best friend looked ready to collapse.

"Upstairs," I said. "Come on."

I led her through the back and up the narrow stairs to my apartment. It wasn't much. Just a living room, tiny kitchen, bedroom, and bathroom. But it was mine, and it was safe, and now I was bringing someone from my past into it.

Lily stopped in the doorway of the living room, taking it in. The worn couch I'd bought secondhand. The bookshelf overflowing with mysteries and fantasy novels. The window overlooking Main Street with its view of the mountains beyond. The five cat trees strategically placed around the room.

"It's perfect," she said, and her voice cracked. "Alexis, it's perfect. You built this. A real life."

"Sit," I said, pointing to the couch. "I'll make tea."

I brewed chamomile, my hands moving through the familiar motions while my mind raced. When I turned back with two mugs, all five cats had joined Lily on the couch. Even Gus had relented, perching on the armrest with the air of someone grudgingly admitting defeat. Millie was curled in Lily's lap, and Sage was attempting to climb up her shirt.

"You always had a way with animals," I said, settling into the armchair across from her. I needed the distance. Needed to think.

Lily wrapped her hands around the mug, breathing in the steam. For a long moment, we just sat there. Two women who used to know everything about each other, now separated by years and secrets and fear.

"I left the coven three months after you did," Lily said finally.

My heart stuttered. "What?"

"I couldn't stay. Not after what they did. Not after what they tried to make us do." She looked at me, and her eyes were fierce. "You left without telling me why, without saying goodbye. That hurt, Alexis. It hurt so badly. But then I figured it out. You ran because you knew what they were becoming. What they wanted us to become."

"Lily..."

"Let me finish." She took a sip of tea, hands still trembling slightly. "A week after you disappeared, Margot started asking questions. Where had you gone? Did I know how to find you? Had you mentioned anything about leaving?"

Margot. The coven leader. The woman who'd taken us in when we were lost and searching and desperate for belonging. The woman who'd slowly, carefully, turned that belonging into control.

"I told her I didn't know," Lily continued. "And I really didn't. You never told me. I had no idea where you'd gone." Her voice broke. "That's when I understood. You were protecting me. If I'd known, they would have gotten it out of me eventually."

My throat was tight. "I wanted to tell you. Wanted to bring you with me. But I knew if I did, you'd be in danger."

"I know that now." Lily set down her mug. "But at the time, I was just hurt and confused. Then Margot started pushing harder. More demanding rituals. More dangerous magic. She wanted us to bind someone. Fully bind them. Take away their free will."

My stomach turned. "Did you..."

"No." Lily's voice was sharp. "I refused. That's when I realized you were right to run. That's when I understood why you didn't tell me where you were going. So I left too."

"You could have led them here." The words came out harsher than I meant them. "Margot could have followed you. The whole coven could be on their way right now."

"I was careful." Lily leaned forward. "Alexis, I was so careful. I backtracked. I laid false trails. I used every trick we ever learned. No one followed me. I made sure of it."

"You can't be certain."

"I can. I am." She reached out like she wanted to touch me, then pulled back. "I felt the magic here. The ley lines, the convergence points. The magical energy here is thick, like a fog. It masks our presence. That's probably why you felt drawn here, even if you didn't realize it consciously."

I stared at her. I'd learned about the convergence points from Maeve and Hazel's letter, but hearing Lily explain it made it feel more real, more protective. "You really think we're safer here?"

"I'm sure of it. I've been to seven different states over the past four months, following leads. Nowhere felt like this. Larkspur Valley is special. The magic here... it's like a shield."

The tension in my shoulders eased, just a fraction. "And you're sure no one followed you?"

"I'm sure."

I wanted to believe her. Wanted to feel relief instead of this gnawing fear. But a year of hiding, of constantly looking over my shoulder, of building a life on the foundation of running away, that didn't just disappear because my best friend showed up and told me it was okay.

"Why now?" I asked. "Why keep searching for me? You got out. You were free. Why risk coming after me?"

Lily's eyes filled with tears. "Because you're my best friend. Because I've been alone for four months, and I was alone before that, even when I was still in the coven. Because when you left, I realized I'd lost the only real family I ever had." She wiped at her eyes angrily. "And maybe because I was hoping you'd be happy to see me. That maybe you'd missed me too."

The words hit me like a physical blow. I'd been so focused on fear, on danger, on protecting what I'd built, that I hadn't let myself feel it.

But now I did.

I'd missed her. Desperately. The way you miss a part of yourself that you thought was gone forever.

I set down my mug and crossed to the couch. Sat next to her, careful not to disturb the pile of cats. Took her hand in mine.

"I missed you every single day," I said, my voice breaking. "Every single day, Lily. I wanted to tell you I was leaving. Wanted to bring you with me. But I knew if I did, you'd be in danger. That they'd use you to find me. That staying away from you was the only way to keep you safe."

"I know," she whispered. "I understand now. I do."

We sat like that for a while, hands clasped, years of separation slowly knitting back together. Outside, Larkspur Valley went about its Tuesday afternoon business. Inside, the cats purred and the light shifted toward evening, and two witches began to remember what it felt like to not be alone.

Finally, I pulled back. "You can't stay at a hotel. Well, you could. We have the Ridge View Motel and a couple of bed and breakfasts. But you shouldn't. Not when it's been this long and we need to properly catch up."

Lily laughed, surprised and relieved. "You're offering me your couch?"

"The couch pulls out. It's not fancy, but..." I gestured around the small apartment.

"It's perfect," Lily said firmly. "If you'll have me."

"I'll have you." The decision felt right, settling into my chest like a warm weight. "But we need a cover story. A reason you're here. People in this town notice things."

"Old colleagues?" Lily suggested. "We worked together years ago in Chicago, lost touch, you mentioned you'd moved to Larkspur Valley, so I decided to visit and reconnect?"

"That could work." I thought it through. "We could say you're thinking about moving here. Looking for a change. I could introduce you around, help you find an apartment."

"Are you offering me a town and a job in one day?"

"The café could use help." The words surprised me, but once I said them, I knew they were true. "It's been busy. More than I can handle alone sometimes. And if you're here, if we're together..." I trailed off, not quite ready to say it out loud.

But Lily said it for me. "If we're together, we're safer. Two witches are harder to catch than one. And if they do find us, we face them as a team."

"As a team," I echoed. Then, because she needed to know, because it might make a difference: "And there are others."

Lily's eyes widened. "Others?"

"Other magical people in Larkspur Valley. Maeve, who owns the bookshop. She's a Seer. Atticus, the park ranger, talks to animals but doesn't realize it's magic. And there's a little girl, Ella. She's only six, but she can sense things. Hear the cats sometimes." I paused. "We're not as alone as I thought we were."

"A magical community," Lily breathed. "That's... that's incredible, Alexis."

"It's small. Quiet. Most of them don't even know about each other. But they're here. And if the coven comes..." I met her eyes. "We won't face them alone."

Poppy chose that moment to voice her opinion. "I like her. She can stay. But she has to learn that I get fed at six AM sharp. No negotiations."

I laughed, the sound startling me with how genuine it felt. "Poppy says you can stay."

"Oh good. I was worried about the calico."

We spent the next hour catching up, trading stories of the past months. Lily had been to seven different states, following leads that mostly went nowhere. She'd worked odd jobs to earn money. Waitressed in Denver. Cleaned houses in Albuquerque. Read tarot cards at a Renaissance faire in Texas. She'd kept moving, kept searching, until the rumors led her to Colorado. To Larkspur Valley. To me.

"I walked into your café and I knew," she said. "Before I even saw you. I felt your magic, your presence. And I just... I knew I'd found you."

"I'm glad you did," I said, and meant it.

As the light faded toward evening, I showed her the bathroom, pulled sheets from the closet for the couch, and tried to remember what it felt like to share my space with someone who understood. Someone who knew what I was, who I'd been, what I'd run from.

But as I lay in bed that night, unable to sleep, staring at the ceiling and listening to Lily's soft breathing from the living room, the fear crept back in.

What if she was wrong? What if someone had followed her?

What if bringing her into my life meant destroying everything I'd built?

"Stop spiraling," Gus told me, his warm weight settling on my chest. "The new person is fine. Smells like good magic. Smells like friend."

"But what if she brought danger?" I asked.

"Then we deal with it. Together." He kneaded my chest with his paws, claws pricking through my shirt. "You're not alone anymore. That's good. Being alone is terrible."

He would know. I'd found him abandoned in an alley, starving and scared. Being alone was the worst thing he could imagine.

Maybe he was right. Maybe being found, being known, being not-alone was worth the risk.

I fell asleep with that thought, with Gus purring on my chest and Rocky sprawled across my feet, and for the first time in four months, I dreamed of something other than running.

I dreamed of standing my ground.

The next morning, I woke to voices in my kitchen.

For a moment, I was disoriented. Then I remembered.

Lily.

I pulled on jeans and a soft sweater and padded into the living room. Lily was in my tiny kitchen, and she'd somehow found the coffee maker and the coffee beans I kept stocked for the café downstairs.

"Morning," she said, turning with a smile. "Hope you don't mind. I'm useless without coffee."

"That's fine." I slid onto one of the two stools at my breakfast bar. The cats were already gathered, watching this new morning routine with interest.

"So, what's the plan?" Lily poured coffee into two mugs. "Do we open the café like normal? Do I just... exist in the background? How do we do this?"

I thought about it. "We open like normal. You can help if you want. I'll introduce you as my old colleague from Chicago. People will ask questions, but that's okay. Curiosity is better than suspicion."

"And later?"

"Later, we figure it out. One day at a time."

Lily nodded slowly. "I can do that. One day at a time."

We finished our coffee, Lily chattering about how peaceful Larkspur Valley felt, how she could feel the magic humming beneath everything. I listened, letting her voice fill the spaces that had been quiet for too long.

At six, I headed downstairs to start my morning routine. The adoptable cats in the viewing room needed feeding first. Then my five needed breakfast, which involved careful negotiations with Poppy about portion sizes and Gus's complaints about his joints.

At seven-thirty, I started prepping the café for opening. Grinding beans, arranging the pastries that Flo had dropped off earlier from her diner next door, making sure everything was perfect.

Lily joined me around seven-forty-five, watching as I moved through my routines.

"You've really built something here," she said quietly.

"I've tried." I wiped down the counter. "It's not fancy. It's not glamorous. But it's mine."

"Ours," Lily corrected gently. "If you'll let me stay. If you'll let me help."

I met her eyes. Saw the hope there, the fear, the desperate need to belong somewhere after months of running and searching and being alone.

I knew that feeling intimately.

"Ours," I agreed.

At eight, I unlocked the front door.

Within minutes, the morning regulars started trickling in. Horace, looking for his first coffee of the day. Mabel ordering her usual Lavender Dreams tea and sitting with her crossword puzzle book. Young Timothy from the hardware store, grabbing a muffin before his shift.

And everyone, absolutely everyone, noticed Lily.

"New hire?" Horace asked, his eyes twinkling.

"Old friend," I corrected. "Lily and I used to work together in Chicago. She's visiting, thinking about relocating."

"To Larkspur Valley?" Mabel looked delighted. "Oh, how wonderful! We could use more young people in town. And Alexis could certainly use the help. This place has gotten busy since she opened."

Timothy was more direct. "You seem nice. You should definitely move here. It's a good town."

Lily handled it all with grace, smiling and answering questions and learning the espresso machine like she'd been doing it for years. Maybe she had been. I realized I didn't actually know what she'd been doing for work before the coven, or during the coven, or after she left.

There was so much we needed to catch up on. So much to learn again about each other.

But we had time now. That was the thing. We had time.

The bell over the door chimed, and we both looked up.

A man walked in. Tall and lanky, with strawberry blonde hair that looked like he'd forgotten to comb it and freckles across his nose that made him look younger than his forty-six years. He wore a graphic t-shirt with some superhero I didn't recognize and carried the easy confidence of someone who'd never learned to guard himself.

"Lionel," I said, smiling despite myself. "Your usual?"

"Please." He settled at his favorite table by the window, pulling out a worn paperback. "And one of those lemon scones if you have any left."

"For you? Always." I started preparing his Dandelion Root Revival. Lily was watching me with interest.

"Friend?" she murmured.

"Regular," I said. Then, more honestly, "Maybe friend. I'm still figuring that out."

Lionel owned the comic shop three doors down. He came in almost every morning, ordered the same thing, read for an hour, and left. We'd struck up an easy friendship over the past few months. He'd invited me to his Friday game nights at the shop, and I'd actually gone a few times, surprised by how much I enjoyed the casual atmosphere and friendly people. He brought me graphic novels sometimes, choosing ones he thought I'd like with uncanny accuracy.

But there was something in the way he looked at me sometimes, something hopeful and patient, that made me keep my distance. I wasn't ready for more than friendship. Wasn't sure I'd ever be ready.

I brought his coffee and scone over. "Lionel, this is Lily. She's visiting from Chicago."

"Lovely to meet you." He stood, shaking her hand with genuine warmth. His green eyes were kind. "Friend of Alexis's?"

"Old colleagues," Lily said smoothly. "Catching up after too long apart."

"Well, any friend of Alexis's is welcome here." He smiled at me. "There's a new graphic novel series that just came in. Urban fantasy with a witch protagonist. Thought you might like it. Want me to set aside the first volume?"

"Please."

After he settled in with his book, Lily gave me a knowing look. "He likes you."

"He's just friendly."

"Alexis. He stood up to shake my hand. He's setting aside graphic novels about witches for you. He likes you."

I felt my face heat. "It's not... I'm not..."

"You're not ready," Lily finished softly. "That's okay. But maybe someday?"

Maybe. But not now. Not when I was still figuring out how to have my best friend back. Not when the fear of the coven finding me still woke me up in the middle of the night.

The door chimed again. A woman in her fifties entered, elegant and composed in a way that suggested warmth and confidence. Florence Hendry, one of the town's founding family members and one of my first customers.

"Alexis, dear," she said, beelining for the counter with her usual energy. "I'll have my regular Chamomile Calm Latte, please. And don't tell me you're out of those chocolate croissants I brought over this morning. I know I made extras."

"Never out for you, Flo." I started on her latte. "This is my friend Lily. She's visiting from Chicago. Lily, this is Florence Hendry.

She owns Flo's Diner next door and supplies all our wonderful pastries."

Flo's face lit up as she turned to Lily. "How delightful! Are you thinking of moving to our little town?"

"I'm considering it," Lily said.

"Oh, you must. We'd love to have you." Flo leaned in conspiratorially. "Tell you what, there's a Founder's Day party this Sunday at my home. You should both come. It's the social event of the season. I'm presenting my family's heirloom necklace to my daughter. Five generations of Hendry women have worn it."

I hesitated. Parties weren't really my thing. Crowds, small talk, being on display. But Flo had been nothing but kind to me since I'd arrived. She'd been one of my first customers, had talked me up to everyone in town, had basically ensured The Cozy Purrch's success through sheer force of enthusiasm.

"We'd love to," I heard myself say.

Flo clapped her hands together. "Wonderful! Sunday, two in the afternoon. I'll text you the address." She took her latte with a delighted smile. "This is going to be such fun. I'll see you girls then!"

After she left, Lily raised an eyebrow. "We're going to a party?"

"Apparently."

"You hate parties."

"I know."

"But you said yes anyway."

"She's been good to me. To the café. I owe her." I sighed. "Besides, it'll be good for you to meet people. If you're going to live here."

"You've decided I'm staying?"

"I think I decided the moment you walked through my door yesterday." I looked around the café, at the customers reading and chatting, at the cats lounging in the window, at the life I'd built. "This feels right. Like you're supposed to be here."

"I'm glad," Lily said, and her voice was thick with emotion. "Because it feels right to me too."

The rest of the day passed in a blur of customers and questions and Lily fitting seamlessly into my routines. By the time we closed at six, I was exhausted but content in a way I hadn't been in months.

We headed upstairs, ordered pizza from the place on the edge of town, and spent the evening watching terrible reality TV and laughing at things that weren't even funny. It was perfect. It was normal. It was everything I'd been missing.

That night, after Lily had gone to bed on the pull-out couch and the apartment was dark and quiet, I stood at my bedroom window and looked out at Larkspur Valley. The mountains rose dark against the star-filled sky. The street lamps cast warm pools of light on the sidewalks. Everything was peaceful.

But beneath that peace, I felt it. The hum of magic Lily had mentioned. The convergence points. The protection that came from this place, this town that had become my home.

Maybe she was right. Maybe we were safer here than anywhere else.

Or maybe I was fooling myself. Maybe danger was coming, drawn by Lily's presence, by our combined magic, by the fact that two witches from the same coven had found each other again.

I didn't know.

But for the first time since I'd run, I wasn't facing it alone.

And that, I thought as I finally crawled into bed, was worth every risk.

"You're thinking too loud," Poppy complained from her spot on my pillow. "Go to sleep."

"Sorry," I told her.

"The friend-person will still be here tomorrow. So will the café. So will we." She kneaded the pillow, her purr rumbling. "Tomorrow is tomorrow. Tonight is sleep."

Wise words from a cat.

I closed my eyes and let sleep take me, Poppy's warmth against my head, Rocky sprawled across my legs, Gus on the nightstand keeping watch.

Whatever tomorrow brought, whatever the future held, at least I wouldn't face it alone.

Not anymore.

Never again.

Chapter Two

Wednesday morning arrived with the kind of bright, clear light that made Larkspur Valley look like something out of a postcard. I woke to the smell of coffee brewing and the sound of someone humming softly in my kitchen.

For a moment, still half-asleep, I forgot where I was. Forgot that I'd been alone for over a year. The familiar comfort of another person moving through the morning routine pulled me back to the coven house, to mornings when Lily and I would take turns making breakfast, comfortable in that easy sisterhood we'd built.

Then I remembered. Lily was here. Really here. Sleeping on my couch, her few belongings tucked neatly in the corner, her presence filling the apartment with warmth I hadn't realized I'd been missing.

I padded out to the kitchen in my pajamas and found her at the stove, making scrambled eggs while my coffee pot burbled on the counter. She'd pulled her dark hair back in a messy bun, and she was wearing the spare pajamas I'd lent her last night, the ones that were too big on her.

She looked like she belonged here.

"Morning," she said without turning around. "I made coffee. Yours is the blue mug."

I picked up the mug and took a sip. Perfect. Just the way I liked it, with a tiny touch of cinnamon that only someone who really knew me would remember.

"You didn't have to make breakfast."

"I know. But I wanted to." She glanced over her shoulder, smiling. "Plus, I figured if we're going to work together all day, we should probably eat something besides pastries from the display case."

"You're doing the nervous thing again," Poppy said from her perch near the window. The calico was watching me with those knowing amber eyes. "The friend-person will be fine."

"Unless she's terrible at making coffee," Gus added from the armchair where he'd settled for the morning. The tuxedo cat had appointed himself as Lily's primary skeptic. "Then we're all doomed."

"She smells nice," Rocky offered, sprawled across my feet in direct violation of personal space. The orange tabby had no concerns about anything ever. "Like flowers and rain."

"They're talking about me, aren't they?" Lily said, flipping the eggs onto two plates.

"Gus thinks you might poison the coffee."

"Gus is a pessimist." She set the plates on my small kitchen table and sat across from me. "Tell him the coffee is fine and he should trust me."

"You can tell him yourself. They understand us perfectly."

"Right. I keep forgetting." Lily turned toward Gus, who was perched on the back of the couch with narrowed eyes. "Gus, the coffee is safe. I promise I didn't poison it."

Gus's tail flicked, and I could feel his grudging acceptance through our bond. Lily smiled, sensing the shift even though she couldn't hear his actual response.

"He's warming up to me," she said.

"Give him time."

We ate in comfortable silence, the kind that only comes from years of friendship. It had been like this at the coven, before everything went dark. Lily and I sharing space, sharing quiet mornings, understanding each other without needing to fill every moment with words.

I'd missed this. Missed it so much I hadn't let myself think about it.

"Thank you," I said quietly. "For finding me. For being here."

Lily reached across the table and squeezed my hand. "Where else would I be?"

At seven-thirty, we headed downstairs to open the café. Lily had borrowed one of my sweaters, soft green wool that made her eyes look warmer. We moved through the opening routine together, and I was surprised by how naturally we fell into step. She learned the quirks of the espresso machine while I set out the pastries. She filled the display case while I counted the register.

"This place suits you," she said, looking around the café as morning light started filtering through the windows.

"It's home," I said simply.

"I can see why." She tied on an apron and smiled. "So. Where do you want me today?"

I showed her the details. How to work the espresso machine without the temperamental quirk that made it spit steam if you didn't hold the handle just right. Where we kept the pastries Flo brought over from her diner. How to arrange yesterday's leftovers alongside the fresh ones since they were still perfectly good.

She learned fast. Of course she did.

At eight o'clock, I unlocked the front door and flipped the sign to Open. Within minutes, the regulars started trickling in. Maeve arrived first, as she usually did, her silver hair catching the morning light. She studied Lily with those sharp eyes that saw too much. "You must be the friend who just arrived recently."

I shouldn't have been surprised that Maeve knew. She always seemed to know things, to sense things. The same way she'd known I was different from the moment we met.

"Maeve, this is Lily. We worked together in Chicago. Lost touch for a while, but she's in town now." The cover story felt strange on my tongue, but Lily nodded along with an easy smile.

"Old colleagues reunited," Lily said. "It's wonderful to see Alexis again after all these years."

Maeve studied Lily with those sharp eyes that saw too much. Then she smiled. "Welcome to Larkspur Valley. Any friend of Alexis's is welcome here."

After Maeve left, the morning rush continued. More customers arrived, curious and friendly. Lily charmed them all with her warm smile and genuine interest in their stories.

During a brief lull around nine-thirty, while we were both behind the counter restocking cups, I leaned close to Lily and whispered, "Maeve knows who you really are."

Lily glanced toward the window where Maeve had disappeared down the street, then nodded. "I figured as much. I could read her energy when we shook hands. She's like us. Different flavor of magic, but it's there."

"She is. We worked together on some spells last month." I kept my voice low. "She's a Seer. Probably knew you were coming before you even arrived in town."

"Good." Lily smiled. "It'll be nice to have more allies."

By mid-morning, we'd fallen into an easy rhythm, moving around each other in the small space behind the counter like we'd been doing this for years instead of hours. Lily handled the register while I made drinks, and we traded off on pastries and refills.

"She's good with people," Poppy observed. "Better than you."

"I'm good with people," I protested.

"You tolerate people. She likes them. There's a difference."

Poppy had a point.

During a lull around ten, Lily wiped down the counter and said casually, "So. Apartment hunting. I should probably start looking."

I felt a small pang at that. The past two nights of having her in my apartment had felt right. Like coming home to something I hadn't realized I'd lost. Waking up to another person in the space, sharing coffee, falling back into that easy rhythm we'd had at the coven.

But I also understood. We both needed our own spaces. Our own places to retreat to. The coven had taught us that, too. You could love someone, trust them completely, and still need a space that was entirely yours.

"There's a place two blocks away that just opened up," I said, trying not to sound too eager. "Small one-bedroom above the yarn shop. Cordelia mentioned it yesterday."

"Perfect. Can we look at it this afternoon?"

"I can close early today. Small town privilege." I smiled. "Around three?"

Lily grinned. "Then it's a date."

"Not a date," Gus muttered. "Friends looking at apartments. Totally normal. Nothing suspicious here."

"You're paranoid," Rocky said.

"I'm cautious. There's a difference."

The apartment was perfect. Hardwood floors, big windows that let in the mountain light, a tiny kitchen that reminded me of my own upstairs space. The rent was reasonable and Cordelia was delighted to have a tenant.

She came bustling up the stairs to show us around, her reading glasses hanging from a beaded chain around her neck. "Oh, I'm so pleased!" she said, beaming at Lily. "Any friend of Alexis's is a friend of mine. And it'll be wonderful to have someone upstairs again. The place has been empty too long."

"When can you move in?" Cordelia asked Lily.

"Is tomorrow too soon?"

Cordelia beamed. "Tomorrow is perfect."

Walking back to the café, Lily bumped my shoulder with hers. "Thank you. For helping me find this. For letting me stay."

"You're my friend," I said simply. "Where else would you go?"

"I don't know. I just know I had to find you." She was quiet for a moment. "Are you really okay with this? Me being here?"

I thought about the question. Thought about the fear that still lived in my chest, the worry that the coven might follow, the thousand what-ifs that kept me up at night.

Then I thought about last night. About not being alone. About having someone who understood the truth of what I was, what I could do.

And I thought about something else, too. Something I'd been avoiding but couldn't ignore anymore. The coven could find me whether Lily was here or not. If they were looking, they'd search. If they were determined, they'd track me down eventually. My running hadn't made me invisible. It had just made me isolated.

I'd rather face them with a friend at my side than alone.

"Yes," I said. "I'm really okay with it."

Thursday morning, Lily arrived with boxes she'd picked up from the post office just that morning. Not many. She'd been traveling light, same as I had when I'd run.

But when we got to her new apartment that afternoon to help her unpack, we weren't alone.

Cordelia was there with a set of mismatched dishes and a reading lamp. "From my storage room," she said. "Been gathering dust for years. They deserve a good home."

Flo arrived with a coffee table and two throw pillows. "Had these in my garage. Lee helped me load them this morning."

Maeve showed up with a small bookshelf already filled with novels. "Every home needs books," she announced. "Consider it a housewarming gift."

And Pearl from the crochet circle appeared with a crocheted afghan in shades of blue and green. "Made it last winter. Was waiting for the right person to give it to."

Lily stood in the middle of her apartment, looking overwhelmed as furniture and household items accumulated around her. "This is too much. I can't accept all of this."

"Nonsense," Pearl said firmly, settling the afghan over the back of a slightly worn but comfortable-looking couch that had somehow appeared. "Not charity, dear. Larkspur Valley takes care of its own, and you are now one of us."

Lily's eyes filled with tears. She looked at me, and I nodded. This was what community looked like. What belonging looked like.

We spent the afternoon unpacking her few belongings and arranging the gifts from the town. By evening, her apartment looked lived-in. Warm. Like home.

It felt strange, helping her create a space that wasn't mine. Part of me wanted to keep her in my apartment, keep that warmth of shared space, of waking up to someone who understood me. But I also knew this was right. We both needed the breathing room, the independence. We could be close without being on top of each other.

"You'll come over for dinner," I said as we arranged her few books alongside Maeve's donations on the shelf by the window. It wasn't a question.

"Obviously. And you'll come to mine." Lily smiled at me. "Just because I have my own space doesn't mean we're not together in this. We're still us. Still sisters."

That word settled something in my chest. Sisters. Not by blood, but by choice. By shared experience and trust built over years.

"Still sisters," I agreed.

By Friday, it felt like she'd always been here.

The café was busier than usual. Word had spread about the new barista, and people kept stopping by to meet her. Lily handled it all with grace, remembering names and preferences, making small talk that felt genuine instead of forced.

She also started experimenting with drinks.

"Try this," she said around two o'clock, sliding a lavender-colored latte across the counter.

I took a sip. The flavors bloomed across my tongue. Honey and lavender and something else. Something that made me think of summer afternoons and peaceful moments.

"That's incredible. What is it?"

"Honeyed Harmony. Honey lavender latte with a touch of vanilla and a tiny bit of magic to make people feel calm." She said the last part quietly, just for me. "Thought it might be nice. People seem stressed lately."

Within an hour, three people had requested it. By the end of the day, it was our most popular drink.

"The friend-person makes good things," Rocky announced, having convinced Lily to give him extra treats. "I approve of her."

"You approve of anyone who feeds you," Gus grumbled, but even he seemed to be warming up to Lily. She had a way with animals, same as me. The cats were responding to her gentle presence.

Millie, my shy tortoiseshell, had even been sitting with Lily and let her pet her. That was practically a declaration of trust.

Around four o'clock, Piper came in with her daughters. Eva, the nine-year-old, was carefully carrying a to-go cup from Flo's diner next door, while six-year-old Ella skipped ahead, dark curls bouncing. There was something about Ella that always caught my attention. Something in the way her eyes tracked the cats, the way she tilted her head like she was listening to conversations no one else could hear.

I'd noticed it before. Filed it away as interesting but not urgent. Kids were sometimes more sensitive to magic than adults.

But today, with Lily here, Ella's attention sharpened.

She sat at one of the small tables near the window while Piper ordered tea and Eva requested hot chocolate, her gaze fixed on Poppy. The calico was sunbathing, tail wrapped neatly around her paws, eyes closed in contentment.

Then Ella looked at Gus, who was judging everyone from his favorite perch by the cat room window. Then Rocky, who was being his chaotic self in the viewing area, trying to steal a dropped toy mouse.

"Mom," Ella whispered, tugging on Piper's sleeve. "They're talking to each other."

Piper laughed, the sound fond and indulgent. "What are they saying, sweetheart?"

Ella's face scrunched up in concentration. "Poppy likes the sunshine. It makes her fur warm. And Gus wants more treats. He thinks Alexis is being stingy."

My hand stilled on the mug I was wiping.

Because Ella wasn't just sensing vague emotions anymore. She was hearing specific thoughts. Complete sentences. That was new. That was stronger than what I'd witnessed before.

I'd known about Ella's gift since shortly after opening the café. She'd always been able to pick up on the cats' general moods, their basic wants. But this? This level of clarity? This was her power growing, developing, becoming more precise.

And she was only six years old.

Lily caught my eye across the counter. Her expression was carefully neutral, but I could see the concern there. The recognition of what this meant.

Piper was still smiling, oblivious. "Your imagination is wonderful, honey. Now drink your hot chocolate before it gets cold."

Ella's face fell. "It's not imagination. I can really hear them."

"Of course you can, sweetheart." Piper's tone was indulgent, patronizing in that well-meaning way parents had when they thought their children were playing pretend.

Ella crossed her arms, her small jaw set in frustration. Then she looked directly at me, her eyes pleading. Help me. Tell her it's real. Tell her I'm not making it up.

My chest tightened. I wanted to. I wanted to tell Piper that her daughter had a gift, that she was special, that she needed guidance and understanding, not dismissal. But I couldn't. Not without revealing myself. Not without putting both Ella and myself at risk.

I gave her the smallest nod. A silent promise. I see you. I believe you. We'll talk when it's safe.

Ella's shoulders relaxed just a fraction. She picked up her hot chocolate and took a sip, but her eyes stayed on me for a moment longer before she turned back to watch the cats.

After they left, Lily and I cleaned up in silence for a few minutes. Then she said quietly, "Her abilities are getting stronger."

"I know." I wiped down the counter, my mind racing. "A few months ago, she could only sense general emotions from the cats. Happy, scared, hungry. Now she's hearing complete thoughts. Specific details."

"That's a significant jump in a short time." Lily's voice was gentle but worried. "As her power grows, it's going to get harder for her to hide it. Harder for her to control."

"And if she mentions the wrong thing to the wrong person..." I didn't finish the sentence. We both knew the dangers.

"Then we teach her. Soon." Lily met my eyes. "Before someone notices what she can do. Before she accidentally reveals too much."

"Carefully," I agreed. "So no one realizes what we're doing."

The suggestion settled into my chest, warm and right and terrifying all at once. Because teaching Ella meant revealing ourselves. Meant taking a risk. Meant building something here that was bigger than just survival.

"I'll think about it," I said.

"Of course." Lily smiled. "Just know that I'm here. If you decide to do this, you won't be alone."

Thursday had brought Ella's demonstration of her gift. Friday brought a different kind of complication.

Lionel stopped by around noon, same as he did most days. His dark brown hair was slightly messy like he'd been running his hands through it, and his green eyes lit up when he saw me. He'd met Lily on Wednesday when he'd come in for his usual coffee, and they'd hit it off immediately, bonding over their shared love of fantasy novels.

Today he carried a paper bag that smelled like fresh bread from the bakery and a comic shop bag.

"Brought you lunch," he said, setting the paper bag on the counter. "Figured you might not have time to eat with the café being so busy."

Inside the bag was a turkey sandwich, my favorite kind, and a chocolate chip cookie still warm from the oven.

"Lionel, you didn't have to do this."

"I know. I wanted to." He pulled a graphic novel from the comic shop bag and set it on the counter. "New release. Mystery series set in a magical bookshop. Thought you might enjoy it. Reminds me of you."

Then he was gone, the door chiming behind him.

I stared at the book. It was a cozy mystery set in a small mountain town, featuring a protagonist who solved crimes while running a bookshop.

"He's interested," Lily said, not bothering to hide her amusement.

"We're friends."

"He wants more."

I didn't know how to respond to that. Lionel was kind and thoughtful and we'd become friends over the past few months. But anything more than friendship felt impossible. Too complicated. Too risky.

"I'm not dating anyone," I said finally.

Lily just smiled and went back to work.

Friday afternoon brought Dr. Colton Dover.

He showed up around three o'clock, ostensibly to check on the cats. He'd been their vet since I'd opened the café, professional and competent and occasionally lingering a little longer than necessary when he talked to me.

Today was no exception.

He examined each cat with practiced ease. Poppy tolerated it with dignity. Gus complained the entire time. Rocky tried to play with the stethoscope. Millie hid until Colton coaxed her out with gentle patience.

"They're all healthy," he said, packing up his bag. "Sage is doing great. That kitten is thriving."

"Thanks to you."

"Thanks to you. You're the one who rescued her. You're the one who's giving her a good home." He paused, his hazel eyes meeting mine. "How have you been? Big week with your friend arriving."

"It's been good. Really good."

"I'm glad." He hesitated, then said carefully, "Would you ever want to grab coffee? Outside the café? Maybe dinner sometime?"

The question hung in the air between us. Direct. Honest. No pretense.

"The café keeps me pretty busy," I said, defaulting to the excuse I always used.

Colton smiled, unfazed. "I'm patient. The offer stands whenever you're ready."

After he left, Lily appeared at my elbow. "Two suitors now. You're popular."

"I'm not dating anyone," I said firmly.

"But you could. Maybe. Someday." She wasn't teasing now. Her voice was gentle, understanding. "You're allowed to have a life, Alexis. You're allowed to be happy. To let people in."

"I let you in."

"You did. And look how well that's going." She bumped my shoulder with hers. "Just think about it. That's all I'm asking."

I thought about it. All through the rest of Friday and into Saturday morning. Thought about Lionel's thoughtful gifts and easy friendship. Thought about Colton's direct honesty and patient interest. Thought about the possibility of being something more than just the café owner who kept to herself.

The idea was terrifying and tempting in equal measure.

Saturday was chaos.

The café was packed from the moment we opened. Everyone was talking about Founder's Day, the big celebration happening tomorrow. Apparently it was one of Larkspur Valley's biggest events, honoring the families who'd founded the town over a century ago.

Flo Hendry came in around three, looking elegant and excited. Her silver hair was perfectly styled, and she wore a cream sweater with a delicate gold necklace.

"Just wanted to remind you both about tomorrow," she said, accepting the tea I'd already started preparing. "Two o'clock at my house. I'm so glad you'll both be there for the presentation."

"We wouldn't miss it," Lily said.

"Wonderful! It's going to be quite the event. I've hired caterers, rented tables and chairs. The whole town will be there." Flo's eyes sparkled with excitement. "Five generations this necklace has been in my family. Now it's Piper's turn."

After she left, I looked at Lily. "Are you sure about going tomorrow? Parties aren't really my thing."

"I know. But Flo's been kind to you. And besides," she smiled, "we're building a life here. That means showing up sometimes."

"The friend-person is right," Poppy said. "You should go. The fancy-lady-person has been kind to you."

"Plus, there will probably be good food," Rocky added hopefully.

"You're not invited," Gus informed him.

"Yet," Rocky countered.

That evening, as we closed up the café, Lily and I stood in the quiet space, surrounded by the evidence of our work. Clean counters, swept floors, five cats settled in their favorite spots.

"We did it," Lily said softly. "Built lives worth living."

"For now."

"What do you mean?"

I looked out the window at Larkspur Valley settling into evening. Lights coming on in windows. People heading home to their families. Normal, ordinary lives.

"The coven might still come," I said. "They might find us."

"Let them." Lily's voice was fierce. "We have something worth fighting for now. We have this place. These people. Each other."

She was right. In less than a week, my life had shifted. I wasn't alone anymore. I had a partner, a friend, a person who understood.

And maybe, just maybe, I was starting to build something real here. Something worth defending.

Whatever came next, whatever dangers waited in the future, at least I wouldn't face them alone.

"Tomorrow," Poppy said sleepily from her window perch. "Big party. Fancy people. Important necklace."

"What could possibly go wrong?" Gus muttered.

As it turned out, everything.

But we didn't know that yet.

Chapter Three

The November air bit at my face as Lily and I walked toward Flo's house. I'd layered a thick cardigan over my dark green dress and wrapped a scarf around my neck, but I could still feel the cold seeping through. Beside me, Lily had done the same, her blue dress mostly hidden under her wool coat.

"Think it'll snow?" she asked, glancing up at the gray sky.

"Probably." I pulled my scarf tighter. "Welcome to November in Colorado."

As if on cue, the first few flakes began to drift down, light and lazy. They caught in Lily's dark hair and melted on my nose. By the time we reached the historic district, the snow was falling in earnest, turning Larkspur Valley into something out of a winter postcard.

Flo's Victorian house glowed with warm light from every window. Cars lined both sides of the street despite the weather, and I could see people hurrying up the front walk, bundled in coats and scarves. Through the windows, I caught glimpses of movement and color. The party was clearly in full swing inside.

"Here we go," Lily murmured, linking her arm through mine.

We climbed the porch steps and knocked. The door opened immediately, releasing a wave of warmth and the sound of conversation and music. A server in black and white took our coats, and suddenly we were inside, surrounded by people and heat and noise.

The house had been transformed. The formal living room and dining room had been opened up, furniture rearranged to create flow. Rental tables draped in white linens lined the walls, laden with elegant appetizers and champagne flutes. Servers moved through the crowd with trays. A small string quartet played in the corner. Everything looked sophisticated and warm and welcoming.

And there were so many people.

Flo spotted us almost immediately and hurried over, her silver hair perfectly styled and her cheeks flushed with excitement. She wore an elegant cream dress and her eyes were bright with nervous energy.

"You're here!" She pulled us both into quick hugs. "I'm so glad. Come in, warm up. Food and drinks are everywhere, the house tours start at three, and I'm just so happy you could make it."

"It's beautiful, Flo," I said, meaning it. "You've outdone yourself."

"Thank you." She touched her collarbone briefly, a protective gesture even though the necklace wasn't there. "I keep thinking something will go wrong, but so far everything's perfect. The caterers are amazing, everyone's having a good time." She took a breath. "I think my great-great-grandmother would be proud."

A server appeared at her elbow with a question about the wine service, and Flo excused herself with an apologetic smile.

Lily and I stood near the fireplace, watching the crowd.

"This is a statement," Lily murmured, keeping her voice low.

I knew what she meant. The elegance, the professional catering, the abundance. It spoke of wealth and history and pride. Some people would see it as Flo honoring her family's legacy. Others would see showing off.

"Look at this spread," a man said to his companion as they passed near us. His tone was admiring but carried an edge I couldn't quite name.

Lily caught my eye. She'd heard it too.

At two-fifteen, a man arrived who immediately caught my attention.

He was in his early fifties, maybe five-foot-five, with graying hair and a face that looked like it had forgotten how to smile. He wore an uncomfortable-looking suit and stood stiffly near the entrance, observing the party rather than participating.

Flo spotted him and hurried over, her hostess smile firmly in place. "Warren! I'm so glad you came."

"Wouldn't miss Founder's Day," he said, his voice tight and controlled. "Important to remember who built this town."

There was the slightest emphasis on "who built," barely noticeable unless you were listening for it.

"Of course," Flo said warmly. "Help yourself to food and drinks. The first house tour starts at three if you'd like to see the upstairs."

Warren nodded and moved away, his gaze sweeping the property with an expression I couldn't quite read. Calculation? Resentment?

"Who's that?" Lily whispered.

"Warren Jacobs. His family was one of the original founding families."

"Ah." Lily's eyes tracked him as he moved through the crowd. "There's something..."

"What?"

"Old anger. Deep resentment. Like embers that never quite went out."

I filed that information away and tried to focus on mingling. But everywhere I looked, I saw new faces. Townspeople I'd served coffee to but never really talked to. Connections I hadn't made yet. It was overwhelming.

At two-thirty, another man arrived. Zeke Hargraves, according to the name I'd heard Flo greet him with. He was stocky with a construction worker's build and calloused hands, looking more comfortable in his flannel shirt and work jeans than many of the other guests in their party clothes. He moved through the party with more ease than Warren, but there was still an edge to him.

I overheard him talking to another guest near the appetizer table, his voice carrying just enough to be heard. "My grandfather Josiah laid the foundation for half these buildings," he said, gesturing toward the windows. "Some contributions get remembered more than others, though. The Hendrys always get the glory, but it was Hargraves sweat and skill that built this town as much as anyone's."

The other guest nodded uncomfortably and moved away. Zeke didn't seem offended, just resigned. Like he'd said these words many times before and expected nothing to change. The comment hung in the air, neither hostile nor friendly. Just... noted.

Lily touched my elbow. "Another one with resentment."

Zeke must have noticed us watching because he made his way over, a beer in one hand. Up close, I could see the weathering on his face, the permanent squint of someone who'd spent decades working outdoors.

"You're the new café owner," he said to me, his voice friendly enough. "Alexis, right? The Cozy Purrch?"

"That's me. And this is Lily, my... colleague."

"Zeke Hargraves." He shook both our hands, his grip firm and calloused. "Haven't made it to your place yet, but I've heard good things. People say the coffee's decent, and the cats are entertaining."

"They're the real draw," I said, warming to his easy manner. "The coffee just gives people an excuse to visit them."

He smiled, and it softened his whole face. "Smart business model." He glanced around the elegant room, his expression shifting to something more complicated. "Flo knows how to throw a party. I'll give her that. The Hendrys always did have a flair for... presentation."

There was something in the way he said "presentation" that caught my attention. Not quite bitter, but not entirely neutral either.

"You grew up here?" Lily asked, her tone conversational.

"Born and raised. Fourth generation Larkspur Valley. My great-great-grandfather Josiah came here same time as Simon Hendry. Built half the town together." He took a swig of beer. "Course, you wouldn't know that from the historical markers or the town museum. According to official history, Simon Hendry did it all by himself."

"That must be frustrating," I said carefully.

"It's history." He shrugged, but I could see the tension in his shoulders. "Can't change what's written in the books. My family knows what we contributed. That's what matters, right?"

The words said one thing, but his tone said another. This was a wound that had never quite healed.

"Are you working on something to document it?" Lily asked. "Your family's contributions?"

His face lit up, genuine enthusiasm replacing the resignation. "Actually, yeah. I'm writing a book about the architecture of early Larkspur Valley. Documenting which families built what, the construction techniques they used, the craftsmanship. Most of the original buildings are still standing, which is remarkable. I've been photographing them, researching the property records, tracking down descendants who remember the stories."

"That sounds fascinating," I said, and meant it.

"It is. And maybe when it's published, people will understand that this town was built by more than just one family." He glanced at his watch. "I should find Flo. Want to thank her for the invitation before the tours start. Nice meeting you both."

He walked away, and I watched him go with a strange mix of sympathy and unease.

"He's angry," Lily murmured. "But he's also genuine. That love for the architecture, the craftsmanship... that's real. Not just about resentment."

"Which makes him harder to read," I said.

"Exactly."

"How many founding families were there?"

"I'm starting to think too many."

At two-forty-five, a thin, elegant man with nervous energy approached Flo directly. He had a jeweler's hands, careful and precise, and he carried a camera bag over one shoulder.

"Flo," he said, his intensity immediate. "May I see the necklace? My great-great-grandfather crafted it. I'd love to photograph it for family records."

Flo's smile remained warm. "Of course, Grayson! I'm doing house tours starting at three. The necklace will be upstairs in my display case. You can see it and photograph it then."

"Thank you." His relief was palpable, almost excessive. "It means everything to document our family's work. To preserve that history."

After he moved away, Lily leaned close. "That one's obsessed."

"With the necklace?"

"With legacy. Family pride. Proving something." She frowned. "But there's something else underneath. Desperation, maybe? Hard to read clearly with so many people around."

The party continued, the noise level rising as more guests arrived and the champagne flowed. Servers circulated with trays of elegant appetizers. The string quartet played softly in the background. It should have been perfect.

But that feeling of unease kept growing.

At three o'clock exactly, Flo gathered a group of about ten people for the first house tour. Warren Jacobs was among them. I watched them climb the stairs, Flo's cheerful voice explaining the history of the Victorian architecture as they ascended.

"Should we go on a tour?" Lily asked.

"Later maybe. Right now, I need some space."

We moved toward a quieter corner of the living room. That's when a tall man with intense energy pushed through the crowd toward Flo. His wife hurried after him, her face apologetic.

"Flo!" he called out, his voice carrying. "We need to talk. About my father and yours."

Flo had just emerged from leading the first tour. She turned, her hostess smile slipping slightly. "Theo. Not today. This is a celebration."

"It's never the right time." Theo Vincent's voice rose, drawing attention. "You keep avoiding this conversation. Someone needs to tell the truth about what happened between our families."

His wife touched his arm. "Theo, please."

He pulled away. "My father was cheated. Everyone knows it. The Hendrys destroyed him."

The conversations around us had stopped. People were watching now, the festive atmosphere cracking.

Flo's face remained calm, but I could see the strain around her eyes. "I promise we'll talk, Theo. Just not now. Not at the party."

"When?" he demanded. "When will you finally acknowledge what your family did?"

"Theo." His wife's voice was firmer now. "You're making a scene."

Something in that seemed to reach him. He looked around at all the staring faces and his expression shuttered. Without another word, he stalked off toward the back rooms of the house, radiating anger.

The party slowly resumed, but the damage was done. The perfect afternoon had a crack in it now.

"That was intense," Lily murmured.

"That was rage." I watched Theo disappear through the dining room. "Old grief turned into something dark."

About ten minutes later, I found myself near the back sunroom, looking for a quieter space away from the crowd. That's where I found Theo Vincent standing alone, staring out the windows at the snow-covered garden. His wife was nowhere in sight.

His shoulders were hunched, hands shoved deep in his pockets. The rage from earlier had burned down to something else. Exhaustion, maybe. Or regret.

I almost backed away without saying anything, but he must have heard me because he turned.

"I know," he said before I could speak. "I made a scene. My wife's furious with me. Hell, I'm furious with me." He ran a hand through his hair. "But I can't seem to help myself when it comes to the Hendrys."

"Why?" The question slipped out before I could stop it.

He laughed, but there was no humor in it. "You really want to know?"

"I wouldn't have asked if I didn't."

He studied me for a moment, then seemed to make a decision. "My father was Simon Hendry's business partner. Nearly thirty years, they worked together. Built something real. Or so my father thought." His voice went flat. "When they dissolved the partnership in the eighties, my dad thought everything was fair. Equal split, clean break, both men set up for success."

"But it wasn't?"

"Simon thrived. My father... didn't. Every business venture failed. Every investment turned sour. By the time he died in the mid-nineties, he was broke, bitter, and convinced Simon had cheated him somehow. That the accounting had been manipulated, that the split hadn't been equal, that he'd been pushed out so Simon could take all the success for himself."

"And you believe him?"

Theo's jaw clenched. "I watched my father wither away. Watched the light go out of his eyes. Watched him spend his last years obsessed with proving he'd been wronged. It destroyed him. Destroyed our family. My mother left him. My sister stopped speaking to him. I was the only one who stayed, and by the end, I'm not sure he even knew I was there."

There was such raw pain in his voice that I felt it in my chest. Whatever anger he carried, it came from a place of deep hurt.

"So, you're trying to prove what he couldn't," I said quietly.

"I've been researching. Going through old documents, partnership agreements, financial records. And I'm finding...

discrepancies. Things that don't add up. Things that suggest my father was right." His hands curled into fists. "But no one wants to hear it. The Hendrys are Larkspur Valley royalty. My father was just a failed businessman who couldn't accept his own mistakes."

"Is that what you think? That he made mistakes?"

"I don't know what I think anymore." He turned back to the window, his reflection ghostly in the glass. "Maybe he was cheated. Maybe he wasn't. Maybe the truth is somewhere in the middle. But I owe it to him to find out. Even if it makes me look crazy. Even if everyone thinks I'm just carrying on a ridiculous grudge."

"I don't think you're crazy," I said.

He looked at me sharply. "You don't know me."

"No. But I know what it's like to carry something heavy. To feel like you're the only one who sees the truth, even when everyone else thinks you're wrong."

Something in his expression shifted. Softened, just slightly. "Thanks for that. Most people just think I'm an asshole."

"You were kind of a jerk earlier," I pointed out.

He laughed, and this time it was almost genuine. "Fair. Flo doesn't deserve my anger. She wasn't even alive when it happened. But she's a Hendry, and sometimes that's all I can see."

His wife appeared in the doorway, relief flooding her face when she saw him. "There you are. I've been looking everywhere." She came over and touched his arm gently. "Are you okay?"

"I'm fine," he said, though his voice said otherwise. "Just needed a minute."

She looked at me, gratitude in her eyes. "Thank you for talking with him. He's been... it's been a difficult time."

"I understand," I said.

"Come on," she said to Theo. "Let's get some food. You haven't eaten anything since breakfast."

He nodded, gave me a small, weary smile, and let her lead him back toward the party.

I stood in the sunroom for a moment longer, watching the snow fall in the garden, thinking about the weight of family history. How it could twist people up inside, make them do things they'd later regret.

Theo Vincent wasn't just an angry suspect. He was a man trying to make peace with his father's ghost.

That made him human. And it made him dangerous.

"Most overtly suspicious of everyone here." Lily said, coming to stand beside me.

"Maybe. Or maybe just the most honest about his resentment."

At three-thirty, Lionel appeared at my elbow, holding two glasses of champagne. Lily had drifted off to talk with Pearl from the crochet circle, leaving me standing near the fireplace.

"Thought you might need this," he said, offering me one. His dark hair was slightly messy and his green eyes were warm. "Big party."

"Thank you." I took the glass, grateful. "How are you?"

"Good. Shop's closed today so I actually have time to socialize." He stood close, comfortable in that easy way we'd developed over the past months. "You look nice, by the way."

Heat rose in my cheeks. "Thanks."

We talked for a while, Lionel asking about the café and Lily's integration into town. He was genuinely interested, not just making small talk. After a bit, he said casually, "There's a new bookstore opening in Silverpine next weekend. They're having a grand opening event. Would you want to check it out? Maybe grab dinner after?"

My heart did a strange little flip. "Like... just us?"

"If you want. Or we could invite Lily too. No pressure. Just thought it might be fun."

"Maybe," I said, deflecting without quite refusing. "I'll let you know."

"Sounds good." Lionel smiled, unfazed. "No rush."

After he walked away, Lily reappeared at my side. "He's courting you."

"We're friends."

"He wants more. I can see it in his aura."

Before I could respond, someone else approached. Dr. Colton Dover, looking polished in dark slacks and a button-down shirt. His hazel eyes found me immediately.

Lily excused herself with a knowing smile. "I'll go find Pearl again."

"There you are," he said. "I've been looking for you."

"Hi, Colton." I was very aware of how different his energy was from Lionel's. More direct. More confident. "Enjoying the party?"

"It's impressive. Flo really went all out." He glanced around the crowded room, then back at me. "It's getting loud in here. Want to find somewhere quieter to talk? Maybe the library? Flo mentioned it's not part of the tour route."

I hesitated. That felt more intimate than standing in the middle of a crowd.

"Just to talk," he said, reading my hesitation. "I'd like to know you better, Alexis. You're interesting. Different."

Against my better judgment, I agreed.

We made our way to Flo's library, a cozy room lined with bookshelves and furnished with comfortable chairs. It was quieter here, insulated from the party noise. Through the window, I could see the snow falling steadily outside.

"Can I be honest with you?" Colton asked.

"Usually a dangerous question."

He smiled. "I'd like to take you to dinner. A real date. Get to know you outside of coffee shop transactions and cat checkups."

My breath caught. "Colton..."

"You don't date. I know. You've made that clear." He leaned against one of the bookshelves. "But everyone dates. You just haven't met the right person yet."

It was bold. Assuming. And yet there was something appealing about his directness.

"I'm not good at this," I admitted. "Relationships. Letting people in."

"Then practice with me." His smile was warm. "No pressure. Just dinner. Coffee. Whatever makes you comfortable."

"I'll think about it."

"That's all I'm asking."

We walked back to the party in comfortable silence. But my mind was spinning. Two men. Two very different approaches. Both interested in something more than friendship.

And I had no idea what I wanted.

Around four o'clock, I excused myself to find a bathroom. The downstairs powder room had a line, so I headed upstairs where Flo had told guests they could use the guest bathroom at the end of the hall.

The second floor was quieter, insulated from the party noise below. I found the bathroom and afterward, as I was washing my hands, I heard a soft sound from the bedroom across the hall.

A meow. Quiet and uncertain.

I dried my hands and peeked into the guest bedroom. "Paisley?"

Two blue eyes peered out from under the bed, reflecting the dim light from the hallway.

I crouched down, making myself small and non-threatening. "Hey, sweetie. I know, it's scary down there, isn't it? All those people and noise."

Paisley crept forward slightly, her cream and chocolate coat disheveled. She was a beautiful Ragdoll, one of my first adoptions when I'd opened the café. She'd been an owner surrender after her elderly owner passed and the surviving family couldn't keep her. Flo had fallen in love with her immediately.

"What are you doing in here?" I kept my voice soft and soothing. "I thought Flo put you in the study."

"Too loud," Paisley said, her mental voice trembling. "Closed door. Scratched. Got out. Hiding here now. Safer."

"That makes sense. You're a smart girl." I extended my hand for her to sniff. She bumped her nose against my fingers, then retreated back under the bed. "You stay here where it's quiet, okay? The party will be over soon."

"Strange men upstairs," Paisley said. "During tours. Don't like them. Smell wrong."

My attention sharpened. "What do you mean, smell wrong?"

"Old. Like paper and smoke. Like... angry." She couldn't quite articulate it better than that, and I didn't want to push. She was already frightened.

"I understand. You're doing great by staying hidden. Keep being safe, Paisley."

I stood and headed back downstairs, my mind turning over what she'd said. Strange men. Old paper and smoke. Anger.

It probably meant nothing. Just a stressed cat's perception of unfamiliar people in her territory.

But something about it nagged at me anyway.

Lily found me at the bottom of the stairs. "You okay?"

"Fine. Just needed a minute." I glanced back up toward the guest bedroom. "Paisley's hiding upstairs. She's scared."

"Poor thing." Lily followed my gaze. "Did she say anything interesting?"

"Maybe. I'm not sure yet."

At four-thirty, Piper emerged from the kitchen with Eva and Ella. The girls spotted me immediately and came running over.

"Alexis!" Ella threw her arms around my waist. "You came!"

"Of course I came. Wouldn't miss your grandma's big day."

Ella looked up at me with those perceptive six-year-old eyes. "You have sparkles around you. So does Miss Lily."

"Ella," Piper said gently. "Let's not bother them with that."

"It's not bothering," Ella insisted. "It's real. They have magic sparkles. Good ones."

Eva rolled her eyes affectionately. "She's been saying that all week."

"Your imagination is wonderful, honey," Piper said.

But Ella crossed her arms, frustrated. "It's not imagination. I can see things others can't."

I caught Lily's eye. We'd need to address this soon. Help Ella understand what she was sensing before she said too much to the wrong person.

"I believe you," I told Ella quietly, crouching down to her level. "Some people can see things others can't. That's special."

Her face lit up with relief and vindication.

Lily smiled warmly at Ella, but when the girl turned to watch the cats again, Lily leaned close to me and whispered, "Dangerous to acknowledge. But necessary." She approved, even as she warned.

I nodded. We'd need to be careful. But Ella deserved to know she wasn't alone.

The party continued through the afternoon, tour groups rotating through the upstairs every thirty minutes. By five o'clock, the snow outside had picked up, creating a beautiful backdrop through the windows. Inside, the warmth and celebration continued. Servers began setting up the dining tables for dinner service. Everything was flowing according to Flo's careful plan.

At five-twenty, Flo stood near the fireplace and clinked a glass to get everyone's attention.

"Thank you all for coming," she called out, her voice strong and clear. "In just a few minutes, we'll begin dinner service. But first, I'd like to gather everyone here for a special presentation."

The crowd quieted, pressing closer.

"For five generations, the women of my family have worn a very special necklace. A family heirloom passed from mother to daughter, representing our family's history in Larkspur Valley. Today, it's my honor to present this necklace to my daughter, Piper."

Applause rippled through the room. Piper stepped forward, her face flushed with emotion. Eva and Ella stood close by, watching with pride.

"Let me just run upstairs and get it from my display case," Flo said, already moving toward the stairs. "I'll be right back."

She hurried up the stairs, her heels clicking on the hardwood.

The crowd waited, murmuring softly. Anticipation hung in the air.

While we waited, I noticed Warren Jacobs standing near the staircase, his gaze fixed on the second floor. His expression was hard to read. Intent, maybe. Or calculating. When he noticed me watching, his face went carefully blank and he turned away, moving toward the windows.

Something about that moment nagged at me, but I couldn't pinpoint why.

One minute passed.

Then two.

Then three.

Piper glanced toward the stairs, a small frown creasing her forehead. "She's taking a while."

"Maybe she can't find it in the box," Henry joked, trying to lighten the mood. Flo's son stood beside his sister, his hands in his pockets. He was younger than Piper, maybe mid-twenties, and unmarried. Lee, Piper's husband, put a reassuring hand on her shoulder.

But something in my chest tightened. That feeling that had been building all day suddenly crystallized into certainty.

Something was wrong.

I moved toward the stairs. Lily followed without question.

We'd just reached the bottom when Flo's voice rang out from above. Not loud, but everyone heard it. The panic in it carried.

"It's gone."

People rushed up the stairs, crowding into the hallway and bedroom doorway. I pushed through until I could see.

Flo stood by her dresser, the antique display case open in front of her. Her hands were shaking. Her face had gone pale.

"The necklace," she whispered, looking around wildly. "It's gone."

Piper pushed into the room. "Mom, what? No. It has to be there."

Flo touched the empty space in the velvet lining where the necklace should have been. Other pieces of jewelry sat undisturbed. Only the locket was missing.

"It was right here," Flo said, her voice breaking. "I checked it this morning before the party. It was right here."

"Someone took it," Lily said quietly, speaking the truth everyone was thinking.

The room erupted in confusion. People talking over each other, asking questions, making theories. But all I could focus on was Flo's devastated expression.

Five generations. A family legacy. A symbol of everything the Hendrys had built in Larkspur Valley.

Gone.

Stolen from her own home during her own party.

And somewhere in this crowd of guests, someone had it.

Chapter Four

The room erupted into chaos.

Everyone tried to talk at once. Questions, theories, accusations flew through the air like sparks from a fire. Flo stood frozen by the display case, her hand hovering over the empty space where the necklace should have been.

"Everyone, quiet!" Sheriff Iris Scott's voice cut through the noise like a blade.

The room fell silent immediately. Iris had that effect on people. She stood just inside the doorway, her gray eyes sharp and assessing, taking in the scene with the kind of practiced efficiency that came from years of law enforcement.

"This is now a crime scene," she said. Her voice was calm but firm. "No one leaves until I've talked to each of you. Understood?"

Murmurs of agreement rippled through the crowd.

"Good. Everyone back downstairs. Now. Flo, Piper, Alexis, Lily, you stay here."

I blinked, surprised to be singled out. Lily shot me a questioning look.

The crowd began to shuffle out, voices rising again as soon as they reached the hallway. Iris waited until the last person had left before turning her attention to us.

"Before anyone asks, I want you four here because you're the ones who know this house, know Flo, and were paying attention during the party. Alexis, you helped solve the Hazel Blaine case. You notice things. Lily, you're observant too. I need fresh eyes on this, people who care about Flo and might have seen something others missed."

That made sense. It also made my stomach knot with responsibility.

"Tell me exactly what happened."

Flo's voice shook as she spoke. "I came up to get the necklace for the presentation. It was supposed to be at five-thirty. I'd checked it this morning before the party. It was right there in the display case. But when I opened it just now..." She gestured helplessly at the empty space.

"When did you last see it?" Iris pulled out a small notebook.

"During the last house tour. Maybe four-thirty? I always show it to the guests. It was right there in the case."

"And the display case was locked?"

"Yes. The key is on my keyring. I've had it with me all day." Flo pulled a small ring of keys from her pocket, holding them up with a trembling hand.

Iris examined the display case carefully, not touching anything. The glass door hung open, the lock intact. No signs of forced entry. "Someone used a key. Or picked the lock."

"Who would do this?" Piper's voice was thick with tears. She stood beside her mother, one arm around Flo's shoulders. "Who would steal from us like this?"

"That's what I'm going to find out." Iris's expression softened slightly. "I know this is difficult, but I need you all to think carefully. Who went upstairs today?"

"Everyone," I said quietly. All eyes turned to me. "Flo gave four house tours. Eight to ten people on each tour. Plus people using the bathrooms upstairs. There were dozens of people who had access to this room."

Iris's jaw tightened. "That's going to make this harder. But not impossible." She turned back to Flo. "I'm going to need a list of everyone who was at the party."

"Of course. Whatever you need."

"Good. Now, all of you, go downstairs. I need to examine this room before anyone else disturbs it."

We filed out, leaving Iris to her work. The hallway felt colder than it had before, or maybe that was just the weight of what had happened settling over everything.

Downstairs, the party atmosphere had completely evaporated. Guests stood in small clusters, talking in hushed voices. Some looked genuinely concerned. Others looked... uncomfortable. Guilty, even.

Or maybe I was just seeing suspicion everywhere I looked now.

"I can't believe this," Piper said, sinking into one of the dining room chairs. "Mom worked so hard on this party. Everything was supposed to be perfect. And now..."

Ella appeared at her mother's side, her young face worried. "Grandma Flo's okay, right?"

"She's okay, sweetie." Piper pulled her daughter close. "Just sad. Someone took something very important to our family."

Ella looked at me, her dark eyes wide and knowing. I saw the question there, the same one she'd silently asked me earlier when she'd seen the sparkles around Lily and me.

You can help, can't you?

I gave her the smallest nod. Her shoulders relaxed a fraction.

Lily appeared at my elbow. "She's counting on you," she murmured, so quietly only I could hear. "They all are."

"I know." The weight of it pressed down on my chest. Flo had been one of the first people in Larkspur Valley to make me feel welcome. She'd adopted Paisley from the café, supported my business, invited me into her home. And someone had violated that home, that trust, right under all our noses.

Including mine.

Iris came downstairs twenty minutes later, her expression grim. She positioned herself near the front door and raised her voice. "All right, everyone. I'm going to need statements from each of you before you leave. This will take some time, so please be patient."

A collective groan went through the crowd, but no one protested. This was a small town. People might complain, but they'd cooperate. That was the way things worked here.

"I'll start with those who went on the house tours," Iris continued. "If you went upstairs at any point during the party, I need to talk to you first. Everyone else can wait in the living room or dining room, but don't leave the house."

The crowd began to reorganize itself. People who'd been on the tours moved toward Iris. Others settled into chairs or stood in corners, arms crossed, faces drawn with a mixture of curiosity and impatience.

I spotted the four men I'd noticed earlier. The ones who'd stood out for different reasons.

Warren Jacobs stood near the fireplace, his arms crossed, his expression closed off. He looked angry, but then, he'd looked angry since he'd arrived. Something about the set of his shoulders, the tightness around his mouth.

Zeke Hargraves, the stocky man with the construction worker build, leaned against the wall near the dining room entrance. He kept glancing toward the front door, like he wanted nothing more than to leave.

Grayson St. Martin hovered near Flo, speaking to her in low, urgent tones. Even from across the room, I could see the intensity in his expression. He gestured with those elegant jeweler's hands, his whole body radiating nervous energy.

And Theo Vincent paced near the windows, his wife trying and failing to get him to sit down. He looked like a caged animal, all wound-up tension and barely controlled rage.

Four men. All roughly the same age, all roughly the same height. All had been on the house tours.

All had opportunity.

"What are you thinking?" Lily's voice pulled me back to the present.

"That we need to pay attention," I said quietly. "Watch who gets nervous. Who can't maintain eye contact. Who seems too eager to leave or too insistent on staying."

"The guilty flee when none pursue."

"Something like that."

Iris called the first name. "Warren Jacobs."

Warren's head snapped up. For just a second, something flickered across his face. Fear? Guilt? It was gone so fast I couldn't be sure. He straightened his shoulders and walked toward where Iris had set up at the dining room table, his movements stiff and formal.

"The rest of you, wait here," Iris instructed.

Warren's interview took about fifteen minutes. When he emerged, he looked shaken, his face pale. He didn't meet anyone's eyes as he grabbed his coat from the rack near the door. Iris had given him permission to leave, but the way he hurried out suggested he couldn't get away fast enough.

Zeke went next. His interview was shorter, maybe eight minutes. He seemed more confused than anything, kept shaking his head like he couldn't believe this had happened. When he left, he looked sad more than suspicious.

But instead of heading straight for the door, he paused near where Lily and I were standing.

"This is terrible," he said quietly, shaking his head. "Flo worked so hard on this party. And now someone's gone and ruined it for her." He glanced back toward the dining room where Iris was conducting interviews. "Sheriff asked if I'd been upstairs during the tours. Course I was. Went on the three o'clock tour. But I didn't take anything. Wouldn't do that."

"I'm sure Iris is just being thorough," Lily said gently.

"I know. Still feels bad, being questioned like that. Like suddenly everyone's suspicious of everyone." He pulled on his coat, his movements heavy. "My book project... I've been taking photos of the historic buildings all over town. The sheriff asked if I'd been taking photos here today. I hadn't, but now I'm wondering if people will think that's what I was doing. Scoping the place out."

"Anyone who knows you knows better," I said.

"Maybe." He didn't sound convinced. "Anyway. If you talk to Flo, tell her I hope they find it. That necklace means a lot to her family."

He left, and I felt a pang of sympathy. Zeke Hargraves might have grievances about his family's place in history, but his concern for Flo had seemed genuine.

"He's not our thief," Lily said once he was gone.

"You're sure?"

"Not one hundred percent. But close enough. His energy reads clear. Frustrated, yes. Angry at history, yes. But not guilty of theft."

I hoped she was right.

Grayson's took longer. Nearly twelve minutes. When he emerged, his face was flushed, his movements agitated. He grabbed his coat and left without a word to anyone.

Then Theo, whose interview ran the longest so far. Fifteen minutes that I could hear his raised voice from the other room at least twice. When he finally came out, he was even more wound up than when he'd gone in, radiating barely controlled fury.

"We're leaving," he announced to no one in particular. Then his eyes landed on me, and he stalked over.

Oh no.

"You," he said, pointing at me. "You talked to me earlier. In the sunroom. You listened."

His wife hurried after him. "Theo, please—"

"I need to say this." He looked at me intently, his voice low and urgent. "That sheriff in there? She thinks I took it. I can tell. She kept asking about my 'feelings toward the Hendry family' and my 'history of confrontation with Flo.' Like I'm some kind of unhinged lunatic who'd steal from her."

"Did you?" The question came out before I could stop it.

"No." The word was sharp, definitive. "I'm angry, yeah. I've got grievances. But I don't sneak around stealing family heirlooms. If I wanted to make a point, I'd do it publicly, not by sneaking around like a coward." He ran his hand through his hair, the anger draining to leave only exhaustion. "I've been researching the business partnership. Going through documents. Building my case. Stealing jewelry doesn't prove anything about what happened between our fathers."

"Then you have nothing to worry about," Lily said calmly.

"Don't I?" His laugh was bitter. "You didn't see how that sheriff looked at me. I'm suspect number one because I made a scene earlier. Because I've got the most obvious motive." He looked at me again. "For what it's worth, I hope they find it. Flo's a Hendry, and I've got issues with that name, but she's also a person. And this party meant something to her."

His wife tugged his arm gently. "Come on, honey. Let's go home." This time he let her lead him away. I watched them go, my mind spinning.

"What do you think?" I asked Lily quietly.

"I think he's telling the truth. His anger is real, but so is his integrity. He wouldn't steal. Too straightforward." She frowned. "But Iris doesn't know that. And right now, he looks very guilty."

"So, we need to prove he didn't do it."

"If he didn't do it," Lily corrected. "Don't get too attached to anyone's innocence yet."

She was right. But I couldn't shake the feeling that Theo Vincent, for all his rage and pain, wasn't our thief.

The interviews continued. Most were quick, efficient. Iris would ask what they'd seen, where they'd been at specific times, whether they'd noticed anything unusual. Some took five minutes, others ten, depending on whether they'd been on the house tours or had relevant information. No one took longer than fifteen minutes.

Iris was thorough but not wasteful. She knew how to get information quickly, how to read people, when to push and when to let them go.

Lionel approached me while I waited. He'd been on the four o'clock tour, and Iris had already spoken with him and let him go, but he'd stayed, helping Flo's family clean up, being useful in that quiet, steady way of his.

"Hey." His voice was soft, concerned. "You doing okay?"

"I'm fine. Just... it's a lot."

"Yeah." He glanced toward where Flo sat with her family, her face drawn and pale. "This is awful. I can't imagine how she's feeling right now."

"Devastated." The word felt inadequate, but it was the only one that fit.

"You'll help figure out what happened, won't you?" His green eyes searched my face. "I know you're good at... noticing things."

I opened my mouth to deflect, but he held up a hand.

"You don't have to say anything. I just wanted you to know that if you need anything, information, someone to talk to, whatever, I'm here. Okay?"

"Thank you, Lionel. That means a lot."

He smiled, that warm, genuine expression that made something flutter in my chest. "Let me know when you're ready to head out. I can walk you home. Roads are getting slippery."

Before I could respond, Lily appeared at my elbow, and the moment shifted.

More people filed out as Iris completed their interviews. The crowd thinned steadily until only a handful remained. Those who hadn't been on the tours were questioned more briefly. What had they seen? Heard? Noticed anything unusual?

No one had noticed anything. Or if they had, they weren't saying.

By seven-thirty, only Flo's immediate family, Lily, and I remained. And Dr. Colton Dover, who'd been one of the last to be interviewed because he'd arrived late and hadn't been on any tours.

"You're free to go," Iris told us. "Except you, Flo. I need to go over some things with you about the timeline and the guest list."

Flo nodded wearily. "Of course. Whatever you need."

Piper stood. "Mom, I'll stay with you."

"No, sweetheart. Take the girls home. It's been a long day and they have school tomorrow." Flo's voice was firm despite her obvious exhaustion. "Henry will stay with me, right, Henry?"

Henry, Piper's brother, nodded immediately. "Of course, Mom. Go, sis. Get the girls to bed."

Reluctantly, Piper gathered her daughters. "Call me when you're done. I don't care how late it is."

"I will."

They left, Ella casting one last worried glance over her shoulder at me. I gave her what I hoped was a reassuring nod.

Lily and I pulled on our coats, preparing to head out into the cold. The snow had picked up while we'd been inside. Through the windows, I could see fat flakes swirling in the glow of the streetlights.

"Let me walk you home," Colton said, materializing at my elbow. "It's dark and the roads are getting slippery."

"That's really not necessary—" I started to say, but Lily cut me off.

"That would be lovely, Dr. Dover. Thank you."

I shot her a look, but she just smiled innocently.

Across the room, I caught Lionel's expression shift. Just for a moment, something flickered across his face. Disappointment? Frustration? He'd offered to walk me home too, but Colton had beaten him to it. Our eyes met, and I saw the question there.

I gave him a small, apologetic smile. *I'm sorry.*

He nodded, just slightly, understanding. Then he turned and reached for his own coat, pulling it on with movements that were just a fraction too sharp, too controlled.

"Please, call me Colton. We're not at the clinic." Colton held the door open for us, seemingly unaware of the small tension that had just played out. "After you. Both of you."

We stepped out into the cold November night.

The snow crunched under our feet as we made our way down Flo's front path. The party, which had started with such promise just hours ago, now felt like something from a different lifetime. The elegant decorations visible through the windows seemed garish now, out of place.

"I can't believe someone actually stole it," Colton said as we reached the sidewalk. "Right during the party. That takes some serious nerve."

"Or desperation," Lily murmured.

"Either way, it's bold." He glanced at me. "Iris mentioned you were the one who solved Hazel Blaine's murder last month. That you notice things other people miss."

Oh no. Here we go.

"I just asked some questions," I said carefully. "Got lucky."

"I don't think it was luck." His voice was thoughtful. "I think you're observant. Perceptive. And I think you care about people here, even though you try to keep your distance."

I didn't know how to respond to that, so I said nothing.

We walked in companionable silence for a block. The snow continued to fall, soft and steady, muffling the sounds of the town. Larkspur Valley looked peaceful under its white blanket, like nothing bad could ever happen here.

But something bad had happened. And it was up to us to fix it.

"This is me," Lily announced as we reached her apartment building. She turned to Colton with a smile. "Thank you for the escort, Dr. Dover. Very gentlemanly of you."

"My pleasure." He returned her smile. "Get some rest."

"Oh, I will." She looked at me, something knowing in her expression. "See you tomorrow morning, Alexis. Bright and early."

"Six o'clock," I confirmed.

"Can't wait." She squeezed my hand briefly, then disappeared into her building, leaving Colton and me alone on the snowy sidewalk.

The silence felt different now. Heavier somehow.

"Shall we?" Colton gestured down the street toward my café.

We walked the remaining two blocks without speaking. I was acutely aware of his presence beside me, the comfortable way he matched his pace to mine, how he stayed on the street side of the sidewalk like it was the most natural thing in the world.

"I meant what I said earlier," Colton said quietly as we neared my building. "At the party. About wanting to take you to dinner."

"Colton—"

"I know the timing is terrible. And I'm not trying to pressure you. But I also don't want to pretend I'm not interested. Because I am. Very interested. And I think you might be too, even if you're not ready to admit it."

He was right. That was the problem. There was something about him that drew me in, something solid and steady that made me feel safer than I had in years. But safety was an illusion. And getting close to people, letting them in, that only led to pain.

"I don't know what I am," I said honestly. "My life is... it's complicated. And I can't give you what you want."

"What do I want?"

"Something real. Something without secrets. Someone who can be fully present in a relationship." I met his eyes. "And I can't be that person."

He studied me for a long moment, snow catching in his dark hair. "Because of your past?"

I'd told him, weeks ago during Hazel's investigation, that I'd left Chicago because of an abusive situation. It wasn't the whole truth, but it was close enough to make him understand why I kept my distance from people.

"Because of a lot of things."

"Fair enough." He didn't push, which I appreciated. "But for the record, everyone has secrets. Everyone has complications. That doesn't make you undateable. It just makes you human."

We'd reached The Cozy Purrch. The café windows were dark, but I could see the glow of lights from my apartment windows on the second floor. We stopped at the bottom of the outside stairs. I had two ways into my apartment, through the café or up these stairs, and tonight I was grateful for the private entrance.

"Thank you for walking us home," I said. "You didn't have to do that."

"I wanted to." He was standing close, close enough that I could see the snowflakes caught in his dark hair, the warmth in his eyes. "Be careful, Alexis. Whoever took that necklace, they were bold enough to do it with dozens of people around. That means they're confident. Maybe overconfident. And confidence can make people dangerous when they feel threatened."

"I'll be careful."

He leaned in, slowly, giving me time to pull away. His eyes asked the question his lips hadn't.

I should let him. I should let myself have this one moment of normal, of connection, of possibility.

But I couldn't.

I stepped back, just before his lips could reach mine. "I'm sorry. I'm not ready."

He stopped immediately, straightening. If he was disappointed, he didn't show it. Instead, he just nodded, understanding. "That's okay. I appreciate your honesty."

"I just... I can't. Not yet. Maybe not ever."

"But maybe someday?" There was hope in his voice, gentle and patient.

"Maybe." It was all I could offer.

He smiled, and it reached his eyes. "Then I'll be here when you are. No pressure. No expectations. Just... here."

"Thank you." My voice came out smaller than I intended.

"Goodnight, Alexis."

"Goodnight, Colton."

I watched him walk away, his figure growing smaller as the snow swirled around him. When he turned the corner and disappeared from view, I finally climbed the outside stairs to my apartment, my hands trembling as I unlocked the door.

Inside, my apartment felt warm and safe. The cats greeted me immediately, twining around my legs, demanding attention and explanations. I shed my coat and kicked off my boots, letting the familiar comfort of home settle over me.

But my mind kept replaying the evening. The theft. The violated trust. The worry on Flo's face. The tears in Ella's eyes.

And Colton, standing in the snow, offering me something I wasn't sure I deserved or could accept.

Connection. Community. Belonging.

I'd spent years running from those things, convinced they'd only lead to pain. But maybe Lily was right. Maybe living in fear of the past wasn't worth giving up the possibility of having a future.

Maybe.

But first, we had a thief to catch.

51

Chapter Five

Monday morning arrived too early.

I'd barely slept. Every time I closed my eyes, I saw Flo's devastated face. The empty display case. Five generations of history, gone.

When my alarm went off at five-thirty, I was already awake, staring at the ceiling while Poppy purred on the pillow beside me.

"You're doing the worry thing again," she observed.

"I know."

"The friend-person will be here soon. You can worry together."

She had a point.

I dragged myself out of bed and into the shower, letting the hot water wash away some of the exhaustion. By the time I'd dressed and started the kettle heating, it was five-fifty.

The knock came exactly at six o'clock.

Lily stood outside my apartment door, bundled in a heavy coat and scarf, her cheeks pink from the cold. Snow still covered the ground from last night, making Larkspur Valley look like a winter postcard.

"Morning," she said, stepping inside and immediately shedding her coat. "Please tell me you have coffee."

"Just started." I gestured to the kitchen where the kettle was heating. "And I'm making eggs."

"Bless you." She collapsed onto one of my dining chairs. "I did not sleep well."

"Me neither." I cracked eggs into a bowl, whisked them with milk. "Kept thinking about yesterday. About Flo's face when she realized the necklace was gone."

"And about Colton?"

I shot her a look over my shoulder. "How did you know?"

"Please. You have that conflicted expression you get whenever you're thinking about him. Or Lionel. Or any form of human connection that might require emotional vulnerability."

"Told you!" Poppy called from her perch by the window.

"I don't have an expression."

"You absolutely do." She accepted the mug of coffee I handed her, wrapping both hands around it. "For what it's worth, I think you handled it well last night. Being honest. Telling him you're not ready."

"I hurt him."

"Maybe a little. But you didn't lead him on. That's worse." She sipped her coffee. "And who knows? Maybe someday you will be ready."

"Maybe." I poured the eggs into my skillet, added cheese. "But right now, we have bigger problems."

"The theft."

"The theft."

My other four cats appeared one by one, drawn by the sounds and smells of breakfast. Gus positioned himself near the table, hoping for scraps. Rocky wound between my legs, nearly tripping me. Millie watched from her safe spot near the fern in the living room. And Poppy remained on her perch by the window, observing everything with those knowing amber eyes.

"Good morning, Rocky," Lily said, reaching down to scratch his orange head. "Still causing trouble, I see?"

"I cause adventure, not trouble," Rocky announced proudly. "Me and Sage."

"Speaking of Sage," I said, glancing toward the living room where a tiny gray and white blur was currently attacking one of Millie's toys, "she's getting as chaotic as you are."

"That's what I've been teaching her," Rocky said, puffing up with pride. "She's an excellent student."

"The little one has energy," Gus observed dryly. "Too much energy. At ten weeks old, she should still be sleeping most of the day. Instead, she's racing around like a tiny tornado."

"Hey! I was teaching her important skills," Rocky protested.

"You were teaching her how to knock things off tables," Millie said from her safe spot.

"Exactly. Important skills."

I smiled despite my exhaustion, setting plates on the table. Lily and I ate in comfortable silence for a few minutes, the familiar sounds of the cats moving around us, the warmth of coffee and food helping to chase away the worst of last night's sleeplessness.

"We need to get Paisley near each of the suspects," I said finally, mopping up egg yolk with my toast. "She said she'd recognize the smell. Old paper and tobacco."

"Cigarette tobacco, specifically." Lily nodded. "That's distinctive. Not many people smoke anymore. And old paper suggests books or documents."

"Warren was at the library yesterday morning. According to what customers were saying at the party."

"Researching town history." Lily's expression turned thoughtful. "What was he looking for?"

"That's one of many questions we need answered." I pulled out my phone, opened my notes app. "Let's make a list. Everything we know, everything we need to know."

We spent the next thirty minutes building profiles of our four suspects, writing down every detail we could remember from the party. Their behavior, their comments, what Lily had read in their auras.

Warren Jacobs: Resentful, bitter, emphasized "who built this town," family history of being overlooked.

Zeke Hargraves: Sad more than angry, financial troubles, construction work slow, commented about contributions being forgotten.

Grayson St. Martin: Obsessed with the necklace, wanted to photograph it, family designed it originally, nervous energy.

Theo Vincent: Most overtly suspicious, confronted Flo about their fathers, rage and grief in his aura, couldn't control his anger.

"Any one of them could have done it," Lily said, studying the list. "They all had motive. They all had opportunity."

"But only one actually took it." I checked the time. Seven-fifteen. "We should head downstairs. Get the café ready to open."

We cleared our plates and moved downstairs together, Poppy following at our heels. The café felt cold and dark after the warmth of my apartment, but I quickly turned on lights and adjusted the thermostat. The stone fireplace on the far wall caught my eye, and I flipped the switch to start the gas flames. Immediately, the space felt more welcoming, the firelight casting a warm glow that contrasted beautifully with the icy cold and snow visible through the windows.

The six adoption cats stirred in the viewing room as we entered, stretching and yawning and demanding attention. Butterscotch, the long-haired orange cat, wound between my legs. Obsidian, the sleek black cat with copper eyes, blinked at us from his bed. Marmalade stretched lazily on her perch. And Cleo, a young black cat with luminous green eyes, watched us from the window seat with alert curiosity. She'd only been with us for about two weeks, found wandering near the highway. Young, maybe eight or nine months old, and far more social than her shy start had suggested.

"Hello, new human," Cleo said to me, padding over to investigate Lily with interest. "She smells like you. Are you sisters?"

"Not by blood," I said softly. "But yes."

Cleo approached Lily carefully, sniffing her outstretched hand, then bumped her head against Lily's fingers and started purring.

"She likes you," I told Lily.

"I can feel it." Lily smiled, scratching behind Cleo's ears. "She's curious but friendly. Very trusting for a cat who was found as a stray."

"That's Cleo for you. Decided within a day that everyone here was safe and she'd never leave."

"Smart cat," Lily murmured, and Cleo purred louder in agreement."

Good morning, everyone," I said to the rest of the cats, moving to refresh their food and water. "Ready for a busy day?"

"There's an interesting smell in here," Obsidian said, his voice thoughtful. "Like worry and determination all mixed together."

"That's just us," I said. "We're worried and determined."

"Humans," Butterscotch sighed. "Always making things complicated."

We moved through the opening routine in practiced tandem. Lily wiped down tables and arranged chairs while I prepped the espresso machine and checked tea supplies. She organized the milk and syrups while I counted the register.

At seven-forty-five, right on schedule, there was a knock at the back door.

Flo stood there, looking exhausted and sad, holding two boxes of pastries from her diner.

"Morning, Alexis." Her voice was hoarse. "I brought your usual order."

"Flo." I opened the door wider, letting her in. "You didn't have to. Not after yesterday. You should be resting."

"I needed to keep moving. Keep doing normal things." She set the boxes on the counter. "If I stay home, all I do is think about the necklace. About who took it. About how I failed my family."

"You didn't fail anyone," Lily said gently, coming over to take the boxes. "Someone stole from you. That's not your fault."

Flo's eyes were red-rimmed, like she'd been crying all night. "I just keep replaying it in my head. The party. All those people in my home. Someone I welcomed, someone I probably smiled at and offered food to, was planning to steal from me the entire time."

I poured her a coffee without asking, added cream and sugar the way she liked it. "We're going to figure out who did this."

"But what if you don't?" Her voice cracked. "What if it's gone forever?"

"Then we'll deal with that when it happens," I said firmly. "But right now, we're going to do everything we can to find it."

She accepted the coffee gratefully, her hands shaking slightly as she wrapped them around the warm cup. "Thank you. Both of you. For caring. For trying."

"Of course we're trying," Lily said. "You've been nothing but kind to us since I arrived. To Alexis since she opened this café. We're not going to let someone get away with hurting you."

Flo stayed for a few more minutes, sipping her coffee and trying to compose herself. Then she left, heading back to her diner for the breakfast rush, her shoulders still slumped with grief.

"She looks terrible," Lily said quietly, watching through the window as Flo walked away through the snow.

"She barely slept. I can tell." I started arranging the pastries in the display case. Muffins, scones, danishes, all fresh from Flo's diner. She'd been bringing them since nearly day one, when I'd first opened The Cozy Purrch. A way to help a new business owner, she'd said. A way to support someone trying to make a life here.

And now someone had stolen from her.

"We have to find that necklace," Lily said.

"We will."

At exactly eight o'clock, I flipped the sign to "Open" and unlocked the front door.

The first customers trickled in right away. Mabel Smalls, punctual as always despite it being Monday instead of her usual Tuesday.

"Chamomile today instead of Lavender Dreams," she announced, settling at her usual table. "Mixing things up. Different drink, different day. Otherwise, life gets stale."

"Good philosophy," I said, preparing her tea.

Then Felix Wren, looking more awake than usual, requesting his Ginger Spark. Then Cordelia Kelder from the yarn shop, her flamboyant scarf trailing behind her as she approached the counter.

And every single one of them wanted to talk about the theft.

"Can you believe it?" Cordelia said, leaning against the counter while I prepared her chai latte. "Right during the party. Someone actually stole it right under everyone's noses."

"It's terrible," I agreed carefully.

"Who would do such a thing? To Flo, of all people. She's been nothing but kind to everyone in this town." Cordelia's bracelets jangled as she gestured emphatically. "It wasn't just theft. It was betrayal. Someone she welcomed into her home."

The conversations continued as more people arrived. Pearl Van came in with two of her book club friends, all of them cooing over the adoption cats in the viewing room before ordering coffee. Jasper Sharpe stopped by on his way to open the general store, his usual gruff demeanor softened by genuine concern for Flo. Maeve arrived shortly after, claiming her favorite corner seat and ordering chamomile tea, but even she looked troubled, her usual serene expression clouded with worry.

Everyone had theories. Everyone had suspicions. Some thought it was an outsider, someone passing through who'd heard about the party. Others were convinced it had to be someone local, someone who knew the house and the necklace's value.

Nobody wanted to believe it was one of their own.

But it was. Lily and I both knew it. We'd seen the four suspects. We'd felt the tension, the resentment, the old grudges bubbling just beneath Larkspur Valley's peaceful surface.

At eight-fifteen exactly, the door chimed and Sheriff Iris Scott walked in.

She looked tired. Dark circles under her gray eyes, hair pulled back in a severe bun, uniform crisp but her expression worn. She'd probably been up most of the night processing the crime scene and interviewing witnesses.

"Morning, Iris," I said, already reaching for the largest to-go cup. "Black coffee?"

"Please." She approached the counter, nodding at Lily. "How are you two holding up?"

"We're okay," I said, pouring her coffee. "Didn't sleep much, but okay."

"None of us did." She accepted the cup, wrapped her hands around it like she needed the warmth. "I've been up since four going through statements."

"Find anything useful?"

"Some things. Nothing definitive." She took a long sip, closed her eyes briefly. "But I'm working on it."

The café was busy, people everywhere, conversations flowing around us. Iris glanced around, then leaned in slightly, lowering her voice.

"I need you to be careful, Alexis. Whoever took that necklace was bold. Confident. They planned this, waited for the perfect moment, and executed it flawlessly. That kind of calculation can be dangerous."

"I'll be careful."

"But also observant." Her gray eyes met mine, sharp and knowing. "Though I know I don't have to tell you that last part."

Something in my chest tightened. She was giving me permission. Maybe even asking me to help, in her own indirect way.

"I notice things," I said carefully.

"You do." She straightened, took another sip of coffee. "And if you notice anything relevant, you know where to find me."

"I do."

She nodded, satisfied, and headed for the door. But she paused before leaving, turning back. "And Alexis? Don't do anything reckless. Notice things, tell me what you notice, but don't put yourself in danger. Understood?"

"Understood."

"Good." She pushed through the door and disappeared into the cold morning, taking her coffee with her.

Lily appeared at my elbow. "That was interesting."

"She basically just deputized me."

"Unofficially, of course."

"Of course." I started making the next order, a cappuccino for one of the regulars. "But she knows I'm going to investigate. She's just making sure I don't get myself killed in the process."

"Very considerate of her."

The morning rush continued for another hour. Coffee after coffee, pastry after pastry, conversation after conversation about the theft. I listened to all of it, picking up fragments of information, building a picture of how the town was processing what had happened.

Most people were sympathetic to Flo. She was well-liked, respected, part of the town's foundation. But there were undercurrents too. Whispers about how much money she'd spent on the party. Comments about showing off. Suggestions that maybe she'd made someone jealous or resentful.

Human nature at its finest.

At nine-thirty, the door chimed again and Flo walked back in.

She still looked terrible. Pale, drawn, eyes red from crying. But she carried another box, this one smaller.

"I forgot the cinnamon rolls," she said, her voice hoarse. "Left them cooling at the diner. Thought you might want them for the lunch crowd."

"Flo, you didn't have to come back." I came around the counter. "You should be resting."

"I can't rest. I can't sit still." She set the box down. "Every time I close my eyes, I see that empty display case. I see my family's necklace, gone. Five generations, and I'm the one who lost it."

Lily pulled Flo into a gentle hug. "You didn't lose it. Someone stole it. That's not your fault."

Flo pulled back, wiping at her eyes with a tissue. "It was supposed to go to my older sister, you know." Her voice was barely above a whisper. "When my great-grandmother passed it to my grandmother, and my grandmother passed it to my mother, there was always this understanding. First daughter gets the necklace. But my sister..." Her voice caught. "She left when I was fifteen. Just... disappeared one day. No explanation. No goodbye. I was supposed to be the second daughter, the spare. But I became the one who got everything by default."

She looked down at her hands, twisting the tissue between her fingers. "I wonder what she'd think. Knowing I lost it. Knowing I failed to keep it safe even though I wasn't the one who was supposed to have it in the first place."

"You didn't fail," I said gently. "Someone stole from you. That's not the same thing."

"Isn't it?" Flo's voice trembled.

Lily reached out and squeezed her hand. "You've carried this necklace for how many years? Honored your family's legacy. Kept the tradition alive. One terrible person taking advantage of your hospitality doesn't erase any of that."

Flo nodded, but I could see she didn't quite believe it. The weight of her absent sister, the weight of being the "wrong" daughter to receive the heirloom, the weight of now losing it - it was all pressing down on her.

I didn't push for more. The pain in her voice when she'd mentioned her sister was too raw, too private. Whatever had happened all those years ago, it still hurt.

"Who could have done this?" Flo finally asked, looking up at us. "Who would steal from me like that?"

"That's what we're trying to figure out," I said quietly.

She looked at me, hope flickering in her tired eyes. "You're going to investigate? Like you did with Hazel's murder?"

"If you want us to."

"Please." Her voice broke. "Please, Alexis. I know it's a lot to ask. I know you have your café to run and your own life to live. But I don't know what else to do. The sheriff is working on it, but... but you notice things she doesn't. You see things differently."

The weight of her expectations settled on my shoulders, heavy and inevitable.

"We'll find it," I promised, hoping I could keep that promise. "Lily and I. We'll figure out who took it."

"Thank you." Flo squeezed my hand. "Thank you so much."

After she left, heading back to her diner for the rest of the morning rush, Lily and I stood behind the counter, watching through the window as she walked away through the snow.

"So," Lily said, leaning against the counter. "How do we test the suspects with Paisley?"

"We need to get them here. Separately. Without making it obvious what we're doing."

"And we need Flo to bring Paisley." Lily frowned. "But how do we arrange that without tipping her off? We can't just ask her to bring her cat every time we have someone over. She'll get suspicious."

I wiped down the espresso machine, thinking. "She visits here sometimes with Paisley. Usually on weekday afternoons when it's quiet. Paisley likes to socialize with the adoption cats."

"So if we invite the suspects during those times..." Lily trailed off. "But we can't control when Flo decides to visit. And what if she doesn't come on the right days?"

"Exactly. And even if we try to arrange it, what if the suspects can't come to the café? What if their schedules don't align with when Flo happens to stop by?"

She was right. This was getting complicated fast.

"We need to be flexible," I said slowly. "Have a main plan, but be ready to pivot if it doesn't work."

"And if that doesn't work?"

"Then we go to Plan B." I set down my rag. "And if that doesn't work, Plan C."

"Which means we'll have to improvise." Lily leaned back against the counter. "Take whatever opportunities present themselves."

"Pretty much." I took a deep breath. "We can't control everything. We'll just have to adapt as we go."

"Better than nothing." She pulled out her phone. "So what's our starting point? How do we get them here in the first place?"

I thought for a moment. "What if I'm gathering information for the café? Doing a local history display or something? I could invite each of them to talk about their family's contributions to Larkspur Valley's founding."

Lily's eyes brightened. "That's brilliant. We play to their egos. Their family pride. Warren especially will jump at the chance to talk about how the Jacobs family has been overlooked."

"Same with Zeke. And Grayson will want to talk about the St. Martin craftsmanship. Theo will see it as another opportunity to air his grievances."

"They'll come," Lily agreed. "The question is: when? And can we get Flo here at the same time?"

"We'll have to see how it plays out. Maybe I mention to Flo I'm worried about Paisley's socialization? Ask if she can bring her by to interact with the adoption cats?" I shrugged. "If the timing works out, great. If not, we figure out another way."

"Improvise."

"Improvise." I nodded. "We can't plan for every possibility. We'll just have to be ready to take whatever chances we get."

It wasn't a perfect plan. It wasn't even close to certain. But it was realistic.

"I'll call the suspects this afternoon," I said. "See who's available to come to the café this week."

"And I'll talk to Flo. Casually. See if I can encourage her to bring Paisley by without making it seem like a big deal."

"Without telling her what we're really doing."

"Without telling her," Lily agreed. "The fewer people who know, the better."

We spent the next hour planning out the details. What questions to ask each suspect, how to keep them talking, backup ideas if our café meetings didn't work out. By the time we were done, we had a starting strategy and a willingness to adapt.

It wasn't foolproof. It wasn't even close to certain. But it was something.

The lunch rush started around noon, pulling us back into café mode. More customers, more conversations, more theories about the theft. I served coffee and pastries and smiled and nodded and listened.

And the whole time, I was planning.

This week, we'd try to test our suspects. Some at the café, some elsewhere, some through sheer luck if the opportunity presented itself.

We'd take whatever chances we could get.

We'd adapt as we went.

And hopefully, by the end of it, we'd know which one of those four men had stolen Flo's necklace.

But first, we had to get through today.

One coffee at a time.

One customer at a time.

One piece of information at a time.

Until we had enough to solve this mystery.

At six o'clock, I flipped the sign to closed and locked the front door. The café emptied quickly, regulars bundling up against the November cold and heading home. Lily wiped down tables while I cleaned the espresso machine, both of us falling into our comfortable rhythm.

"Long day," Lily said, hanging up her towel.

"Very long day." I glanced at the clock. "Want to grab dinner upstairs? I think I have leftover soup from—"

A knock at the front door made us both turn. Through the glass, I could see Maeve standing on the sidewalk, her silver hair catching the streetlight, a knowing smile on her face.

"Maeve?" I unlocked the door, surprised. "Is everything okay?"

"Everything's fine." She stepped inside, brushing snow from her coat. "Though I'm interrupting your evening, I know. I was closing up the bookshop and realized this conversation has been overdue since the day Lily arrived." Her gaze moved to Lily with warm recognition. "May I steal a few minutes of your time? Both of you?"

Lily and I exchanged glances.

"Of course," I said, relocking the door behind her. "Let's sit."

Maeve pulled out a chair at one of the tables, and we joined her. She looked at Lily directly, that gentle knowing smile still on her face.

"I know what you are, dear. I've known since the moment you stepped into Larkspur Valley."

Lily's expression remained carefully neutral, but I could see the tension in her shoulders. "Alexis mentioned you're a Seer. That you know about her."

"I am, and I do." Maeve folded her hands on the table. "And now I know about you too. Two witches in one small town. That's not coincidence. That's family finding each other again."

"Family," Lily repeated softly, and I could hear the weight of meaning in that word.

"The kind that matters," Maeve said. "Not the kind you're born into or bound to by obligation, but the kind you choose. The kind that supports rather than controls." She paused, letting that sink in. "That's what I wanted to talk about. You two are stronger together than apart. You know that already, I'm sure. But what you might not realize is that you're not the only magical beings in Larkspur Valley."

I leaned forward. "You mentioned Atticus Law before. The ranger who can talk to animals."

"Yes. And there are one or two others, keeping their gifts quiet." Maeve's expression grew more thoughtful. "Not many, but enough to form a community. A network."

"A coven," Lily said carefully.

"Not a formal coven. Nothing with hierarchy or binding oaths or the kind of structure that can turn dark." Maeve's voice was firm. "Just an understanding. A mutual agreement to support each other, protect each other, and keep our gifts hidden from those who wouldn't understand."

"An informal coven," Lily said, and I could hear the relief in her voice. "Based on trust and choice rather than obligation."

"Precisely." Maeve smiled. "I've been waiting for the right time to approach you both together. To extend the invitation, so to speak. After what happened at Flo's party, after seeing you two begin to investigate using methods that might attract... attention... I realized the time was now."

"Attention from whom?" I asked, though I suspected I knew the answer.

"From anyone paying attention to magical signatures. From organizations that track unusual phenomena." She paused. "From whatever it is you both ran from. Covens have ways of finding their lost members, if they're determined enough."

Lily and I exchanged glances. The fear we'd been carrying, named aloud.

"We're careful," Lily said quietly.

"I know you are. But being careful alone is one thing. Being careful with support is another." Maeve reached across the table, covering both our hands with hers. "What I'm offering is simple: you're not alone. If you need help with investigations, with magic, with protection, you have people here who will stand with you. No strings. No obligations. Just... community."

The word settled into my chest, warm and unfamiliar. Community. Not the toxic kind I'd fled from, but something gentler. Chosen.

"What would that look like?" I asked. "Practically?"

"Sharing knowledge. Teaching each other. Meeting occasionally to discuss concerns or share information about magical activity in the area." Maeve pulled her hands back. "And perhaps, when the time is right, bringing in others who might need guidance. Young Ella, for instance. Her gifts are growing, and her parents don't understand. Eventually, she'll need people who can teach her. Help her."

My chest tightened. "We've been talking about that. About how to approach it."

"It's important," Maeve said, her voice taking on a weight that made me pay attention. "More important than you might realize. A young person with magical gifts, dismissed by those around her, told her experiences aren't real..." She shook her head. "That's how lost souls are created. That's how they go searching for acceptance, for community, for someone who will tell them they're not crazy. They don't understand what they're searching for until it's too late."

Like I did. The thought hit me hard, a punch to the sternum. I'd been eighteen, desperate, isolated, convinced there was something wrong with me because I could hear animals think. And then the coven had found me. Had told me I was special. Had made me feel like I belonged. By the time I understood what they really were, what they wanted from me, I was already in too deep.

"Lost souls turn to dark covens," Maeve continued quietly. "And dark covens turn them to dark magic. It's a cycle that's repeated throughout history. Young witches, desperate for understanding, falling into the wrong hands."

"We won't let that happen to Ella," Lily said firmly, and I could hear the echo of her own experience in those words. We'd both been lost souls once. Both been caught by the same darkness.

"I know you won't." Maeve's expression softened. "That's why I'm bringing this up now. You two understand what she's going through in a way her parents never could. You can guide her, teach her, help her understand her gifts without frightening her or her family. It's a delicate balance, but it's crucial."

"We'll find a way," I said, and meant it. Ella deserved better than what Lily and I had gotten. She deserved to grow up knowing her gifts were real, were manageable, were nothing to fear. She deserved guidance from people who would protect her, not use her.

"I know you will," Maeve said. "But that's a conversation for another day. First, you two need to decide if you want to be part of this network."

I looked at Lily. She looked back at me. We'd been alone for so long. Isolated by choice and by fear. The idea of letting others in, even others like us, felt risky.

But it also felt right.

"Yes," I said. "We're in."

"Absolutely," Lily agreed.

Maeve's smile widened. "Good. Then welcome, officially, to Larkspur Valley's magical community. Small as it is." She stood, pulling a card from her pocket and setting it on the table. "My number. If you need anything, call. Day or night."

"Thank you," Lily said, picking up the card. "This means more than you know."

"I think I have some idea." She pulled her coat back on, preparing to head out into the cold. "And be careful with your investigation. Using Paisley to track scents is clever, but make sure no one sees the pattern."

"How did you—" I started.

"I'm a Seer, dear. I see things." She winked. "Good luck finding that necklace. Flo deserves to have it returned."

After she left, Lily and I sat in silence for a long moment, the café quiet around us except for the soft sounds of the cats settling in for the night.

"We have allies now," Lily finally said, wonder in her voice.

"We do." I ran my thumb over Maeve's card, feeling the embossed lettering. "A network. Protection. People who understand."

"Not a coven like before."

"No. Something better. Something we choose."

Lily smiled, and it reached her eyes. "I like the sound of that."

"Me too." I stood, pocketing the card. "Come on. Let's have that soup. And maybe start planning how we're going to test our suspects."

"With our new safety net," Lily added.

"With our new safety net," I agreed.

And for the first time since arriving in Larkspur Valley, the weight on my shoulders felt just a little bit lighter.

Chapter Six

Tuesday morning arrived with the kind of gray November sky that made the café's warm lights feel especially welcoming. I unlocked the door at six and started the espresso machine, going through the familiar motions of opening.

Lily arrived a few minutes later, right on schedule. We'd fallen into a comfortable routine over the past week, meeting early to have breakfast together before the café opened.

"Ready for this?" she asked, tying on her apron.

"As ready as I'll ever be." I started grinding coffee beans. "First day of actual investigation."

"Think any of them will show up today?"

"I don't know. I was planning to call them this afternoon, see if I could get them to come in under the pretense of the historical display." I pulled out mugs and began arranging them. "Though I'm not sure how convincing I'll sound."

Poppy stretched on her window perch, yawning wide enough to show all her teeth. "Big day ahead."

"Just a normal Tuesday," I told her, trying to sound more confident than I felt.

"Normal Tuesdays don't involve investigating theft suspects," Gus grumbled from his favorite chair. The tuxedo cat had claimed the armchair closest to the fireplace as his personal throne.

Rocky bounded over, orange tail high, with Sage tumbling after him. The gray and white kitten had grown considerably in the past few weeks, all long legs and boundless energy. At ten weeks old, she was healthy, bouncy, and completely devoted to following Rocky everywhere.

"This is exciting!" Rocky announced. "Are we catching a bad guy today?"

"Catching! Catching!" Sage chirped, pouncing on Rocky's swishing tail.

"We're gathering information," I corrected. "That's all."

"Information gathering sounds boring." Rocky batted at the hem of my jeans while Sage attempted to climb up his back. "I want action."

"There will be no action," I said firmly, gently detaching Sage from Rocky's fur. The kitten immediately tried to climb my leg instead.

"Nothing. Just enjoying watching you have a full conversation with yourself from my perspective."

I felt heat creep up my neck. "Right. Sorry."

"Don't apologize. It's kind of adorable." She pulled out coffee beans and started grinding them. "Though I do wonder what they're saying."

"Rocky wants action. Gus thinks this is all unnecessary. Poppy's being cryptic."

"So normal cat behavior, basically."

"Exactly."

The door chimed at seven thirty. Flo Hendry swept in, carrying a large white box from her diner. Despite everything that had happened Sunday, she looked composed in a navy cardigan and pearls, though her smile didn't quite reach her eyes.

"Morning, girls." She set the box on the counter. "Brought maple scones today. Piper made them this morning. She said baking helps her think."

"How is everyone?" I asked, accepting the box carefully. "Sunday was..."

"Awful." Flo's smile finally faded. "Just awful. The girls cried themselves to sleep Sunday night, and yesterday wasn't much better. Henry's been on the phone with the insurance company since Monday morning. And Piper..." She shook her head. "Well, she's heartbroken. That necklace meant everything to her."

Her voice caught slightly. "It meant everything to me too. It was supposed to be my sister's, you know. But she left, and I became the keeper of it by default. And now..." She pressed her lips together. "Now I've lost what she should have had."

"Flo," I said gently. "You've honored that necklace for years. You kept it safe, cherished it, protected it. What happened isn't your fault."

Flo nodded, but I could see she didn't quite believe it. The weight of her absent sister, combined with the theft, was crushing her.

"Anyway," Flo said, straightening her shoulders with visible effort. "Piper said baking helps her think. Maybe it'll help me stop thinking."

"We're so sorry," I said softly.

"Sheriff Iris is doing everything she can." Flo straightened her shoulders again, composing herself. "She took statements from everyone at the party Sunday. Said she'd be following up this week." Her eyes met mine. "Any progress on your end?"

"We're still piecing things together," I said carefully.

She nodded, understanding. "Iris mentioned you two were very observant. Asked good questions." A pause. "Keep asking them."

"We will."

"Well, I should get back. The morning rush waits for no one." She was already moving toward the door. "Let me know if you need anything. Anything at all."

After she left, Lily pulled out two scones and handed me one. "No pressure or anything."

"None at all," I agreed dryly.

"Is there a difference?" Lily took a bite of scone and closed her eyes. "Oh, that's good. Piper might be heartbroken, but her baking hasn't suffered."

The morning rush started around eight, a steady stream of regulars picking up coffee on their way to work. Felix Wren ordered his usual Ginger Spark and spent ten minutes speculating about the theft before hurrying off to his studio. Cordelia Kelder came in with even more dramatic flair than usual, her purple shawl billowing behind her.

"The whole town is talking about it," she announced, not bothering to lower her voice. "Poor Flo! To have something so precious stolen right from under her nose. And during such a lovely party, too."

"It's terrible," I agreed, making her chai latte exactly how she liked it.

"Mark my words, it's someone with a grudge." Cordelia leaned across the counter conspiratorially. "The Hendry family has done very well for themselves over the years. Not everyone is happy about that."

"You think it was personal?"

"What else could it be? That necklace would be nearly impossible to sell. Too distinctive, too well-known in these parts." She accepted her drink with a theatrical sigh. "No, whoever took it wanted to hurt Flo. That's what makes it so cruel."

After she left, Lily raised an eyebrow. "She's not wrong."

"No," I admitted. "She's not."

The morning continued with more of the same. Everyone had theories. Some thought it was an outsider, someone who'd crashed the party. Others, like Cordelia, believed it was personal. A few even suggested the necklace hadn't been stolen at all, that perhaps Flo had misplaced it and was too embarrassed to admit it.

I didn't believe that for a second. I'd seen Flo's face when she realized it was gone. That wasn't embarrassment. That was heartbreak.

Around ten thirty, the door chimed again.

Warren Jacobs walked in.

I recognized him from the party, though we hadn't spoken. Mid-fifties, about five foot five, with thinning brown hair and wire-rimmed glasses. He wore a button-down shirt tucked neatly into pressed khakis, and he carried a leather laptop bag over one shoulder.

"Good morning," I said, putting on my professional smile. "Welcome to The Cozy Purrch."

He nodded stiffly. "The wait at Mountain Brew is sometimes too much, and I've heard good things about your place."

Mountain Brew was the larger coffee shop on Main Street, always packed with tourists. We got the locals who preferred a quieter atmosphere.

"Well, we're happy to have you. What can I get for you?"

"Black coffee. Large." He pulled out his wallet. "Nothing fancy."

"Coming right up."

While I poured his coffee, I watched him from the corner of my eye. He moved with precision, every gesture controlled and deliberate. When I handed him the cup, he accepted it with a brief nod and carried it to the table by the window, setting up his laptop with the same careful attention.

The smell hit me then. Just a whiff as he'd leaned forward to pay. Cigarette tobacco.

My heart jumped.

I turned away quickly, busying myself with wiping down the espresso machine. Beside me, Lily was organizing pastries in the display case, but her posture had changed subtly. She'd noticed something too.

Warren settled into his work, fingers flying over the keyboard. Whatever he was doing, he was focused. Intense. Every few minutes he'd pause to sip his coffee, but his eyes never left the screen.

"He smells like the necklace thief," Poppy observed quietly from her perch. She'd moved closer to Warren's table, her amber eyes fixed on him with unnerving focus.

I didn't respond. Couldn't respond. Not with him right there.

Millie crept out from the adoption room, her Siamese blue eyes wide. "That man feels angry."

Sage tumbled out behind her, then froze when she saw Warren, her kitten instincts telling her something wasn't quite right about him. She scampered back to Rocky, pressing against his orange fur.

"Of course, he feels angry," Gus muttered. "Everyone's angry about something these days."

The café stayed quiet for the next twenty minutes. A few customers came and went, but Warren remained absorbed in his work. I made drinks, served scones, and tried not to stare at him too obviously.

Then his phone rang.

Warren glanced at the screen, his jaw tightening. For a moment I thought he might decline the call, but instead he answered, his voice clipped.

"This isn't a good time."

I couldn't hear the other side of the conversation, but whatever the person said made Warren's expression darken.

"I told you, I'm working on it." His voice rose slightly. "These things take time."

More silence. His free hand curled into a fist on the table.

"You don't understand the situation." The words came out harsh, sharp enough that the elderly couple in the corner glanced over. "The Hendry family has controlled this town's narrative for generations. They've written the Jacobs family right out of history. My grandfather was Simon Hendry's equal partner, and what did he get? Nothing. Less than nothing. Erasure."

My pulse quickened. This was about the founding families. About the old resentments Iris had mentioned.

"I don't care what the historical society says." Warren was fully angry now, his voice carrying across the small café. "They're wrong. I have proof. My grandfather's journals, property deeds, contracts. It's all there in black and white. The Jacobs family built this town just as much as the Hendrys did, and it's time people knew the truth."

The person on the other end must have argued, because Warren's face flushed.

"No, you listen to me." He stood abruptly, the chair scraping against the floor. "I am not letting this go. Not now. Not ever. Our family deserves recognition. Our name deserves to be remembered. And if the historical society won't acknowledge that, then I'll find another way."

He ended the call and stood there for a moment, chest heaving, clearly trying to regain his composure. The café had gone completely silent. Everyone was staring.

Warren seemed to realize it all at once. His face went from red to pale, and he quickly closed his laptop, shoving it into his bag with unsteady hands.

"Sorry," he muttered, though he didn't meet anyone's eyes. "Family business."

He left without finishing his coffee, the door chiming behind him with jarring cheerfulness.

For a long moment, nobody moved.

Then the elderly woman at the corner table leaned toward her husband. "My goodness. That poor man seems quite upset."

"The Jacobs family has always been bitter about the founding families recognition," her husband replied quietly. "My father used to say Warren's grandfather was a difficult man too. Always claiming he deserved more credit than he got."

They paid and left, the café settling into a quiet lull. I started wiping down tables while Lily restocked the pastry display. She'd gone very still, her aura-reading abilities clearly picking up something from the residual emotions Warren had left behind.

"So," Lily said quietly. "That was interesting."

"That was damning." I kept my voice low. "He's obsessed with the Hendry family. With recognition. With proving his family's worth."

"Strong motive for stealing Flo's necklace." Lily glanced toward the window where Warren had sat. "What better way to strike back at the Hendrys than to take their most precious family heirloom?"

"And he smells like cigarette tobacco."

"Part of what Paisley identified." Lily pulled out her phone, typing notes. "She said old paper and tobacco. I wonder if she'd smell the old paper on him too, or if that only comes through when he's around his documents and research."

"Either way, we need confirmation. One conversation and a partial scent match isn't proof."

"No, but it's a start." I thought about Warren's face, the raw fury in his voice. "He said he'd find another way if the historical society wouldn't listen. What if stealing the necklace was that other way?"

"Revenge? Leverage?" Lily looked up from her phone. "Either way, it's motive."

The door chimed. A young couple came in, looking for morning coffee. I smiled and took their order, the conversation with Lily paused but not forgotten.

Poppy jumped down from her perch and wound between my legs. "That man is dangerous."

I bent down to scratch behind her ears, keeping my voice too low for anyone outside to hear. "How dangerous?"

"The kind that believes they're right. The kind that can't see reason anymore." She butted her head against my hand. "Be careful with him."

"We will," I promised.

Lily was watching me again. "What did Poppy say?"

"That he's dangerous. That he believes he's completely justified."

Lily tucked her phone away. "We need to tell Iris about the phone call."

"Agreed. But we still need to get Paisley close to him. To confirm the scent match."

"So much for a controlled first meeting," Lily said quietly.

"I was going to call him this afternoon. Try to set up something here where we could manage the conversation." I shook my head. "He came in before I had the chance."

"And now he's gone before we could get Paisley anywhere near him." Lily's frustration matched mine. "Missed opportunity."

"Then we go to Plan B."

"Which is?"

Lily smiled, but there was no humor in it. "We get creative."

The rest of the morning passed normally, though I couldn't stop thinking about Warren. About the fury in his voice, the obsession with his family's legacy. It fit too well. Too perfectly.

Around noon, Sheriff Iris Scott walked in.

She ordered her usual black coffee and waited until the café was empty before leaning against the counter.

"Warren Jacobs was here this morning," she said without preamble.

I shouldn't have been surprised. This was a small town. News traveled fast.

"He was," I admitted.

"And?"

"He took a phone call. Got very angry. Said some things about the Hendry family and the founding families recognition. About how the Jacobs family deserves more credit than they've gotten."

Iris's expression didn't change, but I could see the wheels turning behind her eyes. "What exactly did he say?"

I repeated the conversation as accurately as I could remember, watching Iris process each word.

"Interesting," she said finally. "Very interesting."

"Is it enough to..."

"To what? Arrest him?" Iris took a sip of her coffee. "The Jacobs family has been angry since the beginning of time about not being credited as the founding family the way the Hendrys have been. Warren's grandfather was obsessed with it. Warren's father was obsessed with it. Now Warren's carrying the torch. Getting angry about historical recognition isn't a crime. Being bitter about your family's legacy isn't evidence of theft."

"But combined with everything else..."

"It's suspicious. I'll give you that." Iris set down her cup. "I'll be watching him more closely. But Alexis, you need to be careful. Just keep your eyes and ears open. Like you are. But don't go looking for trouble."

"I won't."

"Good." She picked up her coffee to leave, then paused. "And if you do happen to notice anything unusual, you'll let me know."

It wasn't quite permission. But it wasn't a warning to stay out of it either.

After she left, Lily finished making a cappuccino for a customer before coming over.

I looked toward the window where Warren had sat, remembering the controlled fury in his movements, the bitterness in his voice. But also remembering something else. The way his hand had trembled when he'd answered that phone call. The exhaustion in his eyes when he'd talked about his family never getting recognition.

"You're thinking," Lily observed.

"I'm wondering if anger and guilt are the same thing."

"What do you mean?"

"Warren is furious about his family being erased from history. But what if that fury comes from pain, not malice? What if he's just a man who's tired of fighting a losing battle?" I wiped down the counter, thinking. "That doesn't make him innocent. But it makes him human."

"Human people can still steal necklaces," Lily pointed out.

"I know. But we can't let ourselves decide he's guilty just because he's angry. We need actual proof."

Lily nodded slowly. "You're right. We need to test him properly. No jumping to conclusions."

"Next, we figure out how to get him and Paisley in the same room. Because if he is the thief, we need proof."

"And if he's not?"

"Then we move on to the next suspect." I thought about our list from yesterday's planning session. Four names. Four people with means, motive, and opportunity. "But my gut says we're looking in the right direction."

Poppy jumped up onto the counter, which she knew she wasn't supposed to do. "Your gut is usually right."

"Usually isn't always," I told her.

"No," Poppy agreed. "But it's a start."

The afternoon brought more customers, more conversations, more theories about the theft. Around three o'clock, I spotted Zeke Hargraves walking past the café window, his flannel jacket collar turned up against the cold. He glanced in, caught my eye, and gave a small wave before continuing down the street.

"That's one of our suspects," Lily murmured, watching him go.

"Zeke. He was at the party, on the house tours. Founding family like Warren, but different energy."

"Less angry?"

"More sad. Resigned." I thought about his conversation at the party, about his architecture book. "He's writing a book documenting his family's contributions. Trying to preserve the history even if no one officially recognizes it."

"That's actually kind of noble," Lily said.

"Or obsessive." I pulled out my phone. "Either way, we need to test him too. I should call him this week, see if he'll come to the café to talk about his book."

"Add it to the list," Lily agreed.

But my mind kept circling back to Warren Jacobs. To the smell of tobacco I'd caught on him. To whether Paisley would detect old paper too. To the rage barely contained beneath his precise, controlled exterior.

If he'd stolen the necklace, what would he do with it? Would he sell it? Destroy it? Keep it as some kind of twisted trophy?

And more importantly, what would he do if he realized we were investigating him?

By the time we closed at six, I was exhausted from thinking in circles.

Sage was racing around the café in her evening burst of kitten energy, chasing invisible prey and occasionally launching herself at Rocky's tail. The orange tabby tolerated her attacks with patient affection.

"Go home," Lily said, shooing me toward the door while scooping up the zooming kitten. "Rest. We've done enough for one day."

"We haven't done anything."

"We've confirmed Warren is obsessed with the Hendrys. We've confirmed he smells like the thief. We've made him a primary suspect." She squeezed my shoulder. "That's not nothing."

She was right. It wasn't nothing.

But it wasn't enough.

Not yet.

I locked up the café and climbed the stairs to my apartment, my cats following behind me. Poppy led the way with her usual authority, while Sage tumbled up the steps, still learning to navigate them with her growing legs.

From my apartment window, I could see Larkspur Valley settling into evening. Warm windows glowing, smoke rising from chimneys. The mountains dark against the fading sky. You'd never know a theft had happened here. That someone had violated a family's trust, stolen their history.

But I knew.

And I was going to find out who.

Even if it meant getting close to someone dangerous. Even if it meant taking risks.

Because Flo had been kind to me from the very first day. Because this town had given me a home when I'd been running for my life. Because sometimes doing the right thing meant doing the hard thing.

And catching a thief?

That was definitely going to be hard.

But with Lily beside me, with the cats watching my back, with Sheriff Iris keeping an eye on things, I thought we might actually have a chance.

Tomorrow, we'd figure out how to test the other suspects. Tomorrow, we'd start building our case.

Tonight, I fed my cats and tried to quiet my racing mind. Tried not to think about Warren Jacobs's angry eyes and controlled fury.

Tried being the operative word.

Because something told me this investigation was only just beginning.

And the hard part was still ahead.

Chapter Seven

Wednesday morning brought a steady rain that turned Larkspur Valley's streets into a patchwork of puddles and mist. The kind of weather that made people seek out warm cafés and hot drinks.

I was restocking the pastry display when my phone buzzed. A text from Flo.

Girls want to visit the cats this afternoon. Mind if we bring Paisley? She could use some socialization.

I stared at the message, my heart picking up speed. This was exactly what we needed. A natural reason for Paisley to be here. No forced arrangement, no suspicious timing. Just Flo bringing her granddaughters and her cat to visit the café.

Of course! We'd love to see all of you. What time works?

After 3, once the girls are out of school.

Perfect. See you then.

I showed Lily the exchange.

"That was lucky," she said, though her expression suggested she knew as well as I did that sometimes the universe provided exactly what you needed at exactly the right moment. Magic had a way of smoothing paths when you were doing the right thing.

"Now we just need one of the suspects to show up while she's here," I said quietly.

"You could call them. Use that historical display excuse."

I pulled out the list we'd made yesterday. Warren had already come and gone. That left Zeke Hargraves, Grayson St. Martin, and Theo Vincent.

Theo seemed like the best option. He was the most suspicious, the most aggressive. If we could rule him out quickly, we could focus our attention on the others.

I dialed his number before I could second-guess myself.

He answered on the third ring. "Vincent speaking."

"Mr. Vincent, this is Alexis Belrose from The Cozy Purrch Café. We met at Flo Hendry's party on Sunday."

A pause. "I remember."

His tone was clipped, suspicious. Exactly what I'd expected.

"I'm working on a small historical display for the café," I said, keeping my voice light and professional. "Featuring Larkspur Valley's founding families and their contributions to the town. I was hoping to speak with you about your family's role, particularly your father's business partnership with Simon Hendry."

Another pause, longer this time. I could practically hear him deciding whether this was legitimate or some kind of trap.

"What kind of display?"

"Just some photos and brief histories. Nothing too formal. I thought it would be nice for customers to learn about the town's heritage while they enjoy their coffee."

"And you want to include my father."

"Of course. The Vincent family has been an important part of Larkspur Valley for generations."

I heard him exhale, a sharp sound that could have been a laugh or a scoff.

"Fine. I can stop by this afternoon. Around three thirty?"

Perfect. Right after Flo and the girls would be here.

"That works perfectly. Thank you, Mr. Vincent."

He hung up without saying goodbye.

Lily raised her eyebrows. "Suspicious much?"

"Everything about this situation makes him suspicious," I said. "But at least he's coming."

"And if Paisley says he doesn't smell like the thief?" "Then we move on to the next suspect." I tucked my phone away. "Theo's test came back partial. Warren's was inconclusive with all those papers. We still need clean reads on Zeke and Grayson."

The morning passed quickly. The usual customers came and went. Felix Wren stopped by for his Ginger Spark and spent twenty minutes sketching the adoption cats through the viewing room window.

At two forty-five, I started preparing. Made sure the adoption room was tidy, the cats all looking their best. Rocky and Sage were racing around, burning off their afternoon energy, while Gus supervised from his chair with typical grumpy authority. Poppy sat on her window perch, watching everything with those knowing amber eyes.

"Flo's coming soon," I told them. "With Paisley. And we're going to test one of the suspects."

"The angry man?" Millie asked from her hiding spot behind the counter.

"Yes. Theo Vincent."

"I don't like angry men," Millie said softly.

"Neither do I," I assured her. "But we need to know if he's the thief."

The door chimed at a few minutes past three.

Flo walked in with Eva and Ella on either side of her, and Paisley in a carrier. The Ragdoll cat meowed indignantly at being confined, her blue eyes peering out through the mesh door.

"Sorry about the carrier," Flo said. "She's been a bit anxious lately. Thought it would be safer for the walk over."

"No problem at all." I came around the counter to greet them. "Hi, girls."

Eva waved shyly, but Ella's attention was already fixed on the viewing room where the adoption cats lounged.

"Can we go see them?" Ella asked.

"Of course." I gestured toward the open doorway. "They'd love the company."

The girls rushed in with the kind of enthusiasm only children could muster, dropping to the floor to greet the cats. Flo set Paisley's carrier down and opened the door. The Ragdoll stepped out cautiously, whiskers twitching as she surveyed her surroundings.

"Thank you for letting us visit," Flo said. "The girls have been asking to come back all week."

"They're welcome anytime." I watched Paisley pad toward the viewing room, her fluffy tail held high. "How are you holding up?"

Flo's smile faltered. "As well as can be expected. Sheriff Iris has been wonderful, but..." She shook her head. "I just want my necklace back. I keep thinking about Piper, about how much that ceremony meant to her."

"I know," Lily said gently, setting a cup of chamomile tea in front of Flo without being asked. "We're all hoping for good news soon."

Flo wrapped her hands around the cup. "The insurance will eventually pay out, but it's not about the money. It's about the history. The connection to my family." Her voice caught. "My sister should have..." She stopped, pressing her lips together. "You can't replace history."

I didn't push. The pain in that unfinished sentence was too raw.

I glanced toward the viewing room. Ella was sitting cross-legged on the floor, surrounded by cats. Butterscotch was purring in her lap, while Marmalade rubbed against her shoulder. But it was a young black cat, sleek and graceful, who had Ella's complete attention.

The cat sat directly in front of her, staring up with luminous green eyes.

"That's Cleo," I said. "She came in about two weeks ago. Found wandering near the highway. She's young, maybe eight or nine months old. Very sweet."

"She's beautiful," Eva said, reaching out to pet her.

But Cleo didn't move toward Eva. She stayed focused on Ella, her tail curled neatly around her paws.

"Hello," Ella whispered to her.

And then, so quietly I almost missed it, she added, "You want me to take you home?"

Flo didn't seem to notice. She was sipping her tea, watching her granddaughters with soft affection. But I noticed. And from the way Lily had gone very still behind the counter, she'd noticed too.

Paisley padded into the viewing room and immediately began her inspection. She sniffed each adoption cat carefully, methodical and thorough. She'd always been a curious cat, social and friendly. It was one of the reasons she'd been such a good fit for Flo's family.

Rocky bound over to greet her. "Paisley! You're here!"

Paisley touched noses with him. "Hello, Rocky. You've grown."

"I'm very strong now," Rocky announced proudly. "I protect everyone."

Sage tumbled over, trying to insert herself into the conversation. Paisley regarded the kitten with patient amusement before continuing her rounds.

I kept one eye on Paisley and one eye on the door. Three twenty-five. Theo would be here soon.

"Grandma?" Ella's voice was small. "Can I talk to you about something?"

"Of course, sweetheart."

Ella stood, cradling Cleo carefully. The black cat settled into her arms with complete trust, purring loud enough for me to hear from across the room.

"I think Cleo wants to come home with us."

Flo smiled gently. "She's a beautiful cat, honey. But you'd need to talk to your mom and dad about that. We already have Paisley at our house, and your parents would be the ones to decide about adding another cat to your home."

"I know. But..." Ella bit her lip. "Cleo needs me specifically. She told me."

I saw Flo's expression shift, that familiar look adults got when children said things that didn't make sense. Not quite dismissive, but not quite believing either.

"Cats can't talk, sweetheart."

"But she can. She's talking to me right now. She says she's been waiting for someone who could understand her, and that someone is me."

Flo glanced at me, a silent question in her eyes. *Is this normal behavior for a six-year-old?*

I kept my expression carefully neutral. "Some children have very strong connections with animals. It's a good sign. Shows empathy and emotional intelligence."

That wasn't technically a lie. Just not the whole truth.

"Well," Flo said carefully, "why don't we take some pictures of you with Cleo? Show your mom and dad how much you like her. Then we can talk about it as a family."

Ella nodded, though disappointment flickered across her face. She set Cleo down gently, and the black cat immediately wound between her legs, purring.

At three twenty-eight, the door chimed.

Theo Vincent walked in.

He looked worse than he had at the party. His face was drawn, his eyes shadowed with exhaustion. He carried a battered leather briefcase and wore the same suit he'd worn to the party, though it looked more rumpled now.

"Mr. Vincent," I said, putting on my professional smile. "Thank you for coming."

He nodded stiffly, his gaze sweeping the café before landing on Flo.

His expression hardened immediately.

"Mrs. Hendry." His voice was cold. "I didn't know you'd be here."

"I'm just visiting with my granddaughters," Flo said evenly, though I could see tension in the set of her shoulders. "We'll be out of your way in a moment."

"No need to rush on my account." But his tone suggested otherwise.

I gestured to a table near the window, trying to defuse the situation. "Please, have a seat. Can I get you something to drink?"

"Black coffee. Large."

While I made his coffee, Lily moved closer to the counter, her posture alert. She could feel the tension radiating off Theo, the barely controlled anger simmering beneath his surface calm.

I brought his coffee over and sat down across from him, pulling out a notebook to make this look legitimate.

"So," I said, trying to sound casual and interested, "I'd love to hear about your father's partnership with Simon Hendry. I understand they worked together on several important projects in town."

Theo's jaw clenched. "My father and Simon Hendry were equal partners. Equal. For nearly thirty years, they built this town together. My father's construction expertise, Simon's business acumen. They were a team."

"That sounds like an important partnership," I said carefully.

"It was. Until it wasn't." Theo opened his briefcase and pulled out a thick folder. "I have documentation. Contracts. Letters. Financial records. All proving my father's contributions. But does anyone remember him? Does anyone acknowledge what he did?"

He was getting louder, his hands trembling as he flipped through the folder.

"The town square has a statue of Simon Hendry. The library has a wing named after the Hendry family. The historical society's entire founding families exhibit focuses on the Hendrys while barely mentioning anyone else." He slammed the folder down on the table. "My father deserved better."

In the viewing room, Eva and Ella had stopped playing with the cats. They were watching Theo with wide, worried eyes.

"I understand your frustration," I said, keeping my voice calm. "Family legacies are important. Your father's contributions should be recognized."

"But they won't be." Theo's voice rose. "Because the Hendrys control the narrative. They always have. My father gave everything to this town, and what did he get? Nothing. Meanwhile, the Hendrys get parties and necklaces and celebrations."

He was looking at Flo now, his expression twisted with resentment.

"My father died barely acknowledged," he continued. "While Simon Hendry got a statue. Tell me, Mrs. Hendry, how is that fair? How is it right that your family gets everything while mine gets forgotten?"

"Theo," Flo said quietly. "Your father chose to step back. My father reached out many times, tried to include him in town events, but he refused."

"Because he was hurt!" Theo stood abruptly, his chair scraping against the floor. "Because he'd been erased! And now you parade around with your precious family heirloom, celebrating your perfect legacy, while people like me are forgotten."

The café had gone completely silent. Even the cats had stopped moving.

Paisley had emerged from the viewing room now. She was walking slowly toward Theo's table, her movements deliberate.

I needed to keep him talking. Keep him distracted while Paisley got close enough.

"That must have been very painful for your family," I said.

"Painful?" Theo laughed, bitter and sharp. "It destroyed us. My mother left. My sister stopped speaking to me. All because my father couldn't let go of what the Hendrys did to him."

Paisley reached his table. She sat down beside his chair, just a few feet away, and lifted her nose.

Sniffing.

Testing.

Theo was too focused on his anger to notice.

"And now," he continued, his voice breaking, "I'm carrying this burden alone. Trying to prove what everyone already knows but won't admit. That my father mattered. That his work mattered. That the Vincent family deserves to be remembered."

"Theo," Flo said, and there was genuine sadness in her voice. "I'm sorry for what you've been through. Truly. But taking your anger out on my family won't change the past."

"Won't it?" The words hung heavy in the air.

Lily had moved closer, her hand resting on the counter in a way that suggested she was ready to intervene if necessary.

Paisley backed away from Theo slowly, returning to the viewing room with her tail low.

I caught her eye. She looked at me directly, and I heard her voice clear as day in my mind.

"He smells like old paper, but not tobacco. He is also very angry."

My heart sank. Another partial match. Warren had tobacco but we couldn't confirm old paper. Theo had old paper but no tobacco. Neither was perfect.

"Mr. Vincent," I said carefully. "I appreciate you taking the time to share your father's story. But I think perhaps we should continue this conversation another time, when emotions aren't running quite so high."

Theo seemed to realize he'd gone too far. He looked around the café, at the faces watching him with varying degrees of concern and wariness. Some of the fury drained from his expression, replaced by something that might have been embarrassment.

"Yes," he said stiffly. "Perhaps that would be best."

He gathered his folder and stuffed it back into his briefcase with shaking hands. When he stood, he swayed slightly, and I wondered if it was anger making him unsteady or something else.

"I'm sorry," he said, though it wasn't clear who he was apologizing to. "I just... my father deserved better. That's all."

He left without finishing his coffee.

The café remained silent for a long moment after the door closed behind him.

Then Flo set down her teacup with a sharp clink. "That man has been carrying that grudge for twenty years. Ever since his father passed."

"Is what he said true?" Lily asked quietly. "About the partnership?"

"Partially." Flo sighed. "My father Simon and Theodore Vincent Senior were business partners, yes. They did work together on several projects. But the Hendrys didn't erase anyone's legacy. After my father died, Theodore Senior chose to step back from public life. He became reclusive, bitter. We tried to include him in town events, to recognize his contributions, but he refused every invitation."

"And Theo inherited that bitterness," I said.

"Along with his father's debts and failed businesses," Flo added. "Theodore made some poor financial decisions toward the end of his life. Theo's been struggling ever since. I think it's easier for him to blame us than to accept that his father made mistakes."

It painted a clearer picture. A man consumed by resentment, by the belief that his family had been wronged. Desperate to reclaim what he thought had been stolen.

But Paisley said he didn't smell like tobacco. Just old paper.

A partial match. Like Warren.

Which meant we still didn't know for certain.

After Flo left with Eva and Paisley, Ella stayed behind. She stood in the viewing room, still holding Cleo, looking at me with those too-knowing eyes.

"You can hear the cats too," she said. It wasn't a question.

I glanced at Lily, who nodded slightly. This was going to happen eventually. We'd known that from the first moment we'd realized Ella had the gift.

"Yes," I said simply. "I can."

"And Miss Lily?"

"Lily has different gifts. But yes, she understands things that most people don't."

Ella absorbed this with the kind of calm acceptance that only children possessed. "I thought I was the only one. Eva can't hear them. Mom can't. Grandma can't."

"You're not the only one," I promised. "There are people like us. Not many, but we exist."

"And Cleo really is talking to me?"

"She really is."

Ella looked down at the cat in her arms. "She says she needs me. That we're supposed to be together."

"Then maybe you are," I said gently.

"But Grandma thinks I'm making it up. Making it all up in my head."

Lily crouched down next to her. "Your grandmother loves you very much. She wants to protect you. Sometimes adults don't understand things that don't fit into what they think is possible."

"Will she let me adopt Cleo?"

"I don't know," I admitted. "But maybe we can help convince her. Give it a few days. See how things go."

Ella nodded slowly, then carefully set Cleo back down. The black cat meowed in protest but didn't try to follow her.

"Can I come back?" Ella asked. "To practice? To learn?"

"Anytime you want," I promised.

After she left, chasing after her grandmother and sister, Lily and I stood in the quiet café.

"Well," Lily said finally. "That was eventful."

"Theo's smell didn't match perfectly," I said. "Old paper but no tobacco."

"Partial match, like Warren." Lily started cleaning up the cups and dishes. "Could be timing, could be they washed, or a dozen other factors."

"We should tell Iris about his outburst, though. Even if he's not the thief, that level of volatility is concerning."

"Agreed." Lily's expression was thoughtful. "Which means we need to test Zeke and Grayson next. See if either of them is a perfect match."

"And hope one of them is," I said. "Because if none of them match perfectly, we're back to square one."

The rest of the afternoon passed in the usual rhythm of the café. Customers came and went, seeking refuge from the cold rain that had returned with the evening. By five thirty, the café had emptied except for old Horace, who sat in his corner nursing his third cup of coffee and working on a crossword puzzle.

At six o'clock, I started the closing routine. Horace left with a friendly wave, and I locked the door behind him, flipping the sign to closed.

"I should head home," Lily said, untying her apron. "Early morning tomorrow."

"Be careful walking. It's gotten dark early with all these clouds."

"I'll be fine. It's only two blocks." She pulled on her coat and scarf. "See you tomorrow."

I was upstairs washing dinner dishes when my phone rang. Lily.

"Hey," I answered. "You home already?"

"Not yet. I'm standing outside the library, and something weird just happened." Her voice was low, almost a whisper.

I turned off the water. "What kind of weird?"

"Zeke Hargraves is sitting in his truck in the parking lot. The library's been closed for an hour, but he's just sitting there with the interior light on, going through papers."

My pulse quickened. "Papers?"

"Lots of them. Documents, maybe? I can't see details from here, but he's spreading them out on his dashboard, comparing them, taking notes." She paused. "He looked really intense about it. Focused."

"That's strange."

"It gets stranger. He just looked up and saw me watching him."

"And?"

"He shoved all the papers into a folder really quickly, started his truck, and drove off. Fast. Like he didn't want anyone to see what he was doing."

I leaned against the kitchen counter, thinking. "You're sure it was Zeke?"

"Positive. His truck has that construction company logo on the side. Hargraves Building and Restoration."

Through our bond, I felt Poppy's interest perk up from her spot on the couch. "What's happening?"

"Not sure yet," I told her silently.

"Should I follow him?" Lily asked.

"No. Why don't you come back here and we can talk about it. I can make us dinner."

"Okay. Be there in five."

I hung up and stood there, mind racing. Zeke Hargraves, sitting in a closed library parking lot, poring over documents he clearly didn't want anyone to see. Documents he was comparing, studying, taking notes on.

What was he looking for? Or what had he found?

"You're thinking very loudly," Gus observed from his chair by the fireplace.

"Zeke was at the library after closing. Going through papers in his truck."

"The construction man?" Rocky perked up from where he'd been napping. "Is this investigation stuff? Are we doing investigation stuff?"

"Maybe."

"Suspicious behavior," Poppy said definitively. "Hiding suggests guilt."

"Or embarrassment," I countered. "Could be innocent."

"Could be," Gus rumbled. "But probably isn't."

When Lily arrived, her cheeks flushed from the cold walk, I had soup warming on the stove and tea waiting. We settled at my small dining table, and she pulled out her phone.

"I took a photo," she admitted. "Just of his truck, from a distance. Before he saw me."

She showed me the screen. Zeke's pickup truck in the library parking lot, interior light glowing, a figure hunched over the dashboard. Grainy, distant, but clear enough.

"His aura was defensive," Lily said. "Nervous. Like he was doing something he shouldn't be."

"Or like he was afraid of being misunderstood."

"Maybe." She sipped her tea. "But Alexis, why hide research? If it's legitimate family history work, why do it in a dark parking lot after the library closes?"

"Good question."

"Should we tell Iris?"

I thought about it. A man looking at papers in his own truck wasn't a crime. Being nervous when someone watched you wasn't evidence of theft.

"Not yet," I said. "Let's see what happens when we test him. If Paisley identifies his scent, then we mention this. If not, maybe it's just awkward timing."

"Fair enough." Lily set down her empty bowl and stood. "Thanks for dinner. I should get home."

After she left, I sat with my cats, thinking about Zeke Hargraves and his mysterious late-night research session. About Theo Vincent's rage. About Warren Jacobs's cold resentment. About Grayson St. Martin, who we still needed to test.

Four men, each with their own grievances. Each with their own pain. And one of them had stolen Flo's necklace.

"He's hiding something," Poppy said with certainty.

"Everyone's hiding something," I replied. "The question is whether it's the thing we're looking for."

In the viewing room downstairs, Cleo sat by the window, her green eyes watching the empty street.

Waiting for the girl who could hear her.

Waiting to go home.

And somewhere in Larkspur Valley, a thief was waiting too. Hiding secrets in dark parking lots, carrying grudges like precious burdens, nursing old wounds that refused to heal.

The question was: which secret mattered? Which wound had driven someone to theft?

We were getting closer to the answer.

But we weren't there yet.

Chapter Eight

Thursday morning dawned clear and cold, the kind of November day that promised an early winter. I opened the café at six as usual, going through the familiar routine of starting the espresso machine and setting out the pastries Flo had dropped off the night before.

Lily arrived promptly at six fifteen, her cheeks pink from the cold.

"I think we might see more snow soon," she said, unwrapping her scarf. "The air has that feeling."

"Please, no." I handed her a steaming mug of coffee. "Sunday's snow was enough for me."

"You've been in Colorado for over a year. You'd better get ready." She took a grateful sip. "Any plans for testing the remaining suspects?"

"I was going to call Zeke and Grayson today. Try to get them to come in separately over the next few days." I pulled out my phone. "Though I'm not sure how to get Paisley here for both visits without it seeming suspicious."

"We'll figure it out." Lily started arranging the pastries in the display case. "One step at a time."

At eight, I unlocked the door and flipped the sign to "Open." The morning rush started almost immediately. The usual crowd filed in, seeking their caffeine fixes before work. Mabel Smalls arrived shortly after we opened, ordering her Lavender Dreams tea and settling into her favorite corner with a book. She gave me a knowing look as I delivered her drink.

"You're looking thoughtful this morning, dear," she said.

"Just trying to solve a mystery," I admitted.

Her eyes sharpened. "Flo's necklace?"

"Among other things."

"Hmm." She took a delicate sip of tea. "Well, if anyone can figure it out, I expect it's you. You found out who killed poor Hazel, after all."

The reminder sent a small chill through me. Hazel's murder investigation had nearly gotten me killed. I wasn't eager to repeat that experience.

"I'm just keeping my eyes open," I said carefully.

"Of course you are." Mabel's smile was enigmatic. "That's what makes you good at it."

At eight fifteen, right on schedule, Sheriff Iris Scott walked in. She ordered her usual black coffee and waited until I brought it to her before speaking.

"Any progress on your... historical display?" she asked, her tone suggesting she knew exactly what I was really doing.

"Some. I've talked to a few people. Learning a lot about the founding families."

"I bet." She took a sip of her coffee. "It's complicated history. The two founding families besides the Hendrys both feel overlooked, dismissed. And then there's Theo Vincent, carrying his father's business grudge like it's a family heirloom."

"All of them have reasons to resent the Hendrys."

"They do. And they all have motive." Iris set down her cup. "But motive isn't evidence, which is why this case is so frustrating. I know it's one of them. My gut says so. But I can't prove it."

"What about Grayson St. Martin? I haven't met him yet."

"He's been out of town since Sunday night. Left right after Flo's party." Iris's expression hardened. "Claims it's a family emergency. His sister's health took a turn."

The timing made my stomach clench. "He left Sunday night? Right after the theft?"

"Within hours." Iris tapped her pen against her notepad. "Could be coincidence. Could be he needed to get out of town with a stolen necklace."

"To sell it somewhere else?"

"Possibly. Though I haven't found any evidence he tried to sell it. No pawn shops, no jewelers, no suspicious transactions." She sighed. "But he's been gone all week. Convenient timing, if you ask me."

"When does he get back?"

"Tomorrow. And I'll be interviewing him the moment he does." Her jaw tightened. "If he stole that necklace, I'll find out."

"His family designed it, right? Disputed ownership?"

"Exactly. The St. Martins claimed it was theirs, the Hendrys won the lawsuit back in the 1800s." Iris closed her notepad. "So yes,

Grayson St. Martin is a very serious suspect. Especially with that convenient 'family emergency' right after the theft."

After Iris left, I went back behind the counter where Lily was making a cappuccino.

"Did you hear that?" Lily said quietly. "Grayson left town Sunday night. Right after the theft."

"Perfect timing to steal a necklace and leave town." I started wiping down the espresso machine. "If he did it, he's had all week to try to sell it."

"Or hide it. Or get it appraised." Lily's expression was troubled. "That's incredibly suspicious."

"It is. Though Iris said she hasn't found evidence of him trying to sell it."

"Maybe he's waiting. Or maybe he just wanted it for himself. If his family designed it, maybe he thinks it rightfully belongs to him."

"Either way, we need to test him when he gets back. See if his scent matches."

The morning continued with a steady flow of customers. At nine o'clock sharp, the door chimed.

Zeke Hargraves walked in.

I remembered him from the party. He'd introduced himself, made small talk about the café and the cats. He'd even seemed sympathetic after the necklace went missing. But the man walking toward me now looked nothing like that.

And he looked angry.

"Ms. Belrose." His voice was clipped. "I need to speak with you."

"Of course." I put on my professional smile. "What can I get for you?"

"Coffee. Black. Large." He pulled out his wallet with sharp movements. "And an explanation."

I poured his coffee, trying to read his mood. Anger, yes, but there was something else underneath it. Hurt, maybe. Or frustration.

"What is this Theo is telling me about some historical display you're doing?" he asked, his tone accusing.

My heart sank. Of course, Theo had talked to the other suspects. Of course they'd compared notes.

"I'm working on a small display for the café," I said carefully. "Featuring Larkspur Valley's founding families and their contributions to the town."

"And you asked Theo to participate."

"I did, yes."

"But not me." His jaw tightened. "Why did you ask Theo and not me? It's like the Hargraves are just forgotten as always. Third founding family, but nobody remembers. Nobody cares."

There was real pain in his voice. This wasn't just anger. This was years of feeling overlooked, dismissed.

"Mr. Hargraves, I was going to call you," I said quickly. "I've been reaching out to the founding families one at a time. Theo was first because I ran into him at the party and thought of it. You were absolutely on my list."

He studied me, trying to determine if I was telling the truth. "Really?"

"Really. In fact, since you're here now, would you be willing to tell me about your family's role in Larkspur Valley's history? I'd love to include the Hargraves family in the display."

Some of the tension eased from his shoulders. "You would?"

"Of course. The Hargraves family is an important part of this town's heritage."

He took a long sip of his coffee, considering. "Fine. What do you want to know?"

I gestured to a table. "Why don't you sit down? This might take a few minutes."

As he settled into a chair by the window, I caught Poppy's eye. She was on her perch, watching Zeke with that unnerving intensity cats sometimes had. I gave her a subtle nod.

Investigation time.

Zeke set his coffee down and leaned back in his chair. "My great-great-grandfather Josiah Hargraves came to this valley in 1872. Same time as Henry Hendry and Elias Jacobs. The three of them were the original founders."

"Three founders," I said, pulling out my phone to take notes. "I didn't realize there were three."

"Most people don't." The bitterness crept back into his voice. "Because the Hendrys took all the credit. Built that statue in the town square with just Henry Hendry's name on it. Like Josiah and Elias didn't exist."

This was familiar territory. Warren had said almost the exact same thing about his family.

"What did Josiah Hargraves contribute to the town?" I asked.

"Everything." Zeke's voice strengthened. "He was a carpenter. Built half the original structures in Larkspur Valley. The first church, the original town hall, dozens of homes. His craftsmanship is all over this town, but nobody knows it was him."

He pulled out his phone and started showing me photos. Old buildings, historic structures, detailed architectural sketches.

"I've been documenting his work," Zeke explained. "Photographing every building I can confirm he built. Sketching the ones that have been torn down from old photographs. I'm writing a book about it. About preserving his legacy."

"That's wonderful," I said, and I meant it. This wasn't the bitter resentment of Warren or Theo. This was someone trying to honor their family's contributions.

"The Hendrys took enough," he said quietly. "They got the recognition, the statue, the street names. I'm not trying to take that away from them. I just want my family to be remembered too."

Behind him, Rocky had crept closer. The orange tabby was sniffing the air near Zeke's chair, his whiskers twitching. Sage tumbled after him, trying to be stealthy but mostly just being adorable.

In the viewing room, several of the adoption cats had moved toward the doorway. Butterscotch, Obsidian, Marmalade. All of them testing the air, picking up scents.

"Your book sounds like an important project," I said, keeping Zeke's attention on me. "When do you think you'll finish it?"

"Another year, maybe. It's slow work. I'm doing it around my construction jobs, and those have been..." He trailed off, looking uncomfortable. "Well, work's been slow lately."

"I'm sorry to hear that."

"It is what it is." He took another sip of coffee. "The economy's tough right now. But I'll manage. I always do."

Gus had wandered over from his chair, moving with the deliberate slowness of an elderly cat who wanted everyone to think he wasn't interested. But I knew better. He was investigating just as thoroughly as the others.

Millie peeked out from behind the counter, her blue Siamese eyes fixed on Zeke. Even from across the café, I could sense her assessment.

Zeke showed me more photos, talking about his great-great-grandfather's work with genuine pride. This was someone who loved his family's history, who wanted to preserve it. Not someone consumed by bitterness or rage.

But that didn't mean he wasn't the thief.

After about fifteen minutes, Zeke finished his coffee and stood.

"Thank you for listening," he said, his tone considerably warmer than when he'd arrived. "And for wanting to include my family in your display."

"Of course. I'll call you when I'm ready to put it together."

"I'd appreciate that." He hesitated at the door. "And Ms. Belrose? I know people are talking about Flo's necklace. About who might have taken it. I just want you to know it wasn't me. I might be frustrated with how the Hendrys get all the attention, but I wouldn't steal from them. That's not who I am."

"I appreciate you saying that," I said carefully.

After he left, I turned to find all five of my cats had gathered near the counter. The adoption cats were still clustered by the viewing room doorway.

"Well?" I asked quietly, making sure no customers could hear. "What did you smell?"

"Leather and coffee," Poppy said immediately. "Strong scents. Old leather, like a well-worn jacket."

"No tobacco?" I asked.

"No tobacco," Rocky confirmed. "Just leather and coffee and maybe a little bit of sawdust."

"From his construction work," I murmured.

"No old paper smell either," Gus added. "Nothing musty or archival. Just working man smells."

Millie crept closer. "He felt sad. And angry, but not the dangerous kind of angry. More like... disappointed angry."

Sage tumbled over to me, all kitten energy. "He was nice! He didn't try to pet us, but he looked at us kindly."

I processed this information. Another suspect tested. Another smell that didn't match.

Warren: tobacco, no confirmed old paper. Theo: old paper, no tobacco. Zeke: leather and coffee, neither tobacco nor old paper.

We were running out of suspects, and none of them matched perfectly.

Mabel Smalls approached the counter for a refill of her tea.

"How's the historical display coming along?" she asked, her sharp eyes missing nothing.

"It's... progressing," I said carefully.

"I heard Warren Jacobs came by. And Theo Vincent." She pursed her lips. "I hope you're not giving too much weight to the gossip about Warren. Yes, he's obsessed with his family legacy, but the man has his principles."

"His principles?" Lily asked.

"Warren Jacobs is many things. Bitter, resentful, stubborn as a mule." Mabel set down her cup. "But he's honest to a fault. Won't even take a penny if someone miscounts their change. I've known him thirty years, and whatever his faults, theft isn't one of them. He's too proud for that."

After Mabel returned to her table, I caught Lily's eye.

"She makes a good point," Lily said quietly. "Warren's pride. Would someone that concerned with his family's honor actually stoop to theft?"

"Pride can be complicated. Maybe stealing the necklace is about reclaiming honor in his mind, not stealing." But doubt crept in anyway. "Or maybe we're looking at the wrong person entirely."

"Like who?"

"Zeke." I kept my voice low. "Remember what you saw last night? Him sitting in that library parking lot, going through papers after closing. Looking nervous when you spotted him."

"His architectural book research," Lily said, but she sounded uncertain.

"Or that's what he wants us to think." I wiped down the counter, thinking. "He mentioned his construction business is struggling. Money problems. And he was at the party during the theft window. What if all that talk about preserving his family's legacy is a cover? What if he's desperate enough to steal and sell the necklace?"

"But his scent didn't match."

"Neither did anyone's. Not perfectly." I shook my head, frustrated. "We're missing something. Either about the scents, or about one of these men. Someone is lying, and we need to figure out who."

The door chimed, and a customer approached the counter. Lily moved to help them while I busied myself organizing the pastry display, my mind still churning through suspects and motives and insufficient evidence.

I thought about what Millie had said. Sad and disappointed, not dangerously angry. I thought about his book project, his genuine pride in his family's contributions.

But I also thought about what he'd said about work being slow. About managing despite difficulties.

"Maybe," I said. "But that doesn't completely clear him, does it? He could have showered. Changed clothes. The smell Paisley detected was from Sunday. It's Thursday now. People wash, change, cover scents."

Lily nodded slowly. "Good point. We can't eliminate anyone just because they don't smell like the thief days later. Especially if they had reason to clean up."

"And he mentioned his construction business has been slow. Financial pressure could make someone desperate."

"Desperate enough to steal?" Lily's expression was troubled. "He seemed genuine. Like he really cares about preserving his family's legacy."

"I think he does. But that doesn't mean he's not also struggling financially. Both things can be true."

"So we still have four suspects and no definitive proof."

"We need a different approach." Lily started wiping down the espresso machine. "Or we need to catch one of them in a lie. Find some other evidence."

The door chimed. Cordelia Kelder swept in with her usual dramatic flair, purple shawl billowing.

"Alexis! Lily!" She beamed at us. "I'm so glad I caught you both. I wanted to remind you about the crochet circle tonight."

I'd completely forgotten. Thursday evenings at seven was crochet circle day at Cordelia's yarn shop.

"Seven o'clock, right?" I said.

"Seven o'clock sharp." Cordelia ordered her chai latte. "And Lily, you're coming too, yes? You mentioned last week you wanted to learn."

Lily glanced at me. We'd discussed this briefly. The crochet circle was a good way to integrate into the community, to hear the town gossip. Plus, it would give Lily more connections outside of just the café.

"I'll be there," Lily confirmed.

"Wonderful!" Cordelia collected her drink and swept out with her usual flair.

After she left, Lily raised an eyebrow. "Gossip session?"

"Probably. But that might actually be useful. The founding families, the old resentments, who has grudges. We might learn something."

"Then I'm definitely coming." Lily grinned. "Besides, I should probably learn to crochet. It looks relaxing."

"It is. When you're not dropping stitches and cursing your yarn."

"Sounds delightful."

The rest of the morning passed in a blur of customers and coffee.

"Stop thinking so hard," Poppy said from her perch. "You're doing the worry thing again."

"I can't help it. We're running out of leads."

"Then you'll find new ones." Her amber eyes were calm, confident. "You always do."

I wished I had her certainty.

Lunch rush came and went. The afternoon brought more customers, more conversations. By the time six o'clock rolled around, I was ready to close up.

Lily helped me wipe down tables and clean the espresso machine while the cats settled in for the evening.

"We have about an hour before crochet circle," she said, checking her watch.

"Just enough time to feed the cats and change." I locked the front door and flipped the sign to "Closed." "You're still up for it?"

"Definitely. If we're going to learn anything useful about the founding families, tonight's the night."

"Maybe." I looked around the café one more time. Everything was clean, organized, ready for tomorrow. "Though I'm not sure how much more investigating we can do without concrete evidence."

"We test Grayson tomorrow. See if he's a perfect match."

"And if he's not?"

Lily pulled on her coat. "Then we figure out another approach. We always do."

She sounded like Poppy.

We headed upstairs to my apartment where I quickly fed the cats and changed into something more comfortable for an evening of crocheting. Poppy supervised from the back of the couch while Rocky and Sage chased each other around the living room.

"We'll be back in a few hours," I told them.

"Be careful," Poppy said. "People talk when they're comfortable. You might hear something important."

"That's what I'm hoping for."

Lily and I walked the two blocks to Cordelia's yarn shop through the cold November evening. The streetlights cast warm pools of light on the sidewalk, and I could see my breath in the air. Winter was definitely coming.

But first, we had a crochet circle to attend.

And maybe, just maybe, we'd learn something that would help us catch a thief.

Chapter Nine

Cordelia's Yarn Haven glowed warm against the cold November night. Through the large front window, I could see the crochet circle already gathered around the center table, several women bent over their projects under the soft lamplight. The bell chimed as Lily and I stepped inside, and the smell of wool and lavender sachets wrapped around us like a hug.

"Alexis! Lily!" Cordelia swept toward us in a swirl of purple shawl and jangling necklaces. Her silver hair was piled high on her head, secured with what looked like decorative crochet hooks this time instead of knitting needles. "Right on time! Come in, come in."

"Thanks for having us," Lily said, her warm smile easy and genuine.

"My pleasure, dear. Everyone's already here except Maeve, who had book club commitments tonight." Cordelia gestured to the table where several other women were settling in with their projects. "You know most everyone, of course."

I recognized them all from previous circles and from the café. Pearl Van, mid-sixties with neat gray curls and gentle eyes, was working on what looked like a baby blanket in soft yellow. Dorothy Webb, early seventies and always impeccably dressed, had a delicate lace shawl spread across her lap. Beatrice Frost, late fifties with laugh lines and kind eyes, was crocheting a chunky scarf in deep burgundy. Mabel Smalls, seventy-something with sharp eyes and sharper opinions, was tackling an intricate doily pattern.

And there was someone new. A woman in her early sixties with shoulder-length brown hair touched with silver, working on a simple scarf in cream-colored yarn. She looked up as we approached, her expression friendly and a little nervous.

"And this is Loretta Doherty," Cordelia said warmly. "She just started working at the shop this week. Moved to Larkspur Valley from Denver with her husband last month."

"Welcome to town," I said, meaning it. I knew what it was like to be new.

"Thank you." Loretta's smile was genuine. "We were looking for a slower pace than Denver. All our children moved out, took jobs, are living their own lives. We decided it was time for a change."

"Larkspur Valley is definitely slower-paced," Lily said with a grin. "I'm new in town as well."

"Yes, she just moved here from Chicago a few weeks ago," Cordelia said cheerfully. "Chicago is so busy. This is a big change for her too."

"She and Alexis used to work together," Mabel added, her sharp eyes gleaming with that particular look she got when sharing information. Small-town gossip at its finest.

Lily and I exchanged a quick glance, amusement flickering between us. Technically true, if you counted working together in a coven as employment.

"That's right," I confirmed. "Old friends reconnecting."

"That's what we wanted." Loretta's hands moved steadily on her scarf. "Cordelia's been wonderful, teaching me the ropes at the shop. I've worked retail before, but never in a yarn store specifically."

To my surprise, I also spotted Florence, Flo for short, tucked into a chair near the window. She didn't normally attend the crochet circle, but Cordelia had clearly convinced her to come. She was working on a simple dishcloth, her hands moving automatically while her mind was clearly elsewhere.

Dark circles shadowed her eyes, and I noticed her normally perfect hair was pulled back in a simple ponytail rather than her usual elegant style.

"Flo," I said gently. "How are you holding up?"

"As well as can be expected." She managed a tired smile. "Keeping busy helps. Cordelia convinced me to come tonight instead of sitting home dwelling on everything."

"Good for Cordelia," Dorothy said briskly, not looking up from her lace. "Dwelling never solved anything. Better to keep the hands busy and let the mind work through things naturally."

"Exactly what I told her!" Cordelia bustled over with a basket of yarn. "Now, Lily, have you ever crocheted before?"

"Not really. I know the very basics from watching my grandmother years ago, but I'm definitely rusty."

"Perfect! We'll get you sorted." Cordelia pulled out several skeins of yarn in soft jewel tones. "Pick a color that speaks to you, and we'll start with a simple chain stitch. Alexis, your square is coming along nicely. Why don't you work on that while I get Lily started?"

I settled into a chair between Pearl and Beatrice, pulling out my lumpy project. It was supposed to be a simple granny square, but somehow my stitches kept getting wonky in the corners. Still, it was better than the terrible chains I'd started with a few weeks ago.

"Here, dear, sit between me and Alexis," Pearl said warmly to Lily, shifting her chair to make room. "We'll make space."

Lily chose a deep teal yarn and settled in beside me, watching intently as Cordelia demonstrated the basic chain stitch. Her fingers moved smoothly, the hook slipping through loops with practiced ease.

"Just like this, see? Hook in, yarn over, pull through. It becomes second nature after a while." Cordelia placed the hook in Lily's hand. "Now you try."

For several minutes, the only sounds were the soft clicks of hooks and the rustle of yarn. The shop's warmth seeped into my bones, and I felt some of the tension from the past few days start to ease. This was nice. Normal. Just a group of women working on their projects together.

Then Mabel broke the comfortable silence.

"Flo, dear, I still can't believe someone had the audacity to steal your necklace right out of your own house." She shook her head, her doily pattern forgotten for the moment. "In front of fifty witnesses, no less. Takes nerve, that's what it takes."

Flo's hands stilled on her dishcloth. "The sheriff says they're investigating, but I don't know what they can do without any solid evidence." Her voice dropped. "I'll likely never see that necklace again."

"Security cameras?" Pearl suggested gently.

"We don't have any inside the house. Just the doorbell camera, and that only caught people coming and going. Didn't show anyone specifically going upstairs with the necklace." Flo's voice was flat, exhausted. "They could have hidden it in a pocket, a purse, anything."

"Must have been someone on the house tours," Beatrice said, her burgundy scarf growing longer with each stitch. "That's when they would have had access to your bedroom."

"Four tours, eight to ten people each." Flo rubbed her temples. "So many people going through. I can't even remember who was on which tour anymore. It's all a blur."

I kept my eyes on my granny square, trying to appear only casually interested while my mind catalogued every word. Beside me, Lily was concentrating hard on her chain stitch, but I knew she was listening just as intently.

"Well, I have my suspicions," Mabel announced, setting down her hook with decisive finality. "Warren Jacobs, for one. That man has been bitter about the founding families for as long as I've known him."

"Mabel," Cordelia said warningly, glancing at Flo.

"It's all right," Flo said quietly, though her hands had tightened on her dishcloth. "Everyone knows Warren's resentment. It's not exactly a secret."

"His great-great-grandfather Elias Jacobs was co-founder with Henry Hendry back in 1872," Mabel continued, though her tone had softened slightly. "But somehow the Jacobs name got pushed aside in all the history books and town records. Warren's never forgiven that slight."

"Slight?" Dorothy looked up from her lace, one eyebrow raised. "Is that what we're calling it? From what I've heard, the Hendry family actively wrote Elias Jacobs out of the town's founding narrative over the years. Changed documents, altered records, made sure their own family name was the only one that mattered."

Flo shifted uncomfortably. "That was my great-grandfather Henry, not me. I can't be held responsible for what happened over a hundred years ago. I've tried to talk to Warren about adding a plaque or updating the town square memorial, but he won't even discuss it with me. He just..." She trailed off, shaking her head.

"Of course not, dear," Pearl said quickly, ever the peacemaker. "But you can understand why Warren might feel resentful. His family's contributions were essentially erased."

"Understanding resentment doesn't mean condoning theft," Beatrice pointed out. "If Warren did take the necklace, that's still wrong, no matter how justified he feels."

"Oh, I'm not saying he did it," Mabel clarified. "Just that he'd have motive. Along with that Hargraves fellow. Zeke, I think his name is? Another founding family that got overlooked."

"Zeke's different," Pearl said thoughtfully. "I've talked to him at the library. He's writing a book about the early architecture of Larkspur Valley. Documenting his great-great-grandfather's carpentry work. It's actually quite scholarly. He's not trying to tear down the Hendrys, just preserve his own family's legacy."

"Still resentment, though," Mabel insisted. "Just a different flavor of it."

"Then there's Theo Vincent," Dorothy said, setting down her lace to sip her tea. "Now that's a man with real rage. I've seen him confront Flo twice in public about his father's business partnership with Simon Hendry. Claims his father was cheated."

"He was at my party," Flo admitted quietly. "Made a scene about it, actually. In front of everyone."

"What a terrible thing to do," Pearl said sympathetically.

"His father and mine were business partners decades ago," Flo explained. "After they dissolved the partnership, Theodore Senior's businesses failed while my father's succeeded. Theo's convinced there was some kind of conspiracy, that my father somehow sabotaged his. But it's not true. My father offered Theodore help multiple times, tried to include him in new ventures, but Theodore was too proud and too bitter to accept."

"And Theo inherited that bitterness," Beatrice said.

"Along with his father's debts," Flo added. "I feel sorry for him, I really do. But I can't change the past. And I certainly can't be held responsible for business decisions that were made before I was born."

"Four founding families," I said, making it sound like I was just processing information rather than investigating. "That's a lot of history."

"Three founding families, technically," Mabel corrected. "The Hendrys, the Jacobs, and the Hargraves. The Vincents came later, but Theodore Senior's business partnership with Simon Hendry made them influential. And then there's the St. Martins."

"The jewelers," Pearl said. "Grayson St. Martin. Now there's a complicated situation."

"How so?" Lily asked, her tone casual but interested.

Pearl set down her baby blanket. "The St. Martins designed and crafted Flo's necklace back in the 1880s. But there was a dispute about payment and ownership. The Hendrys claimed they'd paid in full and the necklace was theirs. The St. Martins claimed they'd never been properly compensated and wanted it back. It went to court, and the Hendrys won."

"But the St. Martins never accepted the verdict," Dorothy added. "They've maintained for five generations that the necklace rightfully belongs to them. Grayson still believes that."

"Grayson's a gentle soul," Pearl said softly. "His sister has been sick for years. Multiple sclerosis. He's her primary caregiver when he's not working. I can't imagine him doing something like this."

"He did leave town right after the party," Mabel pointed out. "Sunday night, I heard. Family emergency with his sister."

"Which could be legitimate," Pearl said firmly. "His sister's health is fragile. Emergencies happen."

"Or convenient timing," Mabel countered.

The conversation ebbed and flowed, each woman offering her perspective. I kept my hands busy with my granny square, listening, learning, building a fuller picture of each suspect.

Warren Jacobs: bitter, obsessive, collecting documentation to prove his family's erasure from history.

Zeke Hargraves: scholarly, hurt, writing a book to preserve what the town had forgotten.

Theo Vincent: angry, desperate, carrying his father's grudge like a torch.

Grayson St. Martin: gentle, burdened, caring for his sick sister while believing his family had been cheated of their creation.

"The real question," Dorothy said, setting down her lace to accept a fresh cup of tea from Cordelia, "is whether this was planned or opportunistic. Did someone come to the party intending to steal the necklace? Or did they see an opportunity and take it?"

"Planned," Mabel said with certainty. "You don't just pocket a family heirloom on impulse. Whoever took it knew what they were doing."

"I don't know," Beatrice said thoughtfully. "Emotions run high at gatherings like that. People see things that trigger old resentments. Maybe someone saw the necklace during a house tour and acted without thinking."

"Could have been a group effort," Loretta suggested hesitantly, then looked embarrassed for speaking up. "Sorry, I don't know anyone involved. Just speculating."

"No, that's a good point," Pearl said encouragingly. "Multiple people with the same grievance might work together."

"Four people can't keep a secret," Cordelia said with certainty. "Someone would have slipped by now. No, this was one person acting alone. Someone desperate or angry enough to take the risk."

I thought about the four suspects, each with their own grievances against the Hendrys. Warren's cold resentment. Theo's hot anger. Zeke's wounded pride. And Grayson, who'd fled town within hours of the theft.

But appearances could be deceiving. I knew that better than most.

"The other question," Dorothy said, her needle never pausing in its intricate pattern, "is what the thief plans to do with the necklace. It's distinctive, a well-known piece. They can't sell it without raising suspicion."

"Maybe they just want to keep it," Pearl suggested. "As a symbol. Proof that they've reclaimed something for their family."

"Or maybe they're holding it for ransom," Mabel said dramatically. "Waiting to see if the Hendrys will pay to get it back."

"My insurance policy will pay," Flo said tiredly. "But I'd rather have the actual necklace. Six generations of Hendry women wore that." Her voice caught. "Well, five generations. My sister never... it was supposed to go to Piper. It's not about the money."

The conversation continued, speculation swirling around the table like the steam from our teacups. Names were mentioned, timelines discussed, motives debated. Lily asked occasional questions, her tone always interested but never pushy, and I noticed how smoothly she integrated into the group. By the end of the evening, the other women were treating her like she'd been coming to the circle for months instead of this being her first night.

It was a gift, that easy way she had with people. I'd always envied it, back when we were together in the coven. While I kept to the shadows, Lily moved through every social situation with grace and confidence. She made friends effortlessly. People trusted her instinctively.

And here she was, doing it again. Weaving herself into the fabric of Larkspur Valley like she belonged here. Maybe she did. Maybe we both did now.

"What do you think, Alexis?" Cordelia asked, startling me out of my thoughts.

I looked up from my granny square. "About what?"

"About who might have taken the necklace. You see so many people at your café. You must hear things."

All eyes were on me again. I chose my words carefully, aware that anything I said would be repeated and analyzed.

"I think people are complicated. Everyone has their reasons for what they do, even when those reasons don't make sense to others. Whoever took the necklace probably thought they had justification. Whether the rest of us would agree with that justification is another matter."

"Spoken like a philosopher," Dorothy said approvingly. "Or someone who's seen enough of human nature to know better than to judge too quickly."

"Or both," I said with a slight smile.

The conversation shifted after that, moving away from the theft and into more comfortable territory. Beatrice shared a recipe for apple butter. Pearl showed off photos of her new grandchildren. Dorothy complained about the town council's latest budget decisions. Mabel gossiped about tourists she'd seen behaving badly at the hardware store.

Normal conversation. Community conversation. The kind of comfortable chatter that came from years of friendship and shared history.

By nine o'clock, the evening was winding down. Projects were packed away, teacups collected, chairs pushed back from the table. Flo left first, her shoulders still slumped with exhaustion. Pearl and Dorothy followed shortly after, heading home to their respective husbands and evening routines. Beatrice and Mabel lingered to help Cordelia tidy up, and Lily and I stayed to assist as well.

"Thank you for coming," Cordelia said warmly, squeezing both our hands. "It's so lovely to have new energy in the circle. You're both welcome anytime."

"I'd like to keep coming," Lily said. "If you'll have me."

"Of course! And Alexis has been a regular for a few weeks now. You're practically fixtures already." Cordelia beamed at us. "Same time next week?"

"We'll be here," I promised.

Outside, the November air had turned even colder, and I could see my breath misting in the streetlight. Lily and I stood on the sidewalk for a moment, neither of us quite ready to part ways.

"That was enlightening," Lily finally said, her voice low.

"Very. Four suspects, four sets of grievances, and no clear favorite for the theft."

"Warren seems the most likely based on the scent test," Lily said. "The tobacco and old paper match. But Theo has the most obvious anger. Zeke has legitimate hurt. And Grayson has sympathetic motivation."

"Plus, Grayson left town right after the theft. That timing bothers me."

"Which doesn't actually eliminate any of them."

"No." I tucked my hands into my coat pockets. "But it gives us better context. Understanding why they'd steal helps us figure out who actually did."

"We still need to test Grayson tomorrow. Complete the circuit."

"And hope he's either a perfect match or completely ruled out. This ambiguous middle ground isn't helpful."

Lily glanced at the stairs leading up to her apartment above the shop. "I should head up. It's late, and we have an early morning."

"Six o'clock breakfast," I confirmed.

"I'll bring the eggs." She smiled.

"I'll have the coffee ready."

We said our goodnights and I headed down the street toward the café. The walk was short but gave me time to think about everything we'd learned tonight.

I reached the café and unlocked the door to let myself in through the darkened shop. The cats appeared immediately, materializing from their various sleeping spots to greet me.

"How was the gossip circle?" Poppy asked, rubbing against my legs.

"Informative. Everyone has theories about who took the necklace."

"Did you learn anything useful?" Gus's tone was skeptical.

"Maybe. Context, mostly. Background on why the suspects might have done it."

"Motive isn't the same as evidence," Rocky pointed out, surprisingly insightful for once.

"No, but it helps us understand the players better."

Sage, who'd been following Rocky around according to Poppy's earlier telepathic update, peeked out from behind the orange tabby. "Are you going to catch the bad person?"

"We're trying, little one. We're trying."

Upstairs in my apartment, I collapsed onto the couch with a sigh. The evening had been exhausting in its own way. All that careful conversation, making sure I was saying the right things, gathering information without revealing too much.

But it had been rewarding too. Those women were lovely. I could see why the crochet circle mattered to so many of them. It was nice. Normal.

Normal was underrated.

I thought about tomorrow. We'd test Grayson when he returned to town. And if he wasn't a match, we'd be back to Warren. And we'd have to figure out how to prove he took it.

Or we'd accept that maybe we couldn't prove it. Maybe whoever took the necklace covered their tracks too well.

But I didn't like that option. Flo deserved to get her family heirloom back. Piper deserved to receive what should have been hers. Justice mattered, even in small things like stolen necklaces.

I was exhausted, my mind spinning with names and motives and insufficient evidence. Sleep would help. Or at least make the problem less overwhelming for a few hours.

I headed to my bedroom, where Rocky and Sage had already claimed their spots on my bed. Millie appeared moments later, settling near my pillow with a soft purr. Gus took his usual spot at the foot of the bed. And Poppy curled up beside me, her presence warm and comforting.

"You'll figure it out," she said quietly. "You always do."

"I wish I had your confidence."

"You will. Once you stop doubting yourself."

I wanted to believe her. Wanted to trust that somehow, with enough investigation and careful questioning, the truth would emerge. That we'd find the thief, recover the necklace, make things right.

But life had taught me that sometimes the bad guys got away. Sometimes justice didn't prevail. Sometimes you did everything right and still lost.

I just hoped this wasn't one of those times.

Through my bedroom window, I could see Larkspur Valley settling into its evening quiet. Lights glowing in windows, smoke curling from chimneys, the mountains dark against the starlit sky. My town. My home. My community, built carefully over the past year and a half.

And somewhere out there, someone who'd betrayed that community. Someone who'd stolen from a neighbor, violated trust, and was probably sleeping soundly while Flo lay awake grieving her loss.

Tomorrow we'd test Grayson. And then we'd know.

One way or another, we'd know.

Chapter Ten

Lily arrived at six o'clock sharp, just as the coffee finished brewing. She let herself in, carrying a carton of eggs and a loaf of bread from the market.

"Morning," she said, setting everything on the kitchen counter. "Ready to debrief?"

"More than ready." I poured us both coffee while she cracked eggs into a bowl. "Last night was informative, but now I'm not sure what to make of it all."

"Four suspects, four motives, and everyone at the crochet circle had an opinion." Lily whisked the eggs with practiced efficiency. "Though I noticed Flo got quieter and quieter as the evening went on."

"She's carrying a lot of guilt for things her ancestors did." I pulled out plates and silverware. "Things she can't fix, no matter how hard she tries."

"Warren and Zeke won't even talk to her about updating the memorials. That has to hurt." Lily poured the eggs into the heated pan. "Though I can understand their perspective too. Generations of being erased from history, seeing the Hendry name everywhere while their families are forgotten."

I leaned against the counter, cradling my coffee mug. "What did you pick up from everyone's auras last night? Anything that stood out?"

"Flo's exhausted and grieving, but there's no guilt about the theft itself. Just old family shame." Lily stirred the eggs gently. "Mabel genuinely believes Warren is the thief. Pearl is more sympathetic to everyone involved. Dorothy thinks it's all rather dramatic but entertaining. Beatrice just wants everyone to get along."

"And Loretta?"

"New in town, eager to fit in, a little overwhelmed by all the history and drama. She's genuine." Lily divided the scrambled eggs between our plates. "What about you? Did you pick up anything useful?"

"Mostly confirmation of what we already suspected. Warren's obsessed with family recognition. Zeke's hurt but not dangerous. Theo's carrying his father's bitterness like a torch." I set the plates on my small kitchen table. "And Grayson has the most sympathetic reason for his obsession, but also the most suspicious timing for leaving town."

"Right after the theft." Lily sat down across from me. "Family emergency or clever escape?"

"That's what we need to find out today." I took a bite of eggs. "We need to get him near Paisley. Test his scent properly."

"How do we arrange that without being obvious?"

"I could call Flo this morning, ask her to bring Paisley by for another visit. Then call Grayson and invite him to talk about the historical display." I thought it through. "Time it so they overlap."

"That could work. Though what if he's suspicious about the timing?"

"We make it seem natural. Flo's been bringing Paisley regularly. Grayson will think it's coincidence."

Lily nodded slowly. "When do you want to do this?"

"This morning if possible. The sooner we test him, the sooner we know if we need to focus all our attention on Warren."

We finished breakfast quickly in my small apartment kitchen, discussing strategy between bites. Rocky and Sage chased each other around the living room while Poppy supervised from the back of the couch. Gus claimed his usual spot in the sunny window, and Millie hid under the coffee table, content to watch the chaos from a safe distance.

By seven-thirty, we'd washed the dishes and headed downstairs to the café, going through our opening routine. I ground coffee beans while Lily prepped the espresso machine. The cats who'd stayed downstairs overnight emerged from their various sleeping spots in the viewing room, stretching and yawning.

"Big day today," Poppy announced, hopping onto her favorite window perch. "I can feel it."

"Can you feel who the thief is?" Gus grumbled from his chair. "That would be more helpful."

"Doesn't work that way and you know it."

Rocky and Sage tumbled past, engaged in their morning wrestling match. Millie watched from behind the counter, her tail twitching with amusement.

At eight o'clock, I unlocked the front door and flipped the sign to open.

The morning customers trickled in with their usual orders. Felix Wren arrived first, ordering his Ginger Spark and settling by the window with his sketchbook. Mabel came in shortly after, getting her Lavender Dreams tea and crossword puzzle book. Pearl stopped by for a quick coffee before heading to the library.

At eight-fifteen, right on schedule, Sheriff Iris Scott walked through the door.

She looked less exhausted than she had earlier in the week, though still worn around the edges. She walked straight to the counter and waited while I poured her usual large black coffee.

"Morning, Sheriff," I said, handing her the cup.

"Morning, Alexis. Lily." She nodded to both of us.

"Any progress on the investigation?" I asked carefully.

"Some." She took a long sip of coffee. "I'm planning to talk to Grayson St. Martin this morning. He got back into town last night."

"Oh, he's back?" I kept my voice casual, though inside I was already calculating. If Iris talked to him at ten, we could try to get him to the café this afternoon.

"Finally. Been gone since Sunday night, supposedly with his sister. I need to verify that and get his statement about the party." Iris pulled out her phone, checking something. "Planning to stop by his jewelry shop around ten."

"I hope it goes well," I said, trying to sound supportive rather than investigatively interested.

"Me too." Iris glanced around the café, her sharp eyes taking in the morning crowd. "You hear anything useful lately? People talk around coffee."

"Nothing concrete. Just the same gossip about founding families and old resentments."

"That's what I'm dealing with too. Everyone has theories, no one has evidence." She finished half her coffee in one long drink. "Well, I should get going. Thanks for the coffee."

After she left, Lily moved closer to the counter. "So much for arranging a test with Paisley. If Iris is interviewing Grayson at ten, he won't be available."

"Maybe we can catch him after?" I pulled out my phone. "I'll text Flo, see if she can bring Paisley by this afternoon."

But before I could send the message, the bell chimed.

Grayson St. Martin walked in.

He looked exactly as I remembered from the party. Around five foot five, thin and elegant, with jeweler's hands and an air of refined intensity. But today he also looked exhausted. Dark circles shadowed his eyes, and his usually neat appearance seemed slightly rumpled, as if he'd been traveling and hadn't quite caught up on sleep.

"Good morning," he said, his voice softer than I expected. "You're Alexis Belrose, correct? We met briefly at Florence Hendry's party."

"Yes, Mr. St. Martin. This is my friend Lily." I tried not to look too surprised by his appearance. "Can I get you something to drink?"

"Tea, please. Earl Grey if you have it." He glanced around the café, taking in the cozy space. "I heard from Dorothy Webb that you're putting together a historical display about Larkspur Valley's founding families."

Lily and I exchanged a quick glance. News traveled fast in small towns.

"We're considering it," I said carefully, preparing his tea. "Featuring the contributions various families made to building the town."

"I'd like to be involved." He pulled a leather portfolio from under his arm. "I've been documenting my family's history. My great-great-grandfather Silas St. Martin was a master craftsman who came to Larkspur Valley in the 1870s. He created some of the most beautiful pieces this town has ever seen."

"Including the Hendry necklace," Lily said gently.

Grayson's expression tightened, but he nodded. "Yes. Including that." He set the portfolio on the counter. "I have photographs, sketches, historical documents. Stories about Silas and his work. If you're interested, I'd be happy to contribute them to your display."

I set his tea in front of him. "That's very generous."

"It would mean a lot to me." His voice cracked slightly. "To my sister. She's been working on a family history book, and she'd want the St. Martin legacy to be remembered properly."

"How is your sister?" I asked gently.

His hands trembled slightly as he wrapped them around the teacup. "Not well. I was with her all week. She's in hospice care now in Silverpine. The doctors say it's only a matter of weeks."

"I'm so sorry."

"Thank you." He took a steadying breath. "That's why this matters so much. Finishing the book, making sure people know what Silas created. It's her dying wish."

Lily reached across the counter and touched his hand briefly. I felt the subtle shift in energy as she channeled warmth and peace through that simple contact. It was one of her gifts, something she did so naturally most people never realized magic was involved. They just felt suddenly calmer, more centered, as if someone had wrapped them in a soft blanket.

Grayson's shoulders relaxed almost immediately. The tension in his face eased, and when he looked up at Lily, his eyes were clearer. Still sad, but no longer quite so raw.

"We'd be honored to include your family's history," Lily said gently.

"Thank you," he said again, but this time his voice was steadier. He took a sip of his tea, and I noticed his hands had stopped trembling.

Behind the counter, Poppy had appeared, her amber eyes fixed on Grayson. She jumped down and approached him slowly, her movements deliberate.

"You have beautiful cats," Grayson said, noticing her. He held out his hand, and Poppy sniffed it carefully.

Rocky emerged next, bounding over with his usual enthusiasm. Sage tumbled after him, while Millie peeked out from her hiding spot. Even Gus lumbered over, drawn by the unusual visitor.

The cats circled Grayson, sniffing his shoes, his pants, his hands. To anyone watching, it looked like friendly cats greeting a customer. But I could feel them working, analyzing, comparing.

Grayson opened his portfolio and began showing us his research. Photographs of intricate jewelry pieces, sketches of designs, old documents detailing commissions and sales. He talked about Silas's work with obvious pride and deep knowledge.

"This was the necklace design," he said, showing us a detailed sketch. "Silas spent three months on it. Hand-engraved every flower, balanced the locket mechanism perfectly. It was commissioned by Henry Hendry as a gift for his wife in 1875."

"It's beautiful work," I said honestly.

"Silas was a true artist." Grayson's fingers traced the sketch lovingly. "He came to Larkspur Valley from San Francisco, brought his skills and his craft. He trained apprentices, created pieces that are still worn today. But people only remember him for the Hendry necklace."

"That must be frustrating," Lily said.

"It is." He looked up at us. "The necklace disappearing, it's been difficult. Not just for Florence, though I know she's devastated. But for the book. My sister wanted photographs of it, wanted to document it properly. I took a few quick shots during the house tour, but they were rushed, the lighting was poor, and there were people crowding around. Flo had promised me a private viewing after the party to get proper documentation photos. Now we can't."

He seemed genuine in his regret. Sad for Flo, sad for his sister, sad for the lost opportunity to document his ancestor's masterpiece.

The cats had finished their investigation and were dispersing back to their usual spots. Poppy jumped back onto the counter, positioning herself near me.

Grayson spent another twenty minutes showing us his research, telling stories about Silas and other St. Martin craftsmen through the generations. When he finally left, promising to bring more documentation later, he seemed lighter somehow. As if sharing his family's history had eased some burden.

The moment the door closed behind him, I looked at Poppy. "Well?"

"Old paper smell, yes," she said immediately. "And tobacco. But also metal. Sharp chemical smell. Oil."

"Machine oil," Rocky added, appearing beside her. "Like what the mechanic's shop smells like."

"And jewelry cleaner," Millie said softly from her spot. "Sweet chemical smell. Strong."

"Does it match what Paisley described?" I asked urgently. "Old paper and tobacco?"

Poppy tilted her head, considering. "The paper and tobacco are there, yes. But there are other strong smells too. Metal, chemicals, oil. If this is the thief, he carries a lot more scent than what Paisley picked up in the bedroom."

Gus lumbered over. "Could be the same person after a shower and changing clothes. Could be someone different who also smokes and works with old papers."

"So inconclusive," I said, frustrated.

"Not quite," Poppy corrected. "Paisley said the bedroom person smelled like old paper and tobacco. Nothing else. This man has those scents, but also several others that are very strong. If he'd been in that bedroom, Paisley would have smelled the metal and chemicals too. Cat noses don't miss things like that."

Lily was already pulling out her phone, taking notes. "So, Grayson has some of the markers, but also distinct scents from his jewelry work that weren't present at the theft scene."

"Which means he's probably not the thief," I said slowly. "But we can't rule him out completely."

"Three tested, none perfect matches," Lily said. "That leaves Warren as the most likely. He had tobacco but we never got close enough to check for old paper. The test got compromised by all his documents."

I thought about Warren's visit earlier in the week. How he'd sat surrounded by photocopies and journals, so consumed by his family history. My cats had tried to get a read on his scent, but all that old paper had overwhelmed everything else. We'd never gotten a proper test.

"We need to test Warren again," I said. "Properly this time. Without all his documents as interference."

"How do we arrange that?"

Before I could answer, the bell chimed again. Lionel walked in, his usual warm smile in place. He wore a graphic t-shirt featuring yet another comic book character I didn't recognize and carried a stack of what looked like game manuals.

"Morning, ladies," he said cheerfully. "Just stopping by to make sure you haven't forgotten about game night tonight."

"Game night?" For a moment, my mind was so focused on the investigation that I'd completely forgotten.

"Seven o'clock at my shop. We're playing that new cooperative mystery game I mentioned. You both said you'd come." He set the manuals on the counter. "Though if you're too busy investigating stolen necklaces, I understand."

"We'll be there," Lily said before I could deflect. "It'll be good to take a break from thinking about the theft."

"Excellent." Lionel's smile widened. "Colton's coming too. And a few others from town. Should be fun."

After he left, I looked at Lily. "We don't have time for game night. We need to figure out how to test Warren properly."

"We have all day to work on that. A few hours tonight won't hurt." She started wiping down the espresso machine. "Besides, sometimes taking a break helps you think more clearly. And who knows? Maybe we'll learn something useful. Small town, remember? Everyone knows everyone's business."

She had a point. The crochet circle had provided valuable context. Maybe game night would too.

The morning rush picked up, keeping us busy with orders and conversation. Flo stopped by around ten-thirty with a fresh delivery of pastries from her diner.

"Morning, dears," she said, setting the boxes on the counter. "I saw Grayson St. Martin leaving earlier. How did that go?"

"He wanted to contribute to our historical display," I said. "Brought research about his great-great-grandfather's jewelry work."

"That sounds lovely." Flo looked tired but less devastated than she had at the crochet circle. "Did you learn anything useful?"

I chose my words carefully. "He seemed genuine in his grief about the necklace being stolen. Said it meant his sister couldn't have photographs for her book."

"Poor Delilah." Flo shook her head. "Such a tragedy. And here I am mourning a necklace when she's dying."

"Both losses matter," Lily said gently.

"I suppose." Flo's voice wavered. "My sister would have understood. She knew what family legacy meant." She caught herself, pressing her lips together. "Anyway. I should get back to the diner. Lunch rush starts soon."

After she left, I stared at the espresso machine, my mind spinning.

We were missing something. Or someone.

The lunch crowd started filtering in around eleven-thirty. Felix returned for a midday coffee. Cordelia stopped by, gushing about how wonderful it had been to have Lily at the crochet circle. Jasper from the general store grabbed a quick drink before heading back to work.

By noon, the café was bustling with the usual Friday energy. People planning their weekends, discussing upcoming events, sharing gossip and news.

And somewhere among all these normal, everyday conversations, a thief was walking free.

I just had to figure out who.

Around noon, as the lunch crowd began to thin, Flo came back. She'd dropped off pastries earlier, but something in her expression told me this wasn't a social call.

"Everything okay?" I asked.

"Mostly." She hesitated, then lowered her voice. "Theo Vincent was parked outside my house last night. Just sitting there in his car, watching."

My stomach clenched. "For how long?"

"Henry noticed him around eight when he looked out the window. Theo was still there at nine-thirty when I checked before bed." Flo wrapped her arms around herself. "I called Iris, but she said unless he's on my property or threatening me, there's nothing she can do. Public street parking and all that."

"Henry's staying with you?" Lily asked gently.

"Since the theft. He didn't want me alone in that big house, not with all this going on." Flo's voice softened. "It's been nice, actually. Having someone there."

"That must have been unsettling," I said. "Theo just sitting there watching."

"It was. Henry went out and asked if he needed something, but Theo just drove away without saying a word." Flo's hands trembled slightly. "After everything at your café earlier this week, after how angry he was... I don't know what he wants from me."

"Maybe he's trying to work up the courage to apologize?" I suggested, though I didn't believe it.

"Or maybe he's planning something worse." Flo shook her head. "I'm probably being paranoid. He's harmless, right? Just angry and hurting."

"Angry and hurting people can do unpredictable things," Lily said gently.

After Flo left, I caught Lily's eye. She looked as worried as I felt.

"That's escalating behavior," she said quietly. "Confrontation at the café, now surveillance of her home."

"Should we tell Iris?"

"Flo already did. But yes, maybe we should mention it too. Add our concerns about his volatility."

Poppy appeared on the counter, her amber eyes serious. "That man is watching. Waiting. Planning something."

"Or working himself up to do something," Gus added grimly.

I didn't like where this was heading. Theo Vincent wasn't just carrying a grudge anymore. He was actively fixating on Flo, and that made him dangerous.

"We need to test him again," I said. "More carefully this time. Find out if he really is the thief."

"And if he is?"

"Then we stop him before he does something we'll all regret."

The door chimed, and Jasper from the general store walked in, looking agitated.

"Alexis, you got a minute?" He glanced around the café, making sure no one was listening too closely. "I need to tell you something. Not sure if it matters, but..."

"What is it?"

"I was in Silverpine this morning, picking up supplies." He leaned against the counter, lowering his voice. "Saw Zeke Hargraves coming out of that pawn shop on Third Street. You know the one, looks kind of sketchy?"

My pulse quickened. "Are you sure it was him?"

"Positive. I've known Zeke since we were kids. Hard to miss that canvas jacket he always wears." Jasper's expression was troubled. "Thing is, he looked nervous. Kept looking around, and when he saw me across the street, he practically ran to his truck."

Lily had moved closer, listening intently. "Did he have anything with him?"

"That's the thing. He was tucking something into his jacket. Small, wrapped in cloth. Could've been anything, but..." Jasper shrugged uncomfortably. "Look, I don't want to accuse anyone. Zeke's a good guy. But with everything going on, with Flo's necklace missing, it seemed weird."

"Why are you telling me this?" I asked carefully. "Did you tell Sheriff Scott?"

Jasper looked uncomfortable. "That's why I came here first. I wasn't sure if it was enough to bother Iris with, you know? I mean, being at a pawn shop isn't a crime. And you've been asking around about the founding families, doing that historical display research. Figured you might have a better sense of whether this means something or if I'm just being paranoid." He rubbed the back of his neck. "If you think I should tell Iris, I will. I just didn't want to waste her time or throw suspicion on Zeke if it's nothing."

"It could be innocent," I said slowly. "Maybe he needed to pawn something of his own. You said his construction business has been slow."

"That's what I thought at first. But people going in to pawn stuff don't look guilty when they come out. They look embarrassed, maybe, or frustrated. Zeke looked..." Jasper searched for the right word. "Scared. Like he'd been caught doing something he shouldn't."

"You should tell Sheriff Scott," I said. "Even if it turns out to be nothing, she needs to know. Let her decide if it's worth investigating."

"Yeah, you're right." Jasper nodded, looking relieved to have the decision made. "I'll head over to the station after I finish my deliveries. Thanks, Alexis."

After Jasper left, I turned to Lily, my mind racing.

"Zeke was at a pawn shop in Silverpine," I said. "The day after he came here and gave us that whole speech about preserving his family's legacy. About his book project and how he just wants recognition."

"Could be innocent," Lily said, but her tone was uncertain. "Maybe he was researching for his book. Pawn shops sometimes have old items, historical pieces."

"Or maybe he was trying to sell the necklace." I pulled out my phone. "His smell didn't match perfectly, but we said that could be because he showered, changed clothes. What if we were right the first time? What if the partial match was enough?"

"But Poppy said—"

"Poppy said his primary scents were leather and coffee. But people have layers of smells. What if the tobacco and old paper were underneath, just fainter?" I was grasping now, I knew it. "And he mentioned financial problems. His business is struggling. A desperate man might do desperate things."

Lily bit her lip. "Iris will check it out once Jasper tells her. Let her investigate properly."

"You're right." I set down my phone, but I couldn't shake the unease. "But tonight, at game night, if Zeke's there, maybe we can observe him. See if his behavior gives anything away."

"Assuming he shows up."

"Small town. Everyone goes to Lionel's game nights." I looked at the clock. "Five hours until we find out."

Poppy had been listening from her perch. "The construction man carries much pain. But is it guilt or grief?"

"That's what we need to figure out," I said.

I grabbed a rag and started wiping down the counter, needing something to do with my hands. My mind kept replaying Flo's words. Theo sitting outside her house for hours. Watching. Just watching. The image made my skin crawl.

It was one thing to be angry at a historical injustice. It was another to fixate on a specific person, to surveil their home in the dark. That crossed a line from grievance into something far more concerning.

"Stop frowning," Poppy said from her perch. "You'll figure it out."

"When?"

"When you stop trying so hard. Sometimes the answer is right in front of you, but you're looking past it."

I wanted to believe her. Wanted to trust that somehow, the truth would emerge.

"We'll try again," Lily said, reading my expression. "We'll find another way to test Warren properly."

"And if he doesn't match either?"

"Then we expand our suspect pool. But let's not jump ahead." She handed me a rag. "For now, let's finish the lunch rush. Then we can regroup."

She was right. Worrying wouldn't solve anything. We needed to focus, stay methodical, and trust the process.

But as I wiped down tables and served coffee and watched the afternoon sun stream through the windows, I couldn't shake the feeling that time was running out.

The thief had stolen the necklace six days ago. Every day that passed made it more likely they'd successfully hidden it somewhere we'd never find. Or sold it to someone far from Larkspur Valley. Or destroyed it out of spite.

Flo would never get her family heirloom back. Piper would never receive what should have been hers. And whoever had violated the trust of this community would get away with it.

Unless we figured this out soon.

"Tonight," I said to Lily as the lunch crowd thinned. "After game night. We sit down and review everything. Every suspect, every piece of information, every scent test result. There has to be something we're missing."

"Agreed." She glanced at the clock. "Six hours until game night. Let's use them well."

The afternoon stretched ahead of us, full of possibilities and frustrations in equal measure. But we had a plan, even if it wasn't perfect.

And sometimes, that was enough to keep moving forward.

Chapter Eleven

The Rebel Rogue smelled like paper and cardboard and something sweet, probably the cookies Lionel had set out on the counter. The comic shop was more crowded than I'd expected for a Friday night, with people clustered around tables scattered throughout the space. Shelves lined every wall, filled with carefully organized comics, graphic novels, and board games. String lights hung in gentle loops along the ceiling, giving everything a warm, cozy glow.

"Alexis! Lily!" Lionel's face lit up when he saw us walk in, his smile particularly bright when his eyes landed on me. "Welcome. We're just getting set up. Perfect timing."

"Thanks for having us," Lily said with that easy warmth she had.

Dr. Colton Dover looked up from where he was organizing game pieces at a table near the window. He was in jeans and a casual sweater instead of his usual vet scrubs, and he smiled when he saw us.

"Good to see you both again." His gaze lingered on me just a moment longer than necessary. "Ready for some friendly competition?"

"More like friendly cooperation," Lionel said. "We're playing the disease game tonight."

"We've got a full group," he continued, leading us toward the main table. "You remember Esther, Gabe, and Rory from last time, Alexis. But I don't think you've met them yet, Lily."

Esther waved from her seat, already arranging her section of the table with characteristic precision. She was in her late forties, with sharp eyes and the air of someone who'd spent years teaching middle schoolers and wasn't fazed by much. "Lovely to meet you, Lily. Any friend of Alexis's is welcome here."

Gabe, younger and quieter, gave a friendly nod. He worked at the hardware store and had that careful, measured way of speaking that came from years of customer service. "Nice to have you join us."

Rory beamed at us, his freckles standing out against his pale skin. He was the youngest of the group, maybe late twenties, with an enthusiasm that reminded me of an overly friendly golden retriever. "Great to meet you! Are you planning to stay in Larkspur Valley?"

"I am," Lily said with a warm smile. "I'm enjoying it so far."

There were a few other people I didn't recognize scattered at other tables. A couple playing a two-player card game in the corner, three people deep in what looked like a complicated role-playing campaign near the back. The energy in the shop was relaxed and welcoming, the kind of space where people could just be themselves without judgment.

Lionel had already set up our game on the main table, the board spread out with its colorful map of the world divided into regions. Disease cubes in four different colors were organized in neat piles, ready to spread chaos.

"So for those who haven't played," Lionel began, and I could hear the shift in his voice to what I'd started thinking of as his game master mode. Enthusiastic, clear, patient. "This is a cooperative game. We're all working together to stop four diseases from spreading across the world. We win or lose as a team."

He walked through the basics. How to move, how to treat disease, how to build research stations. Lily picked up the mechanics quickly, asking smart questions about strategy and card management. Colton watched the explanation with the kind of focus he probably brought to complicated veterinary procedures.

"Everyone clear?" Lionel asked after his explanation.

A chorus of affirmatives answered him.

"Great. Let's pick roles." He fanned out the role cards. "Lily, since you're new to the game, you pick first."

Lily drew the Scientist card. "What does this do?"

"You only need four cards of the same color to discover a cure instead of five," Lionel explained. "It's one of the most powerful roles."

"No pressure," Esther said dryly, but she was smiling.

I drew next and got the Medic. Appropriate, given everything happening in town. Gabe got the Researcher, Rory the Dispatcher, Colton the Operations Expert, and Lionel kept the Contingency Planner.

"Perfect team," Lionel said, shuffling the infection deck. "Let's get started."

The first few turns focused entirely on the game. Lionel narrated as we went, explaining the strategy behind each move.

"Okay, blue disease breaks out in San Francisco. Red disease hits Cairo. We're starting to see some clustering in Asia with the yellow disease."

Lily proved to be a natural strategist, working with Esther to plan our moves several turns ahead. They had that immediate rapport that sometimes happens between people who think the same way.

"If Gabe trades you those two blue cards," Lily was saying, "and Alexis treats the disease in Tokyo on her next turn, then I can cure blue disease on my turn after that."

"That works if we don't get a bad epidemic draw," Esther cautioned. "But it's our best shot."

The game progressed smoothly for several rounds. We were doing well, managing the disease spread effectively. Then, as often happens with comfortable groups, the conversation started to wander.

"Did anyone else hear about the Morgans?" Esther asked as she moved her pawn across the board.

"The divorce?" Rory said. "Everyone's heard. It's all over town."

"Twenty-three years of marriage," Gabe added, shaking his head. "Nobody saw it coming."

"These things are rarely as sudden as they seem," Lily observed, trading cards with Colton.

"True," Esther agreed. "Though it does make you wonder what else is happening under the surface in this town. We all think we know each other, but do we really?"

"Speaking of things happening under the surface," Rory said, "that Founder's Day party at Flo's diner was supposed to be a celebration. Instead it turned into a crime scene."

And just like that, we'd arrived at the topic I'd been waiting for.

"Poor Flo," Gabe said, genuine sympathy in his voice. "That necklace meant everything to her. Six generations of family history, just gone."

"Do they have any suspects?" Colton asked, looking directly at me. "You see a lot of people at the café. You must hear things."

"Just speculation, mostly," I said carefully, arranging my cards. "The founding families and their old grievances come up a lot."

"Warren Jacobs," Esther said with the confidence of someone stating an obvious fact. "That man has been obsessed with family recognition for years. It wouldn't surprise me if he took the necklace as some kind of statement."

"That's a pretty big leap from resentment to theft," Gabe pointed out, always the voice of caution.

"Is it, though?" Esther countered. "He's been at the library practically every day for months. Pearl says he's completely consumed by it. Going through old documents, making copies, taking notes. It's beyond normal genealogy research."

"What about the other founding families?" Lily asked. "Weren't there three originally?"

"Three, yes," Lionel confirmed, drawing his cards. "The Hendrys, the Jacobs, and the Hargraves. All came to the valley in 1872, all helped build the town. But over time, the Hendry name is the only one that stuck in the public consciousness."

"Zeke Hargraves isn't happy about that either," Rory added. "Though he seems less angry than Warren. More sad, you know?"

"There's also Grayson St. Martin," Colton said. "His family made the necklace originally. I've heard he thinks they should have some claim to it."

"His sister is dying," I said quietly. "Terminal cancer. They've been working on a family history book together. That's why he's so focused on documenting everything."

The group went quiet for a moment.

"Well, that's heartbreaking," Esther said finally. "Though I suppose grief can make people do strange things."

"And then there's Theo Vincent," Gabe added. "He's been furious with the Hendry family for years. Something about his father's business partnership?"

"Speaking of Theo," Rory said, and there was that particular energy in his voice that people get when they have gossip to share, "did you all hear about the fight yesterday?"

My attention sharpened immediately. "Fight?"

"Oh my goodness, yes," Esther said. "Right outside the library. Thursday afternoon. Warren had been inside researching like he always does, and Theo tracked him down."

"I actually saw part of it," Gabe said, setting down his cards. "I was walking past on my way to pick up supplies at the hardware store. Theo was yelling about proof and criminals and going to the sheriff. Warren was shouting back. People were stopping to watch."

"It started inside the library," Rory added, leaning forward. "My friend works there with Pearl. She said Theo came in specifically looking for Warren. Found him at the microfiche machine and started accusing him right there in the middle of the quiet reading area."

"Pearl had to make them take it outside," Esther continued. "My sister was there, saw the whole thing. She said she'd never heard Pearl speak like that in her life. Pearl used what my sister called her librarian voice. You know, the one that makes you feel like you're ten years old and being scolded for talking too loud."

"And Zeke Hargraves was there too," Gabe added. "He came out of the library right after Theo and Warren started arguing outside. Tried to calm them both down, but then Theo turned on him too. Started yelling about how all three founding families had conspired to erase his father from history."

"So Theo was fighting with both Warren and Zeke?" I asked.

"More or less," Esther confirmed. "Though Zeke seemed more confused than angry. Like he didn't understand why Theo was including him in the accusations. Warren was the main target, but Theo was lashing out at anyone connected to the founding families."

"What were they fighting about exactly?" Lily asked, her tone carefully casual as she examined her cards.

"That's the interesting part," Rory said. "Theo was claiming he had proof that Warren stole the necklace. He was waving papers around, saying he'd figured it all out and he was going straight to the sheriff's office."

My pulse quickened. "Proof? What kind of proof?"

"No idea," Gabe said. "But Theo seemed absolutely convinced. Warren was denying everything, of course. Calling Theo delusional, saying he was just carrying on his father's ridiculous grudge against the Hendrys."

"It got pretty heated," Esther added. "My sister said people were gathering on the sidewalk to watch. Eventually Warren just stormed off toward the parking lot, got in his truck and drove away.

Zeke tried to talk to Theo for another minute, but Theo just pushed past him and headed off down the street."

"Toward the sheriff's office?" I asked, trying to keep my voice neutral.

"That's the direction he went," Rory confirmed. "Whether he actually made it there, I don't know. I had to get back to the post office."

This was significant. Theo claiming he had proof against Warren. Theo confronting both Warren and Zeke publicly. Theo threatening to take it to Iris. If Theo actually had real evidence, something concrete, that could break the case wide open.

"Well," Lionel said, picking up the dice with a pointed look at all of us, "hopefully Sheriff Scott gets to the bottom of it soon. Flo deserves to get her necklace back, and whoever took it deserves to face consequences. Now, whose turn is it? Because we've been talking so much we've completely lost track of the game."

That broke the tension, and everyone laughed.

"I think it's mine," Gabe said, studying the board.

The game continued with renewed focus. We managed to win the first game, barely discovering all four cures before the player deck ran out. Everyone cheered, and Lionel insisted on getting a photo of our winning board state.

"For posterity," he said, snapping a picture with his phone. "First win of the night always gets commemorated."

"Do you do this every week?" Lily asked.

"Most weeks," Lionel said. "Sometimes it's board games, sometimes role-playing campaigns. Depends on who shows up and what people are in the mood for. It's really just about having a space where people can gather and have fun together."

"It's nice," Lily said. "I can see why Alexis enjoys coming."

"When she actually comes," Lionel added with a pointed look at me. "Which isn't as often as I'd like."

"I've been busy," I protested.

"You've been hiding," he countered, but his tone was gentle. "Which I understand. But you're allowed to have fun too, you know. Even when life is complicated."

"Wise words from the comic shop philosopher," Colton said, and there was something in his voice. Not quite an edge, but something sharp beneath the casual tone.

Lionel's smile didn't falter. "I contain multitudes."

The second game was more challenging. We drew an early epidemic that cascaded into outbreaks across Asia, and despite our best efforts, we lost when the black disease cubes ran out.

"Devastating," Lionel declared dramatically. "We were so close."

"One more round?" Esther suggested. "Best two out of three?"

"I'm in," everyone agreed.

As Lionel reset the board, Rory pulled out his phone and groaned. "I just remembered I have to be up at five tomorrow. Early mail routes during the holiday season."

"That's brutal," Gabe sympathized. "I should probably head out soon too. Opening shift at the hardware store."

"One more game first," Lionel insisted. "We can play quick. Besides, you can't leave on a loss. That's bad luck."

We started the third game with renewed focus. The conversation stayed mostly on strategy this time, everyone determined to end on a win. Lily and Esther's partnership was in full swing, with the rest of us essentially following their lead.

We won decisively, curing all four diseases with several turns to spare.

"Victory!" Lionel announced. "And on that high note, I think we can call it a successful evening."

Esther checked her phone and sighed. "I really do need to get going. Early morning tomorrow, and I'm not as young as I used to be."

"None of us are," Gabe said, stretching. "But this was fun. Same time next week?"

"Always," Lionel confirmed.

The group began breaking up. Rory and Esther left together, both waving as they headed out into the November night. Gabe followed shortly after. The other players at the back tables were packing up too, the shop slowly emptying.

"We should probably get going as well," I said to Lily. "Early morning at the café tomorrow."

"Of course." Lionel started packing up the game with practiced efficiency. "I'm really glad you both came. It made the evening better."

"It was fun," I said honestly. "Thanks for having us."

"Anytime." He paused in his tidying, looking at me with that open honesty that made my chest feel tight. "Both of you are always welcome. You know that, right?"

"We know," Lily said warmly.

"Actually," Lionel continued, pulling on his jacket, "it's pretty cold out there tonight. Can I walk you both home?"

I saw Colton's expression shift immediately. He'd been gathering his own things, clearly preparing to leave, but now he went still. Something flickered across his face. Disappointment, frustration, maybe a touch of jealousy, though he tried to mask it quickly.

"I was just about to offer the same thing," Colton said, his voice carefully casual. "It's dark out, and I'd be happy to walk you."

The air in the shop changed, became charged with that particular masculine tension I'd only ever witnessed from the outside before. Both of them looking at me, waiting. Both of them trying to appear casual while clearly caring very much about the answer.

"That's kind of you both," Lily said smoothly, stepping in before I had to navigate the awkwardness. "But Lionel asked first. It's only fair."

"It's really no trouble," Colton insisted, and there was something almost plaintive in his voice. "I don't mind at all."

"I've got it," Lionel said, and though his tone stayed friendly, there was unmistakable finality in it. "Besides, I need some air after being inside all evening. Help me clear my head before I close up the shop."

Colton's jaw tightened just slightly. He looked at me, seemed to be weighing whether to push the issue, then apparently decided against it. "Another time, then," he said, and I heard the unspoken question in those words. "Good night, Alexis. Lily. I'll see you around."

"Good night, Colton," I managed, feeling awkward about the entire exchange. "Thanks for playing with us."

He nodded, grabbed his coat, and headed for the door. I saw him glance back once before stepping out into the night.

"Sorry about that," Lionel said quietly as he locked up the shop. "Colton's a good guy. We're actually friends, have been for years. But lately there's been some competition, I guess you'd call it."

"Competition?" I asked, though I knew exactly what he meant.

"For your attention." He looked at me directly, his green eyes warm in the glow of the streetlights. "I know you're not looking for anything. I know you've got a lot going on with the café and your life and now this theft investigation everyone knows you're involved in somehow. But I wanted to be clear about where I stand. I like you, Alexis. Have for a while now. More than just as a customer or a friend."

My heart did something complicated. A flutter mixed with a clench of anxiety. "Lionel, I..."

"You don't have to say anything," he said quickly. "Really. I'm not asking for an answer or a decision or anything like that. I just wanted you to know how I feel. No pressure. No expectations. Just honesty. That's all."

We walked in silence for a moment, our footsteps echoing on the quiet sidewalk. Main Street was nearly deserted at this hour, most shops dark except for a restaurant at the far end still serving late dinners.

"I appreciate your honesty," I said finally. "And I'm flattered. Really. You're wonderful. It's just..."

"Complicated," he finished for me. "I know. Life is complicated. You're complicated. That's part of what I like about you, actually. You're not simple or shallow. There's depth there. Mystery. But also kindness and intelligence and a really terrible sense of humor that somehow makes me laugh anyway."

"My humor is excellent," I protested weakly.

"It's terrible and you know it." He grinned. "But I happen to like terrible humor, so it works out."

We reached the café, and Lily tactfully slipped inside ahead of us, giving us a moment of privacy.

Lionel stopped at the door. For a heartbeat, I thought he might try to kiss me. I could see the want in his eyes, the way they flickered to my lips and then back to my face. But he just smiled, soft and a little sad and very patient.

"Good night, Alexis."

"Good night, Lionel. And thank you. For tonight. For being honest. For being you."

"Anytime." He stepped back, hands in his pockets. "Sweet dreams."

He waited until I was fully inside before heading back down the street toward his shop, his silhouette disappearing into the November darkness.

Upstairs in my apartment, I found Lily already curled up on the couch with a mug of tea. The cats appeared immediately, materializing from their various sleeping spots to demand attention and updates.

"How was the human gathering?" Poppy asked, jumping onto my lap.

"Informative. And actually kind of fun."

"Good," Gus rumbled from his chair. "You needed that. You've been wound too tight."

"That shop human likes you," Rocky observed, appearing on the back of the couch. "The doctor human likes you too. You're stuck between them now."

"Very stuck," I confirmed.

"Humans make everything complicated," Millie said softly from behind the fern. "Cats are much simpler. We like food and sunshine and head scratches. Easy."

"If only life were that simple," I said.

I made myself tea and settled beside Lily. "So. That was interesting."

"Which part? The information about Theo and Warren's fight, or the romantic triangle situation?"

"Both, honestly." She sipped her tea. "Though I was mainly referring to the fight. If Theo really has proof against Warren, that changes everything."

"We don't know if he actually took it to Sheriff Iris or not," I said. "He might have just been making empty threats."

"True. But even if he didn't, he must have found something compelling to confront Warren and Zeke so publicly. Theo doesn't strike me as someone who bluffs."

"No," I agreed, thinking about his anger at Flo's party, his obsession with his father's grievances. "He's absolutely convinced the Hendrys wronged his family. If he thinks Warren is guilty, he won't let it go."

We sat in comfortable silence for a while, drinking our tea while the cats settled around us. Rocky and Sage were already curled up together on their favorite cushion. Gus was snoring softly in his chair. Millie had emerged from her hiding spot to claim the arm of the couch. And Poppy stayed on my lap, purring steadily.

"You know," I said eventually, "you were right about tonight. I needed that. Just a fun, relaxing evening with normal people doing normal things. It helped clear my head."

"Good," Lily said. "Sometimes the best thing you can do for an investigation is step away from it for a few hours. Let your subconscious work while you're not actively thinking about it."

"Want to stay over tonight?" I asked suddenly. "We could have a proper sleepover. Like we used to."

Lily's face lit up. "Really? That sounds perfect. I haven't had a sleepover in years."

"Me neither. Let me grab you some pajamas and we can stay up talking."

"Just like old times."

I found her a comfortable t-shirt and sleep pants, and we settled into my bed with the cats arranging themselves around us. Poppy claimed her spot beside my pillow, Rocky and Sage took the foot of the bed, Gus sprawled across the middle taking up far more space than a cat his size should, and Millie curled up between Lily and me.

"This is nice," Lily said softly. "I'd forgotten how comforting this is. Just being with someone who knows you. Really knows you."

"I'm glad you're here," I said. "Glad you came back."

"Me too."

We talked for a while longer, about nothing important. Books we'd read, shows we'd watched, memories from our time in the coven that didn't hurt to remember. Eventually our voices got quieter, our words further apart, until we both drifted into sleep.

Deep, dreamless, restful sleep. The kind I hadn't had in almost a week.

Lily's breathing evened out beside me. The cats purred in their various spots. The November wind whispered against the windows.

Tomorrow would bring answers. Tomorrow we'd follow up on Theo's proof and figure out our next move.

But tonight, I just slept.

Peacefully and completely, more rested than I'd been since the theft.

Not knowing that tomorrow morning would shatter everything.

Not knowing that the investigation was about to take a turn none of us saw coming.

Not knowing that by tomorrow afternoon, we wouldn't just be looking for a thief.

We'd be looking for a killer.

Chapter Twelve

I woke to sunlight streaming through my bedroom window and the warm weight of cats surrounding me. For a moment, I couldn't remember why I felt so content, so deeply rested. Then I shifted slightly and felt Lily's presence beside me, still asleep with Millie curled between us.

The sleepover. Game night. Lionel's honest confession. The information about Theo's fight with Warren and Zeke.

Everything felt clearer this morning, like my mind had organized itself during sleep.

Poppy lifted her head from beside my pillow. "Good morning. You slept well."

"I did." I stretched carefully, trying not to disturb the other cats. "Better than I have in days."

"That's what happens when you stop carrying everything alone. You let someone help. You played games. You relaxed. Your body remembered how to rest."

"Wise words from a wise cat."

"I'm full of wisdom. Also hungry. It's almost six."

Lily stirred beside me, blinking slowly. "Morning already?"

"Afraid so. We've got a café to open."

She sat up, her hair adorably mussed. "I need to run home and change. Unless you have something I can borrow?"

"I think we're about the same size. Help yourself to whatever's in the dresser."

While Lily rummaged through my clothes, I started the coffee maker and fed the cats. The morning routine felt easy, comfortable. Having Lily here didn't feel like an intrusion. It felt natural, like we'd been doing this for years instead of just reuniting a week ago.

We sat at my small kitchen table with our coffee, the morning quiet except for the cats moving through their own routines around us.

"I've been thinking about yesterday," Lily said, cupping her hands around her mug. "About what we learned at game night. About Theo confronting Warren and Zeke."

"Me too." I'd been thinking about little else, actually. "It has to be Theo. Everything points to him."

"Walk me through it."

I took a sip of coffee, organizing my thoughts. "He had the strongest reaction at Flo's party. The most anger, the most desperation. His smell was a partial match with Paisley's identification. Old paper, even if we couldn't confirm tobacco."

"And he's been escalating," Lily added. "The confrontation at our café. Sitting outside Flo's house watching. Then yesterday, that public fight where he claimed he had proof."

"Exactly. He's obsessed. He's convinced the Hendrys stole his family's legacy, so in his mind, stealing their necklace is justice. Reclaiming what should have been his." I set down my mug. "It fits his pattern. It fits his psychology."

"What about Warren? He had the tobacco smell."

"Partial match, like Theo. And yes, Warren's bitter and resentful, but he's cold about it. Calculated. Theo is hot anger, impulsive rage. Stealing the necklace during a party, in the moment?" I shook my head. "That's Theo, not Warren."

Lily nodded slowly. "And Zeke and Grayson?"

"Zeke's hurt but not vengeful. His architectural book project is about preservation, not revenge. And Grayson?" I thought about his dying sister, his gentle demeanor. "He's grieving and desperate, but desperate for recognition, not retribution. Theo is the only one whose motivation includes punishment."

"So, what do we do?"

"We need to prove it." I stood, carrying my mug to the sink. "We test him again. More carefully this time. Or we find another way to confirm he took it. Because right now, we're ninety percent sure, but we need to be one hundred percent before we can tell Iris."

"And then?"

"Then we make sure he returns it and faces consequences. No one gets away with stealing from Flo. Not even someone carrying his father's grudges."

Lily finished her coffee and stood. "Okay. After we open today, we make a plan. Figure out how to prove Theo is our thief."

"Agreed." I felt better having a direction. "One way or another, this ends soon."

By seven-thirty, we were both dressed and caffeinated.

Lily had borrowed a soft green sweater and jeans that fit her perfectly. We headed downstairs to prep the café for opening.

The morning routine was familiar and soothing. I ground coffee beans while Lily restocked the pastry case with yesterday's delivery from Flo's diner. We worked in comfortable silence, each knowing what needed to be done without discussion.

"Today feels good," Lily said as she arranged blueberry muffins. "Like something's going to break in our favor."

"I hope you're right." I checked the espresso machine, making sure everything was ready. "We need to figure out if Theo actually took his proof to Sheriff Iris."

"Speaking of Iris, she should be here around eight-fifteen for her usual coffee."

At eight o'clock exactly, I unlocked the front door and flipped the sign to open.

And immediately, the door burst open.

"Ella, slow down!" Piper's voice called from outside.

But Ella was already rushing past me, her eyes scanning the café with laser focus. She spotted what she was looking for immediately and made a beeline for the viewing room.

Cleo, the sleek black cat with luminous green eyes, was sitting in her favorite spot by the window. The moment Ella appeared, the cat stood and meowed.

"There you are!" Ella scooped Cleo into her arms, holding her close. "I told you I'd come back. I told you we'd take you home today."

Piper walked in more slowly, followed by Lee and their older daughter Eva. Lee looked sheepish, Eva looked excited, and Piper had the expression of a parent who'd lost a negotiation.

"I'm so sorry for the dramatic entrance," Piper said. "Ella has not stopped talking about that cat since we were here last week. Do you still have her available for adoption?"

"Cleo?" I smiled, watching Ella whisper to the cat. "Yes, she's still available."

"Cleo already knows she's coming home with us," Ella announced with complete confidence. "She told me. She's been waiting."

Lee and Piper exchanged one of those parent looks, the kind that said they weren't sure if they should be concerned or charmed.

"Ella has a very active imagination," Lee said apologetically.

But Cleo was purring louder than I'd ever heard her purr, her green eyes half-closed in contentment as Ella held her. The cat had been friendly with everyone who visited, but with Ella, it was different. There was recognition there. Connection.

"Sometimes animals pick their people," I said carefully. "Cleo seems to have picked Ella."

"Can we really take her home?" Eva asked, reaching out to pet Cleo's head. "Can she be our cat?"

Piper sighed in the way that meant the battle was already lost. "Yes, sweetheart. We're going to adopt Cleo today."

Ella's face transformed with joy. She hugged Cleo closer, and the cat simply nestled against her, completely trusting.

I pulled out the adoption paperwork while Lily started preparing the cat carrier and gathering Cleo's medical records. The process was straightforward, but I took my time explaining Cleo's care needs, her food preferences, the importance of keeping her indoors for the first few weeks while she adjusted.

"She's been with us for about three weeks now," I explained. "She's healthy, fully vaccinated, and very social. She loves sunny spots and feather toys."

"And she needs me," Ella added seriously. "That's the most important part."

"That's very true," I agreed.

While Piper filled out the paperwork and Lee paid the adoption fee, Ella sat on the floor of the viewing room with Cleo in her lap, whispering things I couldn't quite hear. Eva had joined them, gently petting Cleo's sleek black fur.

"Thank you for this," Piper said quietly as she signed the final form. "I know Ella seems overly attached already, but I think this cat really is special to her. She's been different since she met Cleo. More confident. More herself."

"Some animals are meant for specific people," I said. "I think Cleo and Ella found each other for a reason."

Rocky appeared at my feet, watching the adoption with interest. "The small human understands. She'll take good care of Cleo."

"I know she will," I murmured too quietly for the humans to hear.

It took another fifteen minutes to get Cleo into the carrier. The cat went willingly when Ella was the one holding her, but meowed in protest when they had to close the carrier door.

"It's okay," Ella soothed through the wire door. "We're going home now. Our home. You'll love it there. I have a whole room you can explore, and Mom says you can sleep in my bed, and Dad's building you a cat tree."

"I'm building what now?" Lee asked, but he was smiling.

"A cat tree. For Cleo. You said you would."

"I did not say that."

"You will though," Ella said with absolute certainty. "Because Cleo needs one."

The family left in a flurry of thank-yous and excited chatter, Ella carrying the cat carrier with careful reverence while Eva skipped alongside, already making plans for all the ways they'd spoil their new pet.

After they left, the café felt quieter somehow. Emptier.

"That was sweet," Lily said, wiping down the counter. "Ella and that cat really did have a connection."

"They did." I thought about Ella's gifts, about how young she was to already hear the cats so clearly. "I hope having Cleo helps her understand her abilities better. Having an animal companion who understands you back, it makes a difference."

"It really does." Lily glanced at the clock. "Eight-thirty. Your sheriff should be here soon."

But eight-thirty came and went with no sign of Sheriff Iris Scott.

Felix Wren arrived for his morning Ginger Spark. Mabel came in for her Lavender Dreams tea. Pearl stopped by for a quick coffee before heading to the library. The usual Saturday morning crowd filtered in, and I served them all with half my attention, the other half waiting for Iris's arrival.

Eight forty-five. Nine o'clock. Still no sheriff.

"That's strange," I said to Lily as we worked through the morning rush. "She's never this late. She's here every single morning at eight-fifteen like clockwork."

"Maybe she's busy with the investigation?"

"Maybe."

But something felt off. A prickle of unease settled at the base of my spine.

At nine-fifteen, Cordelia from the yarn shop rushed in, her usually calm demeanor replaced by obvious distress.

"Alexis, have you heard?"

"Heard what?"

"About Theo Vincent. They found him this morning." She pressed her hand to her chest, catching her breath. "Dead. Near Aspen Falls."

The world seemed to tilt slightly.

"Dead?" I heard my voice say the word, but it sounded distant. "What happened?"

"Nobody knows yet. Hikers found him early this morning. Sheriff Scott is up there now with half the department." Cordelia accepted the chamomile tea Lily pressed into her hands. "It's just terrible. Absolutely terrible."

Lily and I exchanged a look.

Theo Vincent. The man who'd confronted Warren and Zeke in front of the library just yesterday. The man who'd claimed to have proof. The man who'd threatened to go to the sheriff.

Dead.

"Do they know what happened?" Lily asked carefully. "Was it an accident? A fall?"

"I don't know the details," Cordelia said. "But from what I heard, it doesn't look like an accident." She lowered her voice. "I heard someone say there were signs of a struggle."

The café door chimed again. Esther from last night's game group came in, her face pale.

"Have you heard about Theo Vincent?"

"We just heard," I said.

"It's all over town. They found him near the falls. My sister's husband is with the fire department. He was one of the first responders." Esther sank into a chair. "He said it was bad. Really bad."

More customers filtered in over the next half hour, each bringing more pieces of the story. Theo had been found by morning hikers at Aspen Falls, the scenic waterfall in the local park that fed into Lake Larkspur. He'd been lying at the base of the falls, partially in the water. There were signs of a struggle on the trail above. The sheriff's department had cordoned off the entire area.

"They're saying it might be murder," Mabel said in a hushed tone, her crossword puzzle forgotten. "That someone pushed him."

"Who would do such a thing?" Pearl asked, though her expression suggested she had theories.

"The same person who stole Flo's necklace," Esther said. "Has to be. Theo said he had proof. Someone didn't want him talking."

The café buzzed with speculation, theories, and shocked grief. Larkspur Valley was a small town. Murder didn't happen here. Theft was shocking enough. But murder?

That changed everything.

I worked through the morning in a daze, making drinks, serving food, nodding along to conversations I barely processed. Lily moved beside me with the same mechanical efficiency, both of us operating on autopilot.

By eleven o'clock, the initial rush of shocked customers had settled into a steady stream of gossip and speculation. I left Lily to handle the counter and retreated to the back room, needing a moment to process.

The cats followed me, sensing my distress.

"The angry paper human is dead," Poppy said quietly. "We can all feel it. The town feels different."

"He was murdered," I said, my voice hollow. "Someone killed him."

"Because he knew something," Gus added. "Because he was too loud about it."

"We heard him yesterday at the library," Rocky said. "Through the windows. He was shouting at the tobacco human and the quiet human. Saying he had proof."

"And now he's dead." I sank into the storage room chair, my legs suddenly unsteady. "Less than twenty-four hours later."

Lily appeared in the doorway. "Alexis?"

"He knew who the thief was." The words came out flat, certain. "That's why he's dead. He figured it out and he told everyone he had proof and someone killed him to keep him quiet."

"Warren or Zeke," Lily said. "Or maybe even Grayson, though that seems less likely given his sister's situation."

"Warren." The name felt heavy. "Theo specifically accused Warren. And Warren had the most to lose if Theo actually had proof."

"We don't know that for certain."

"But it makes sense." I stood, pacing the small space. "Warren's been obsessed with his family recognition for years. If Theo could prove Warren stole the necklace, that would destroy any credibility Warren has. It would validate everything Theo's been saying about founding family conspiracies."

"So Warren kills him?" Lily's tone was skeptical. "That's a big escalation from theft."

"People do desperate things when they're cornered." I thought about Warren at the café, so controlled, so precise. "But you're right. We're jumping to conclusions. It could have been Zeke. Or someone else entirely. Someone we haven't even considered."

"We need to talk to Sheriff Iris. Tell her about the fight yesterday, about Theo's claims of having proof."

"She probably already knows. The whole town witnessed it." I ran my hands through my hair, frustrated. "But yes, we should talk to her. Confirm what we know."

We returned to the café proper. The lunch crowd was starting to arrive, and despite the town's shock, people still needed to eat and drink and process their grief over coffee and sandwiches.

I went through the motions, making drinks, serving food, offering sympathetic nods to customers who needed to talk about Theo, about the murder, about how nothing felt safe anymore.

But underneath the shock and grief, I felt something else building.

Anger.

Pure, cold anger.

Someone had stolen Flo's necklace. That was violation enough. But now someone had killed a man to cover it up. Had taken a life to protect their theft.

That was unforgivable.

"You're furious," Poppy observed from her perch. "I can feel it radiating off you."

"I am furious," I confirmed quietly. "Theo was obnoxious and angry and carrying grudges that weren't his to carry. But he didn't deserve to die. No one deserves to be murdered."

"No," Poppy agreed. "They don't."

Lily caught my eye from across the counter. I saw my own anger reflected in her face. She felt it too. The violation, the escalation, the sheer audacity of someone thinking they could kill to protect a stolen necklace.

This wasn't just about returning stolen property anymore.

This was about justice for Theo Vincent.

And whoever had killed him was going to pay.

Chapter Thirteen

By two o'clock, I'd had enough.

The café had been packed all afternoon with people who weren't really there for coffee. They were there to gossip, to speculate, to process their shock about Theo Vincent's death. Every conversation circled back to the murder. Who did it. Why. How. Was it connected to the theft. Were they safe.

I understood the need to talk through trauma. But after six hours of the same conversations on repeat, my patience had worn thin.

"That's it," I said to Lily during a brief lull. "I'm closing early."

"Thank god," she said. "I was hoping you'd say that. I don't think I can hear one more theory about how Theo slipped and fell accidentally."

"He didn't slip and fall accidentally."

"No, he definitely didn't." Lily started wiping down the espresso machine. "Want to make an announcement or just start cleaning up?"

I walked to the door and flipped the sign to closed, then turned to address the remaining customers. "I'm sorry everyone, but we're closing early today. If you need to-go cups, I'm happy to provide them."

A few people grumbled, but most understood. Mabel gathered her things with a sympathetic nod. Felix packed up his sketchbook. Pearl gave me a gentle smile on her way out.

"Take care of yourself, dear," she said. "This has been hard on everyone."

By three o'clock, the café was empty and clean. Lily and I stood in the quiet space, both of us deflating slightly now that the performance was over.

"What do we do now?" Lily asked.

"Honestly? I want to do something normal. Something that has nothing to do with theft or murder or investigations."

"Like what?"

"Should we just go have a nice dinner?" The idea formed as I spoke it. "Get out of here, eat good food, pretend we're normal people having a normal evening?"

Lily's face brightened. "That sounds perfect. Where?"

"Ventura's steakhouse? I've heard good things but haven't been yet."

"That sounds nice."

We headed upstairs to my apartment to freshen up. I changed into a nicer sweater and clean jeans, ran a brush through my hair, added a touch of mascara. Lily borrowed a scarf and some earrings. The cats watched our preparations with interest.

"You're going out again," Poppy observed. "Three nights in a row. This is very unusual for you."

"I'm trying to be more social. Isn't that what you've been encouraging?"

"Yes, but I'm suspicious of sudden personality changes. Are you sure you're feeling well?"

"I'm fine. I just need a break from thinking about dead bodies and stolen necklaces."

"Fair enough. Have fun. Don't talk to strangers."

"I'll try."

By five o'clock, we were walking down Main Street toward Ventura's. The evening was cold but clear, the November air crisp against my face. The sun was setting behind the mountains, painting the sky in shades of orange and pink.

"This is nice," Lily said, linking her arm through mine. "Just walking. Being together. No agenda."

"It really is."

Ventura's steakhouse was located two blocks past Main Street, in a building that had once been a wealthy family's private residence. The restaurant occupied the first floor, with what I assumed were apartments above. It had that upscale but casual mountain town aesthetic: exposed wood beams, stone fireplace, dim lighting, white tablecloths but comfortable chairs, and no formal dress code like some fancy steakhouses. It was come as you are, which fit Larkspur Valley perfectly.

The building sat on the same block as the sheriff's office, which I only realized as we approached and saw the department's parking lot adjacent to the restaurant.

And there, stomping out of the sheriff's office, was Warren Jacobs.

He looked furious. His face was red, his movements jerky with barely controlled rage. He was muttering under his breath, words I couldn't quite make out but that sounded distinctly like cursing.

He spotted us and his expression shifted. Not to friendliness, but to something almost desperate. He changed direction, walking directly toward us.

"You," he said, pointing at me. "You're friends with Flo. You know me. Tell them I didn't do this."

I took an instinctive step back. Lily moved closer to my side.

"Mr. Jacobs—"

"Can you believe this?" His voice was rising, drawing attention from people on the street. "They're accusing me. Me! Of murder! Do they have any idea who I am? What my family has done for this town?"

"Mr. Jacobs, I don't think—"

"I didn't steal anything. I didn't kill anyone." He was breathing hard, his hands clenched into fists at his sides. "Theo Vincent was a lunatic. Everyone knew it. He was obsessed, delusional, carrying on his father's ridiculous vendetta. And now they're trying to blame me for his death just because we had an argument?"

"Warren." Sheriff Iris Scott's voice cut through his rant. She'd emerged from the office, her expression hard. "I told you not to harass people on the street."

"I'm not harassing anyone. I'm trying to make them understand—"

"You're done talking for today." Iris walked toward us with deliberate calm. "Go home. Don't approach anyone else. Don't discuss the case. Just go home."

Warren looked like he wanted to argue, but something in Iris's expression made him reconsider. He shot me one last desperate look, then stalked off down the street toward the parking lot.

Iris watched him go, then turned to us. "Are you two okay?"

"We're fine," I said, though my heart was racing. "He didn't hurt us or anything. Just... ranted."

"He's been doing a lot of that today." Iris rubbed her temple tiredly. "I interviewed both Warren and Zeke this afternoon. They both have alibis for last night, but neither is particularly strong."

"What do you mean?" Lily asked.

" Warren claims he was home alone all evening. No one to verify that. Zeke says he was at a bar in Silverpine until closing, but the bartender can't definitively confirm what time he left." Iris sighed. "I need more information to either clear them or arrest them. Right now, I've got two suspects with weak alibis, a dead man who claimed to have proof, and a whole town full of people who are scared."

"We're here if you need anything," I offered.

"I appreciate that." Iris glanced at the restaurant behind us. "You two going to Ventura's?"

"Yes. We closed the café early. Needed a break."

"I don't blame you. Enjoy your dinner. Try not to think about murder for a few hours." She gave us a tired smile, then headed back into the sheriff's office.

Lily and I stood on the sidewalk for a moment, both of us processing what had just happened.

"What just happened?" Lily said with a nervous laugh.

"I think we just got yelled at by a murderer."

"Allegedly a murderer. We don't know for certain."

"He did it," I said quietly. "I can feel it. The way he was so desperate for us to believe him. That's not the behavior of an innocent man."

"Maybe. Or maybe he's just terrified of being falsely accused." Lily tugged on my arm. "Come on. Let's go eat. We can analyze Warren's behavior over steak and wine."

"Now that sounds like a plan."

Ventura's interior was even lovelier than the exterior promised. The hostess, a young woman with a warm smile, led us to a table near the stone fireplace. The restaurant was about half full, with the dinner crowd just starting to arrive.

I scanned the room out of habit and spotted familiar faces. Pearl sat at a corner table with an older woman I didn't recognize, both of them deep in conversation. And at a larger table near the window sat Mabel Smalls with what had to be her family. A man in his fifties who resembled her, a woman around the same age, and three teenagers at various stages of awkward adolescence.

"Small town," Lily murmured, following my gaze.

"Very small."

We settled into our seats and accepted menus from our server, a friendly man named Marcus who recommended the ribeye and the roasted vegetables.

Once he'd taken our drink orders and left us to decide, Lily leaned back in her chair with a contented sigh.

"This is exactly what I needed. Soft lighting, good food, no murder talk."

"Agreed. Though I think we just broke the no murder talk rule."

"Then let's make a new rule. For the next hour, we talk about anything except theft, murder, investigations, or Warren Jacobs."

"Deal."

The wine arrived, a smooth red that warmed me from the inside. We ordered our meals, both choosing the ribeye, and then settled into the kind of easy conversation I hadn't realized how much I'd missed.

"Remember when we tried to learn illusion magic?" Lily said, her eyes bright with the memory. "And you accidentally made your entire room look like it was underwater?"

"Don't remind me. It took three days to figure out how to undo it. I was so nauseous from the constant motion."

"You slept in my room for a week. We stayed up every night practicing counter-spells."

"And you kept making my books float around like fish. That didn't help the nausea."

"I thought it was funny." Lily grinned. "You were so serious about everything. Someone needed to make you laugh."

"You succeeded. Usually at my expense."

"That's what friends are for."

We traded stories from our time in the coven, carefully editing out specific magical terms and names in case anyone was listening. But the essence of the memories remained. Learning together. Failing together. Supporting each other through difficult lessons and harder realities.

"Do you remember Renatta?" Lily asked, her voice soft.

"The healing specialist? Of course."

"She used to say that real power wasn't in the spells you could cast. It was in the people you could trust." Lily swirled her wine. "I didn't understand that then. I thought she was just being sentimental. But now, after everything, I get it."

"Trust is its own kind of magic."

"Exactly."

Our food arrived, and for a while we just enjoyed the meal. The steak was perfectly cooked, tender and flavorful. The vegetables were roasted with herbs and butter. The bread was warm and soft.

"This place is amazing," I said around a bite of steak. "Why haven't I come here before?"

"Because you're a hermit who never leaves her café?"

"Fair point."

Across the restaurant, I saw Mabel's family celebrating something. The teenagers were laughing, the adults were smiling, and Mabel herself looked more relaxed than I'd seen her in the café. It was nice, seeing people just living their lives despite the darkness that had touched the town.

Pearl caught my eye and gave a little wave. I waved back, and she returned to her conversation with her companion.

"It's strange," Lily said, following my gaze. "How life just continues. Someone dies, something terrible happens, and yet people still go out to dinner. Still laugh. Still celebrate."

"It's resilience. The human capacity to find joy even when things are awful."

"Or maybe it's denial."

"Maybe it's both."

We lingered over dessert, splitting a chocolate cake that was rich enough to be sinful. The conversation drifted to lighter topics. Books we'd read recently. Shows we wanted to watch. Plans for the café.

"I've been thinking," Lily said, scraping up the last bit of chocolate frosting. "After all this is resolved, maybe we should do a special event at the café. Something fun. A poetry reading or open mic night or something."

"That could be nice. Build community. Give people a reason to gather that isn't gossip or tragedy."

"And maybe we should actually do that historical display we've been talking about," I added. "Help the town heal by celebrating what connects them instead of what divides them."

Lily's face brightened. "That's perfect. We already have Grayson's research on the St. Martin family. We could reach out to Warren, Zeke, and the other founding families. Make it inclusive. Show that all their contributions matter."

"Exactly. It might help ease some of those old resentments."

"I love it. Once this is all over, let's make it happen."

By the time we finished, it was nearly eight o'clock. The restaurant had filled up around us, and the noise level had risen to a comfortable buzz of conversation and clinking silverware.

Marcus brought our check, and I insisted on paying despite Lily's protests.

"You've been helping at the café all week. Consider this my thank you."

"Fine. But next time, I'm paying."

"Deal."

We bundled back into our coats and stepped out into the November night. The temperature had dropped considerably, and I could see my breath misting in the air.

"That was perfect," Lily said, linking her arm through mine again. "Thank you for suggesting it."

"Thank you for coming. For being here. For everything."

"Always."

We walked back toward Main Street, our footsteps echoing in the quiet evening. Most of the shops were closed now, their windows dark. Only the restaurants and bars showed signs of life.

At the corner where Lily would turn off toward the yarn shop, we stopped.

"Want to meet up tomorrow?" Lily asked. "I know the café's closed, but we could practice our crochet. Or just have coffee and relax."

"That sounds perfect. Come over around nine?"

"I'll be there." She hugged me quickly. "Sleep well. Try not to think about murderers and thieves."

"I'll try. You too."

I watched her walk down the side street toward her apartment, her figure disappearing into the shadows between streetlights. Then I turned and continued toward the café.

Main Street was quiet at this hour. A few people were scattered about, heading home or to late dinners. The streetlights cast pools of warm light every few yards, with darkness between them.

I was two blocks from the café when I noticed him.

A figure standing across the street, partially hidden in the shadow of a building. At first, I thought it was just someone out for an evening walk. But as I moved forward, the figure moved too. Keeping pace with me. Staying in the shadows.

My heart rate picked up.

I walked faster, keeping my eyes forward but tracking the figure in my peripheral vision. Still there. Still following.

One block from the café now.

The figure crossed the street, angling toward me.

I broke into a jog, my keys already in my hand. The café was right there, just ahead. I could see the sign, the darkened windows.

Behind me, I heard footsteps. Running footsteps.

I reached the café door, fumbling with my keys. My hands were shaking, making it hard to get the key in the lock.

The footsteps were getting closer.

The lock clicked open. I shoved through the door, slammed it behind me, and engaged the deadbolt.

Through the glass, I saw the figure stop just outside. Standing there in the streetlight.

It was Warren Jacobs.

He stared at me through the glass, his expression unreadable. Then, slowly, deliberately, he smiled.

And walked away, disappearing into the November darkness.

I stood frozen in my café, heart pounding, breath coming in short gasps.

Warren had followed me. Had waited for me. Had chased me to my door.

The message was clear.

He knew where I lived. He knew where to find me.

And he wanted me to know that he knew.

Chapter Fourteen

I stood frozen at the door, my hand still gripping the deadbolt. My heart hammered against my ribs so hard it hurt. Through the glass, I could see the empty street where Warren had been standing just moments ago. The streetlight illuminated nothing but pavement and shadows now.

He was gone. But the terror remained.

"Alexis?" Poppy's voice cut through my paralysis. "Are you hurt?"

I turned to find all five of my cats gathered near the counter, their eyes wide and alert. Poppy, Gus, and Millie stood in a protective semicircle. Rocky had positioned himself slightly forward, and between his front paws sat Sage, the kitten's ears flattened against her head. In the viewing room, I could see the adoptable cats pressed against the glass, watching with concern.

"I'm okay," I managed, though my voice shook. "I'm not hurt."

"That man followed you," Rocky said, his usual playful tone replaced with something darker. "We saw through the window. He chased you."

"I know."

"You need to call the sheriff," Poppy said firmly. "Right now. That wasn't normal behavior. That was a threat."

"She already warned him today," I said, even as I was pulling out my phone. "When we ran into him outside Ventura's. She told him not to harass anyone."

"And he did it anyway," Gus growled. "Which means he's dangerous. Call her. Now."

My hands were still shaking as I scrolled through my contacts. I'd added Sheriff Iris's number months ago, just in case. I'd never actually used it.

She answered on the second ring. "Sheriff Scott."

"Iris, it's Alexis. From the café." My voice came out thin and breathless. "I need to report something. Warren Jacobs just followed me home. He chased me to my door."

There was a brief pause, then her voice turned sharp and focused. "Are you safe right now?"

"Yes. I'm inside the café. Doors are locked. He left after I got inside, but..."

"I'm on my way. Stay inside, keep the doors locked. I'll be there in five minutes."

The line went dead.

I sank onto one of the café chairs, my legs suddenly too weak to hold me. The adrenaline that had gotten me through the door was fading, leaving behind a trembling exhaustion.

"Good," Poppy said, jumping onto the table beside me. "She'll handle this."

"He smiled at me," I said quietly. "Through the glass. After he chased me. He just stood there and smiled."

"He's trying to scare you," Gus said. "It's a power play. He wants you to know he can get to you."

"Well, it worked."

"But you're not alone," Rocky added, pressing against my leg while Sage stayed tucked between his paws. "You have us. You have the sheriff. You have friends."

"Rocky's right," Poppy said. "You did the right thing. You got to safety and called for help. That's what you're supposed to do."

I reached down to stroke Rocky's head, taking comfort in his solid warmth. "I hate feeling scared in my own town. In my own home."

"You won't feel scared forever," Millie said softly from her spot near the window. "Once he's caught. Once this is over."

"I hope you're right."

Through the front window, I saw red and blue lights approaching. Sheriff Iris pulled up directly in front of the café, parking at an angle that blocked most of the street. She was out of her vehicle in seconds, hand near her weapon as she scanned the area.

I hurried to unlock the door.

"Are you hurt?" Those were the first words out of her mouth as she stepped inside.

"No. Just scared."

Her jaw tightened. "Tell me exactly what happened. Start from when you left Ventura's."

I walked her through it. The quiet walk back to Main Street. Noticing the figure in the shadows. Realizing he was following me. The moment I started running and heard his footsteps behind me. His face in the streetlight as he smiled at me through the glass.

As I spoke, I noticed lights coming on in the apartments above the other shops on Main Street. Not inside the shops themselves, but in the living spaces above them. People who lived here had seen the police lights, the sheriff's car blocking the street.

Iris listened without interrupting, her expression growing harder with each detail. When I finished, she pulled out a small notebook and had me repeat certain parts, taking notes this time.

Through the window, I could see figures emerging from buildings. Jasper from the general store, pulling a coat over his pajamas. Cordelia from the yarn shop, wrapped in a quilted robe. And Lionel from the comic shop, wearing sweatpants and a hoodie, his dark hair mussed like he'd been sleeping.

They gathered on the sidewalk across the street, talking to each other in low voices, clearly concerned but keeping their distance while the sheriff worked.

"Did he say anything to you?" Iris asked.

"No. He just followed me. And smiled."

"Did he try to open the door or touch the building in any way?"

"Not that I saw. He just stood there for maybe five seconds, then walked away."

Iris closed her notebook with more force than necessary. "I warned him this afternoon. Explicitly. Told him not to approach anyone, not to discuss the case, to go home and stay there." She looked at me, and I saw genuine anger in her eyes. "This isn't just harassment anymore. This is stalking. Intimidation. And given that we're investigating him for theft and possibly murder, this is witness intimidation."

"What does that mean?" I asked.

"It means I'm arresting him tonight. He clearly can't be trusted to stay away from potential witnesses." She glanced toward the window, noting the gathered neighbors. "I need to call this in, get backup. Then we're going to his house. I'll be right outside."

She stepped out onto the sidewalk, and I watched through the glass as she pulled out her radio. The neighbors kept their distance but their attention was clearly focused on the café, on her, on whatever had brought the sheriff here at this hour.

A moment later, Lionel broke away from the small group and approached the café. He opened the door partway, sticking his head in.

"Alexis?" His face was creased with concern. "Are you okay? What happened?"

"Warren Jacobs followed me home," I said quietly. "The sheriff's going to arrest him."

His expression darkened. "Did he hurt you?"

"No. He just followed me from Ventura's, chased me to the door. But he didn't touch me."

"Thank god." He glanced back at Iris, who was still on her radio, then back to me. "Do you need anything? Water? Someone to sit with you?"

"I'm okay for now. The sheriff's handling it."

"Okay. But I'm right here if you need me. I mean it."

"Thank you."

He returned to the sidewalk just as Iris finished her call. She walked back to the café door.

"Deputy Duchamp is meeting me at Warren's house in ten minutes. I'm going to bring him in, hold him overnight at minimum. Probably longer, until he can see a judge Monday morning."

"Thank you," I said.

"Don't thank me. This is my job. Keeping people safe." She studied my face. "Are you sure you're okay? Do you need me to call anyone? A friend to stay with you?"

"I'll be fine. Lily lives just a couple blocks away. I can call her if I need to."

"Good. I'll have a deputy drive by every hour or so tonight, just to check. And I'll call you once we have Warren in custody."

"I appreciate that."

"One more thing." Iris's voice turned serious. "Lock your doors. All of them. Don't open them for anyone unless you know who it is. If you see Warren again, call 911 immediately. Don't hesitate, don't second-guess yourself. Just call."

"I will."

"I mean it, Alexis. This man is dangerous. He's proven that tonight."

She left, and I watched through the window as she drove away, lights still flashing. The small group of neighbors remained on the sidewalk, and as soon as Iris's car disappeared around the corner, they crossed the street toward the café.

Lionel reached the door first. Jasper and Cordelia were right behind him.

"Is it true?" Jasper asked as I let them in. "Warren followed you?"

"Yes. From Ventura's all the way here. He chased me to the door."

"That son of a..." Jasper caught himself, glancing at Cordelia. "Sorry. But that's unacceptable."

"I knew he was unstable," Cordelia said, shaking her head. "The way he went on and on about his family legacy. But this? This is beyond unstable."

"The sheriff's arresting him tonight," I said. "He'll be in custody until at least Monday."

"Good," Jasper said firmly. "He needs to be locked up. What he did tonight, that's not okay."

"Alexis." Lionel's voice was quiet, concerned. "Are you really okay?"

I opened my mouth to say yes, to give the automatic reassurance. But something about the way he was looking at me, the genuine worry in his eyes, made the words catch in my throat.

"Would you two mind heading back?" Lionel asked Jasper and Cordelia. "I want to make sure Alexis is okay, but I don't want to keep you standing here in the cold."

"Of course," Cordelia said immediately. "Alexis, dear, if you need anything at all, I'm right down the street. Just call."

"Thank you."

"I'm serious about Warren being unacceptable," Jasper added. "You did the right thing calling the sheriff."

They headed back to their buildings, still talking to each other in low voices. Lionel remained, his hands shoved in his hoodie pockets.

"Can I come in?" he asked. "Just for a minute. I want to make sure you're really okay."

I stepped back, letting him enter. He seemed to fill the café space with his presence, solid and reassuring and real.

"I'm okay," I said. "Shaken up, but okay."

"You don't look okay." His voice was gentle. "You look terrified."

And suddenly, unexpectedly, tears were burning behind my eyes. I'd been holding myself together through the chase, through calling the sheriff, through giving my statement. But something about Lionel's kindness, his concern, cracked through my defenses.

"He chased me," I said, and my voice broke. "Like I was prey. Like he was hunting me."

"Alexis."

"And he smiled. After I locked the door, he just stood there and smiled at me. Like this was all a game to him."

"Come here." Lionel opened his arms, and I didn't hesitate.

I stepped into his embrace, and he wrapped his arms around me, solid and warm and safe. I pressed my face against his shoulder and let myself shake, let myself feel the fear I'd been suppressing.

He didn't say anything. Didn't offer platitudes or try to minimize what had happened. He just held me, one hand rubbing slow circles on my back, letting me process in silence.

"Thank you," I finally whispered.

"You don't have to thank me." His voice rumbled in his chest, close to my ear. "I'm just glad you're safe."

I pulled back slightly, wiping at my eyes. "Sorry. I didn't mean to fall apart on you."

"Don't apologize. You just got stalked by a potential murderer. You're allowed to fall apart."

A slightly hysterical laugh escaped me. "When you put it that way."

"Do you want me to stay for a bit? I don't have to. But I can, if you don't want to be alone."

I thought about it. About the empty apartment upstairs, the cats who would comfort me but couldn't actually protect me if Warren came back. About how much safer I felt with Lionel standing here in my café.

But I also thought about the confession he'd made last night at game night. About how he had feelings for me, feelings I couldn't return right now. About how letting him stay might send the wrong message.

"I appreciate the offer," I said carefully. "But I think I'll be okay. The sheriff said she'd call once they have Warren in custody. And she's having a deputy drive by regularly tonight."

"Are you sure?" Lionel searched my face. "Because I'm happy to just sit down here for a while. Read a book or play on my phone. You don't even have to talk to me. I just want to make sure you feel safe."

The offer was so genuine, so free of expectation, that I almost accepted. But something in me resisted. I'd spent so long being independent, protecting myself, not relying on anyone. Old habits were hard to break.

"I'm sure," I said. "But thank you. Really. For coming to check on me, for the hug, for the offer. It means a lot."

"Okay." He moved toward the door, then paused. "But if you change your mind, or if you get scared, or if Warren shows up again, you call me. Immediately. I'm three shops down. I can be here in thirty seconds."

"I will."

"Promise?"

"I promise."

He gave me one last concerned look, then stepped out into the night. I watched him walk back to his shop, his figure illuminated and then shadowed by the streetlights. He glanced back once before disappearing inside.

I locked the door behind him and stood in the quiet café. The cats had been remarkably silent during Lionel's visit, which I appreciated.

"You like him," Poppy observed.

"I like him as a friend."

"You let him hug you. For a long time."

"I was scared. He was comforting me."

"You could have accepted his offer to stay," Gus pointed out. "But you didn't."

"Because I don't want to lead him on. He told me last night that he has feelings for me. It wouldn't be fair to accept his help and give him false hope."

"Would it be false hope?" Rocky asked, Sage still tucked protectively between his paws. "You did let him hug you."

"Because I needed comfort. That's all."

"If you say so," Poppy said, but her tone suggested she didn't quite believe me.

I didn't want to analyze my feelings about Lionel right now. I was too tired, too scared, too overwhelmed. So I changed the subject.

"I'm going upstairs. Iris said she'd call when they have Warren in custody."

"We're coming with you," Poppy announced. All five cats moved toward the stairs as one, Sage trotting to keep up with Rocky's longer stride.

"Of course you are."

Upstairs, I changed into comfortable clothes, made myself a cup of chamomile tea, and tried to pretend I was relaxed. The cats weren't fooled.

"Stop pacing," Gus said from his spot on the couch. "You're making me nervous."

"I'm not pacing."

"You've walked from the kitchen to the window four times in the last five minutes."

"I'm just waiting for the sheriff to call."

"She said she'd call. So, she'll call. Sit down before you wear a hole in the floor."

I sat. Then stood again thirty seconds later when my phone rang.

"Sheriff Scott?"

"We have him in custody," Iris said without preamble. "Found him at his house. He tried to argue, but we arrested him without incident. He's at the station now, being processed."

Relief flooded through me. "Thank you."

"I'm charging him with stalking and witness intimidation. The judge will see him Monday morning for arraignment. At minimum, he'll be in custody until then."

"What happens after that?"

"Depends on the judge. But given that we're also investigating him for murder, I can't imagine they'll grant bail. He'll likely stay locked up until trial."

"That's good. That's really good."

"Try to get some rest tonight," Iris said. "And remember, if you need anything, call. We've got deputies doing regular patrols on Main Street, so you're not alone out there."

"I appreciate that."

After we hung up, I relayed the information to the cats.

"Good," Poppy said firmly. "He deserves to be locked up."

"Do you think he'll tell them where the necklace is?" Rocky asked.

"Probably not," I said. "If he admits to stealing it, that's basically an admission of guilt. He'll probably keep denying everything."

"Even though he followed you tonight like a creepy stalker?" Millie asked.

"He'll probably claim he was just walking in the same direction. That it was a coincidence."

"That's ridiculous," Gus huffed.

"Yes, but that's what people do when they're caught. They lie."

I finished my tea and climbed into bed. All five cats arranged themselves around me like furry bodyguards. Poppy curled against my side, Gus took the foot of the bed, Rocky sprawled across my legs with Sage nestled in the crook of his body, and Millie tucked herself against my pillow.

"We're not going to let anything happen to you," Poppy said quietly. "You know that, right?"

"I know."

"We'd fight him if we had to. All of us."

The image of my cats trying to fight a full-grown man was both touching and absurd. But I appreciated the sentiment.

"Thank you. But I don't think you'll need to fight anyone. He's locked up now."

"Good," Rocky said, already half asleep. "Because I'm too pretty to get in fights."

"You're orange," Gus said dryly. "Not pretty."

"Orange is the prettiest color."

"It's really not."

I smiled despite everything, letting their familiar bickering soothe me. Outside, I could hear the occasional car driving past, the sound of the wind picking up, the distant bark of a dog.

Normal sounds. Safe sounds.

Warren was locked up. The investigation was progressing. And tomorrow, Sunday, the café would be closed and I could rest, recover, maybe process everything that had happened this week.

But for now, I closed my eyes and tried to sleep, surrounded by cats and locked doors and the knowledge that my neighbors cared enough to check on me.

It wasn't perfect safety. But it was something.

And something was better than nothing.

Chapter Fifteen

I woke Sunday morning to weak sunlight filtering through my bedroom curtains and the weight of five cats distributed across my bed. For a blissful moment, I forgot about Warren. About being chased. About the terror of seeing him smile at me through the glass.

Then reality crashed back in, and my chest tightened.

"You're awake," Poppy said from her spot on my pillow. "How did you sleep?"

"Better than I expected." I sat up carefully, trying not to disturb Gus at the foot of the bed. "What time is it?"

"Almost eight thirty."

I'd slept later than usual, probably because my body had finally released all the adrenaline from the night before. The apartment was quiet, peaceful. Outside, I could hear the distant sounds of Sunday morning in Larkspur Valley. Church bells. A few cars. The wind rustling through the pines.

"Lily's coming at nine," Rocky reminded me, Sage curled into a tiny ball against his side.

"I remember."

I dragged myself out of bed and into the shower, letting the hot water ease the tension in my shoulders. By the time I'd dressed and made coffee, it was nearly nine o'clock.

The knock came right on time at my apartment door.

"Good morning," Lily said brightly as I let her in. Then she took one look at my face and her smile faded. "What happened? You look exhausted."

"Come in. I'll make coffee and tell you everything."

I made coffee while Lily settled on the couch. The cats arranged themselves nearby, listening with obvious interest. I handed Lily a mug and sat down across from her.

"Warren followed me home last night," I said without preamble.

Lily's cup froze halfway to her mouth. "What?"

I walked her through it. The figure in the shadows. The chase. Warren's smile through the glass. Calling Sheriff Iris. The arrest.

"Oh my god." Lily set down her cup before she could spill it. "Alexis, that's terrifying."

"It was. But he's locked up now. At least until tomorrow morning."

"Tomorrow morning? They're releasing him?"

"He has an arraignment Monday morning. The judge will decide about bail." I wrapped my hands around my coffee mug. "Iris thinks they'll probably hold him given the murder investigation, but there's no guarantee."

"So he could be out by tomorrow afternoon."

"Yes."

Lily was quiet for a moment, processing. Then she leaned forward, her expression intense. "We need to prove he did it. Not just the stalking. The theft. The murder. All of it."

"I know. But how? The scent test didn't definitively prove anything. He has no solid alibi, but that's not proof either. And without the necklace, we can't even prove he stole it."

"What about his research?" Lily asked. "You said everyone knows he's been obsessed with town history, spending hours at the library. What if there's more to it than just innocent family history research?"

"Pearl mentioned he's always on the computers. Everyone thinks he's just looking up old records and family trees."

"But what if he was researching other things too? Things he wouldn't want anyone to know about?"

I sat up straighter. "You mean like how to sell stolen jewelry?"

"Or worse." Lily leaned forward. "If we could see everything he was looking at on those computers, not just the obvious family history stuff..."

"A trace spell," I said.

"A psychometry spell on the computer," Lily said at the same time.

We stared at each other.

"It could work," Lily continued. "If we can get access to the computer he usually uses, we might be able to see echoes of what he was researching."

"But that's not something we've practiced much. And we'd need help." I thought for a moment. "Maeve."

"Perfect. She'd know exactly what to do."

"Let me call her."

I pulled out my phone and dialed Maeve's number. She answered after three rings, her voice warm and slightly amused.

"Alexis. I was wondering when you'd call."

"You knew I would?"

"I had a feeling. Something about urgency and libraries and hidden truths." She paused. "This is about Warren Jacobs, isn't it?"

"Yes. Can we come by? I need your help with something."

"I'll put the kettle on."

Twenty minutes later, Lily and I were sitting in the back room of The Turning Page, Maeve's bookshop. The space was cluttered with books, crystals, and dried herbs hanging from the ceiling. Maeve herself was short and round with wild curly silver hair and perceptive eyes that seemed to see more than most people.

She set tea in front of us and settled into her chair with a knowing look.

"Tell me everything."

I did. Warren's obsession with family history. The theft. Theo's murder. The scent tests that proved nothing definitive. Warren following me last night. His arrest.

"And now," I finished, "we need to prove he planned all of it. That it wasn't just an impulsive theft. That he's dangerous and calculated and needs to stay locked up."

"You want to see what he was really researching," Maeve said. "Not just family history. The truth behind his computer searches."

"Can we do that?" Lily asked.

"With the right spell, yes. Psychometry combined with a revealing charm. Objects hold echoes of their use, especially electronic devices. The computer will remember what it displayed, even if the user deleted the evidence."

"Will it work if other people have used the computer since?" I asked.

"The spell can be targeted to a specific person's energy signature. As long as you have something that belongs to Warren to use as a focus." Maeve sipped her tea. "Do you?"

I thought about it. "No. But I know where he sits in the library. Pearl mentioned he has a favorite spot."

"That might be enough. His repeated presence in that location will have left an imprint." Maeve stood and moved to one of her bookshelves, running her fingers along the spines. "Here. This will help."

She pulled out a slim volume bound in green leather. Inside were handwritten spells, diagrams, instructions.

"This is a psychometry spell specifically for revealing hidden information. It's not easy, and you'll need to maintain focus, but between the three of us, we should be able to manage it."

"Three of us?" Lily asked.

"You don't think I'm going to miss this, do you? I want to see what that man was really up to." Maeve's expression turned serious. "Besides, this spell works best with three. One to anchor, one to channel, one to interpret."

"The library is closed Sundays," I said. "But Pearl works there. She might let us in if I ask."

"Then let's ask."

I called Pearl, explaining that I needed to look up some information for the café, something about historical recipes for an event I was planning. She agreed immediately, offering to meet us at the library in half an hour.

"She doesn't know about the magic," I warned Maeve and Lily as we walked down Main Street. "We'll need to be subtle."

"I'm always subtle," Maeve said with a slight smile.

The library was a beautiful log building near the center of town, with large windows and a stone chimney. Pearl met us at the front door, keys in hand.

"This is so exciting," she said as she let us inside. "I hardly ever get to open up on Sundays. What exactly are you looking for?"

"Historical records about founding families and their recipes," I improvised. "I'm thinking of doing a special historical menu at the café."

"What a lovely idea! The historical section is upstairs, but the computers are down here if you need them." She gestured toward the row of public computers near the reference desk. "I'll be in the back organizing returns. Just call if you need anything."

Once she'd disappeared into the back room, Maeve moved purposefully toward the computers.

"Which one did he use?" she murmured.

"Pearl said he always sat at the end. That one." I pointed to the computer furthest from the main area, tucked partially behind a bookshelf.

Maeve nodded and pulled out the green leather book. "Lily, you'll anchor. Keep the spell stable and contained. Alexis, you'll channel. Focus your energy through the computer. I'll interpret what we see."

We arranged ourselves around the computer. Maeve placed her hands on the keyboard. Lily and I each placed one hand on the desk, creating a connection.

"Close your eyes," Maeve instructed. "Focus on Warren. His presence. His energy. The residue he left behind."

I did as she said, reaching out with my mind the way I did when communicating with cats. But instead of feline consciousness, I was searching for human imprints. Echoes of intention and action.

And there, faint but present, I felt it. Warren's energy. Bitter. Resentful. Obsessive.

"I have him," Maeve murmured. "Opening the channel. Alexis, push through."

I focused harder, pouring energy into the connection. The computer screen flickered to life, but instead of the normal login screen, images began to flash. Search histories. Websites. Documents.

Maeve's voice was steady as she read what she saw. "Hendry family tree. Jacobs family contributions. Historical records 1880s. That's all normal. But then... antique jewelry appraisal. Selling inherited jewelry anonymously. Pawn shops Denver. Removing identifying marks from jewelry."

My stomach tightened.

"More," Maeve continued. "How to research property blueprints. Security systems older homes. Victorian house layouts. And then... Theo Vincent family history. Theo Vincent business records. Theo Vincent partnership disputes."

"He was researching Theo," Lily breathed.

"Wait. There's more." Maeve's expression darkened. "Stolen jewelry value. Theo Vincent address. Theo Vincent daily routine. Aspen Falls trail conditions."

"He planned it," Lily breathed. "All of it."

The images kept coming. Searches about police investigation procedures. How long theft cases stay active. Witness intimidation laws.

And then, near the end, something that made my blood run cold.

"Alexis Belrose," Maeve read. "New resident Larkspur Valley. Alexis Belrose background."

He'd been researching me. Looking for information about me. Trying to find leverage or weaknesses or something he could use.

The spell ended abruptly, the screen going dark. All three of us stood there, shaken.

"He planned everything," I said. "The theft. The murder. Even researching how to intimidate witnesses."

"That's not the behavior of someone who acted impulsively," Maeve said. "That's calculated. Methodical."

"And he was researching you specifically," Lily added, her hand finding mine. "He's fixated on you. That makes him even more dangerous."

"We need to tell Sheriff Iris," I said. "But how do we explain how we know?"

"You can't," Maeve said practically. "She doesn't know about magic. But you can tell her you're certain he'll come for you when he's released tomorrow. And you can offer to help make sure he confesses."

"Like I did with Orla during Hazel's murder investigation."

"Exactly. She trusted you then. She'll trust you now."

We cleaned up quickly, making sure we left no trace of the spell. Pearl emerged from the back room just as we were heading for the door.

"Did you find what you needed?" she asked.

"Yes, thank you so much for opening up for us."

"Anytime, dear. I hope your historical menu turns out beautifully."

Outside, the three of us stood on the library steps, the November wind cold against our faces.

"I'm going to talk to Sheriff Iris," I said. "See if she'll agree to the plan."

"What plan?" Lily asked.

"Warren will be released tomorrow. He'll come for me. I'm sure of it. He wants to intimidate me into silence, or worse." I looked at both of them. "What if we're ready for him? What if we set up a situation where he has to confess?"

"A confession spell," Maeve said slowly. "Risky. But it could work."

"It worked with Orla."

"Orla was already eaten up with guilt. Warren has no such compunction." Maeve considered. "But yes. With the right preparation, the right ingredients, and the right circumstances, we could compel him to tell the truth."

"Then let's do it. Let me talk to Iris first, see if she'll help set it up."

"I'm coming with you," Maeve said firmly. "The sheriff will have questions. She'll be skeptical. Two voices might be more convincing than one."

"And three is better than two," Lily said immediately. "I'm coming with you too."

I looked at both of them, grateful for their support. "Alright. Let's go together."

The sheriff's office was only a few blocks away. The three of us walked there together, the November wind cold against our faces.

Inside, the station was busy despite it being Sunday. A deputy sat at the front desk, and two other officers were moving between desks in the open area beyond. The deputy looked up as we entered.

"Can I help you?" he asked.

"We're here to see Sheriff Scott," I said. "It's about the Warren Jacobs case."

He picked up the phone, spoke briefly, then nodded. "She'll see you. Go on back."

We made our way through the busy station to Iris's office. She was at her desk when we entered, surrounded by case files and empty coffee cups. She looked up, her expression immediately concerned when she saw all three of us.

"Alexis. Maeve. Lily." Her eyes narrowed slightly. "This must be very serious if all three of you are here."

"We need to talk to you about tomorrow," I said.

"Warren's arraignment."

"Yes. He'll probably be released, won't he?"

Iris sighed. "I'm pushing for no bail, but realistically, the stalking charge alone isn't enough to hold him indefinitely. Unless the judge agrees that he's a flight risk or a danger to witnesses." She studied my face. "You think he'll come for you again."

"I know he will. He's obsessed. Desperate. He needs to silence me before I can testify about what he did last night."

"I can put a protective detail on you. Have someone watching the café."

"Or," I said carefully, "you could let him come. And I'll make sure he confesses."

Iris leaned back in her chair, eyes narrowing. "Like how you got Orla to confess to killing Hazel?"

"Yes."

"I still don't fully understand how you did that," Iris said slowly. "Orla was a wreck, yes, but she'd held that secret for over a year. Then twenty minutes with you and she couldn't stop talking." She tapped her pen against her desk. "You have some kind of gift for making people want to confess. I've never seen anything quite like it."

"People carry guilt," I said carefully. "Sometimes they just need someone who will listen without judgment."

"It's more than that," Iris said. "But I'm not going to pry into methods that work."

"So you'll consider it?" Lily asked.

"No." Iris shook her head firmly. "Absolutely not. Do you have any idea how dangerous that would be? Warren already chased you through town and tried to corner you in your apartment. Now you want me to let him come back?"

"With proper precautions—"

"What precautions?" Iris stood, her voice sharp with concern. "You're a civilian, Alexis. It's my job to protect you, not use you as bait."

Maeve stepped forward, her voice calm and steady. "Sheriff, may I?"

Iris glanced at Maeve, then nodded stiffly.

"Warren Jacobs will come for Alexis whether you prepare for it or not," Maeve said reasonably. "He's fixated. Desperate. Cornered.

Men like that don't stop because of protective details or restraining orders. They act."

"Which is exactly why I can't agree to this."

"But what's your alternative?" Maeve asked. "Keep Alexis under protection indefinitely? Hope Warren doesn't find a way past your officers? Or worse, hope the stalking charge is enough to keep him locked up when you and I both know it won't be?"

Iris was quiet, her jaw tight.

"What exactly are you proposing?" she finally asked, her tone still skeptical.

"Warren will come for me whether we plan for it or not," I said. "At least this way, we're prepared. You'll have officers nearby. We'll have witnesses. And I have a method that worked before."

"A method you won't explain."

"I can't explain it," I said honestly. "But I know I can persuade him to talk. Sometimes guilty people really want the truth to come out."

Iris studied me for a long moment, her eyes searching my face. Then she leaned back slightly.

"That's not how the law works. Confessions obtained through... whatever you did... might not be admissible in court."

"They will be if he confesses voluntarily in front of witnesses," Maeve said calmly. "Which he will. He'll want to explain himself, to justify his actions. All Alexis does is... create an environment where the truth comes out."

Iris looked between us, her jaw tight. "You're asking me to put a civilian in danger based on some method I don't understand and can't verify."

"I'm asking you to trust me," I said. "The way you trusted me with Orla."

"That was different. Orla came to you. She was already breaking down. Warren is..." Iris ran a hand through her hair. "Warren is calculating. Dangerous. He planned a murder."

"Which is exactly why we need him to confess," I said. "Otherwise, you might only be able to charge him with stalking. Maybe theft if you find the necklace. But murder? Without a confession or solid physical evidence, he could walk."

The truth of that hung in the air. Iris knew I was right.

"We're not asking you to compromise your integrity," Maeve added. "We're asking you to trust that sometimes, people confess when given the right opportunity. Alexis has a gift for reading people, for making them feel safe enough to unburden themselves. That's all this is."

It wasn't all it was, but it was close enough to the truth.

Iris was quiet for a long moment, clearly wrestling with the decision. She looked at me, really looked at me, and I saw the moment she made her choice.

"If I agree to this," she said slowly, "I need guarantees. My officers will be positioned within seconds of the café. You'll wear a wire so we can hear everything. At the first sign of violence, we come in. No arguments, no waiting."

"Agreed," I said immediately.

"And you tell me right now, honestly, if you have any doubts about this working."

I thought about the spell. About Maeve and Lily's preparation. About how Orla had confessed everything when the truth became too heavy to carry.

"It will work," I said. "I'm certain."

Iris studied me for another long moment, then nodded. "Alright. But I want to be clear. I don't like this. I think it's reckless and dangerous and goes against every protocol I've ever learned." She held my gaze. "But I also know that sometimes, by-the-book approaches don't work. And I saw what you did with Orla. So against my better judgment, I'm going to trust you."

"Thank you," I said, relief flooding through me.

"What do you need from me?" Iris asked.

"Privacy at the café tomorrow afternoon. No obvious police presence, but officers nearby who can hear and respond quickly. And civilian witnesses who can testify to what they hear."

"I can arrange that. What time?"

"After the arraignment. He'll probably come straight to me. Say around two o'clock?"

"I'll be there. Hidden, but close." Iris walked around her desk. "Alexis, are you absolutely sure about this? Last chance to back out."

"I'm sure. He's going to come for me anyway. At least this way, we're prepared. And we'll have proof."

"Alright. Two o'clock tomorrow at the café. I'll have deputies positioned nearby and we'll set up listening equipment." She met my eyes. "You make sure you can deliver on that confession."

"I will."

As we left the sheriff's office, I let out a long breath I hadn't realized I'd been holding.

"She didn't need magic to be convinced," Maeve said quietly. "She needed logic. And she needed to trust her own instincts about you."

"Thank you for coming with me."

"Of course." Maeve's expression turned serious. "Now we have to make sure it works. Because if Warren gets away with this, Iris will never trust either of us again."

"It will work," I said, hoping I sounded more confident than I felt. "It has to."

We walked back to The Turning Page together, all three of us processing what had just happened.

"She actually agreed," Lily said as we entered the bookstore. "I wasn't sure she would."

"Neither was I," I admitted. "Tomorrow at two o'clock."

"Then we have work to do." Maeve moved to her shelves, pulling down jars and pouches. "A confession spell requires specific ingredients. Truth root. Clear quartz. Silver sage. And a binding agent."

"I have some of these at the café," I said. "The healing teas use similar herbs."

"Good. We'll divide the list." Maeve wrote quickly on a piece of paper. "Lily, you gather these from my stores. Alexis, you check what you have at the café. I'll handle the rest. We'll meet back here in two hours to prepare everything."

The rest of Sunday passed in a blur of preparation. Gathering herbs. Grinding ingredients. Inscribing symbols on small stones. Maeve walked us through the confession spell step by step, making sure we understood exactly what to do and when.

"The spell compels truth," she explained. "But it only works if the person is already feeling guilt or fear. Warren has both. He's scared of being caught and he's guilty of two major crimes. The spell will pull those truths to the surface and force him to speak them."

"Will he know what's happening?" I asked.

"Not exactly. He'll feel compelled to confess, like the words are being pulled from him. But he won't know it's magic. He'll probably think it's his own conscience or nerves."

"And if he resists?"

"The more he resists, the stronger the compulsion becomes. Eventually, he won't be able to stop himself."

By evening, we had everything prepared. Small pouches of herbs. Crystals charged with intention. A silver bowl filled with water from Lake Larkspur. Everything we'd need for tomorrow.

"Get some rest tonight," Maeve advised as Lily and I prepared to leave. "You'll need your strength tomorrow. And your focus."

"Thank you," I said. "For all of this. For helping."

"We protect our own," Maeve said simply. "And right now, you need protecting."

Lily walked back to the café with me. At my apartment door, she hugged me tightly.

"We're going to stop him," she said. "Tomorrow, this all ends."

"I hope you're right."

Upstairs, the cats were waiting. I fed them dinner and told them about the plan for tomorrow.

"You're going to confront him," Poppy said. It wasn't a question.

"Yes. With the spell, with witnesses, with Iris nearby. It's the only way."

"We'll be there too," Rocky declared. "All of us. If he tries anything, he'll have to go through us first."

"I'll scratch his ankles," Sage added seriously.

"Rocky, you're a cat."

"A very fierce cat."

Despite everything, I smiled. "I know you are. And Sage, thank you for offering your fierce ankle-scratching services."

I went to bed early, but sleep was elusive. Tomorrow, Warren would be released. Tomorrow, he would come for me. And tomorrow, one way or another, this would all be over.

I just hoped we'd prepared enough.

Chapter Sixteen

Sheriff Iris and Deputy Duchamp arrived at seven-fifteen, while the café was still dark and locked. I let them in through the back door, my hands shaking slightly as I turned the key.

"Morning," Iris said, her expression grim. "We need to set up before you open."

They carried in equipment I didn't fully understand. Small devices that looked like they belonged in a spy movie. Duchamp moved through the café with practiced efficiency, placing them in corners, behind picture frames, under tables.

"Audio only," Iris explained as she worked. "We'll be able to hear everything that happens in here. Deputy Ramsey is already positioned across the street in the general store's second floor. I'll be in the alley behind the building once Warren's released. Duchamp will be in his patrol car two blocks down."

"Will he be able to hear me from that far away?" I asked.

"The equipment is sensitive. As long as you stay in the main café area, we'll hear everything clearly." She adjusted something on a device near the counter. "When he arrives, try to keep him in the center of the room. That's where the coverage is best."

"Okay."

Lily came down from the apartment, fully dressed but looking as nervous as I felt. "Is everything ready?"

"Almost," Iris said. She turned to me, her expression serious. "Alexis, I need to be clear about something. If at any point you feel unsafe, if anything goes wrong, you give us the signal. We'll be inside in less than ten seconds."

"What's the signal?"

"Say the word 'help' or 'stop' and we come in. No questions, no hesitation. Your safety is more important than any confession."

"I understand."

"Good." Iris tested the last device, nodded in satisfaction, then looked at both of us. "The arraignment is at ten. Judge Martin is fair but tough. I'm going to argue for no bail given the stalking incident and the ongoing murder investigation. But there's no guarantee."

"When will I know?" I asked.

"I'll call you as soon as it's over. If he's released, he could be here as early as noon. More likely around two, given how long the paperwork takes." She headed for the back door, then paused. "You're sure about this? About using your method?"

"I'm sure."

She studied me for a long moment, then nodded. "Then we'll be ready. Good luck."

After she left, Lily and I stood in the quiet café, surrounded by hidden listening devices and the weight of what we were about to do.

"The spell is ready?" I asked quietly.

"Everything's prepared. The mixture is in the storage room, charged and ready to use. As soon as he arrives and orders something, we add it to his drink. He won't taste anything different." Lily's hand found mine. "Are you scared?"

"Terrified."

"Me too." She squeezed my hand. "But we can do this. We have to."

At eight o'clock, I unlocked the front door and flipped the sign to open. Within minutes, the regulars started arriving. But their usual morning cheer was replaced with concern and curiosity.

Mabel was first through the door, her expression fierce. "I heard what that man did Saturday night. Following you home like some kind of predator. Are you alright, dear?"

"I'm fine, Mabel. The sheriff arrested him."

"Good. He should be locked up for good." She settled at her usual table, but her sharp eyes kept darting to the door, as if watching for threats. "If he shows his face around here again, he'll have to deal with all of us."

Felix arrived next, his usual quiet demeanor unchanged, but he set a small wrapped package on the counter. "For you. Pepper spray. From my sister in Silverpine. She insists every woman should have one." His ears were slightly pink. "I know you're capable, but... well. Just in case."

"Thank you, Felix. That's very thoughtful."

He nodded, clearly uncomfortable with the attention, and retreated to his corner table with his sketchbook.

Jasper stomped in, dropping a heavy wrench on the counter with a thunk. "Keeping this here. You see that man come near this café, you call me. I'll be at the garage all day. One minute away, tops." He leaned forward, jaw tight. "Man like that shouldn't be walking free. Makes my blood boil."

"The sheriff arrested him that night. He's been in custody since then."

"Good. Should stay locked up, if you ask me." But he didn't take the wrench back, leaving it there like a promise.

By nine o'clock, word had clearly spread through the entire town. Nearly every customer who came in mentioned Warren, asked if I was okay, offered support in various forms ranging from practical to absurd. The community was rallying around me, and while I appreciated it, the constant attention was exhausting.

"You're popular today," Poppy observed from her perch in the window. "Everyone wants to protect you."

"I know. It's sweet. But also overwhelming."

"That's what community is. Overwhelming and sweet in equal measure."

"What's overwhelming?" Sage asked from the windowsill, where she'd been batting at a dust mote in the sunlight. "Is it bad?"

"Not bad," Poppy explained patiently. "Just a lot all at once."

"Oh. Like when Rocky plays too rough?"

"Exactly like that," I said, smiling despite my nerves.

The door chimed again, and Flo bustled in carrying her usual basket of pastries. But her expression was more concerned than usual.

"Alexis, sweetheart." She set the basket down and immediately pulled me into a hug. "I heard about Warren. That must have been terrifying."

"It was. But I'm okay now."

"Are you sure? Because if you need to close for the day, take some time, no one would blame you." She pulled back, studying my face. "You look exhausted."

"I didn't sleep great, but I'll be fine." I gestured to the basket. "What did you bring today?"

"Cinnamon rolls, blueberry muffins, and some of those lemon scones you like." She started unpacking them, arranging them in the display case with practiced ease. "I made extra. Figured people would want comfort food today."

"Thank you. For everything."

"Of course." She finished with the pastries and leaned against the counter, lowering her voice slightly. "I also wanted to give you an update on Cleo."

My attention sharpened. "How is she doing?"

"Wonderfully. Ella is completely devoted to her. They sleep in the same bed, Cleo follows her everywhere when she's home from school. It's like they were meant to find each other." Flo's smile was warm but tinged with something else. Confusion, maybe. Or concern. "The strangest thing, though. Ella keeps insisting that Cleo talks to her. Not out loud, obviously, but... well, you remember that conversation we had at the café."

"I remember."

"Lee and Piper think it's just imagination. You know how kids are, creating elaborate pretend scenarios. But..." Flo shook her head. "Sometimes Ella knows things about Cleo that she shouldn't. Like when Cleo's food bowl is empty even when Ella's at school. Or when Cleo doesn't feel well. She just knows."

"Some people are more sensitive to animals," I said carefully. "It's a gift."

"That's what you said before." Flo studied me. "Do you really believe that? That some people can understand animals in ways others can't?"

"I do."

She was quiet for a moment, processing. Then she smiled, though it was uncertain. "Well, whether it's real or imagination, Cleo is clearly good for Ella. And Ella is good for Cleo. That's what matters."

"Exactly."

After Flo left, I found myself constantly checking the clock. Nine-thirty. Ten o'clock. The arraignment would be starting now. Ten-fifteen. Ten-thirty. What was taking so long?

Lionel arrived around ten-forty-five, and the worry on his face was immediate and obvious.

"Alexis." He didn't even pretend to look at the menu. "I've been thinking about Saturday night. About you being here alone if Warren comes back. I know you said you'd be fine, but I wanted to offer again. I can stay. Work from here today. Just in case."

"That's very kind, but I'm not alone. Lily's here."

"I know, but..." He ran a hand through his hair. "Look, I know you can take care of yourself. I'm not trying to be overprotective or anything. I just... I care about you. And the idea of that man coming anywhere near you makes me want to punch something."

"Lionel—"

"I know. You don't need protecting. You're capable and strong and have been handling this whole situation better than most people would. But caring about someone means worrying about them anyway, even when they don't need it." He met my eyes. "So just know that I'm three shops down. If anything happens. Anything at all. You call me."

"I will. I promise."

He nodded, still looking unconvinced but accepting my answer. "Okay. And if you change your mind about wanting company, the offer stands."

After he left, Lily raised an eyebrow at me. "He really cares about you."

"I know."

"And you care about him."

"As a friend."

"Alexis." Her tone was gentle but firm. "You're allowed to care about people. You're allowed to let people care about you. That's not weakness. That's not letting your guard down. That's just being human."

I didn't have an answer to that, so I busied myself wiping down the already-clean counter.

At eleven-fifteen, the door chimed again. Dr. Colton Dover walked in, and I noticed he wasn't wearing his usual veterinary clinic scrubs. He'd clearly come from home, dressed casually but deliberately.

"Alexis. I heard about what happened Saturday night." He ordered his usual coffee, then leaned against the counter, his easy charm replaced with genuine concern. "I've been debating whether to come by since yesterday. Didn't want to add to the parade of well-meaning people probably driving you crazy."

"It's been a lot," I admitted.

"I can imagine." He accepted the coffee but didn't move to leave. "Look, I know we're not... I mean, we're friends, right? And as your friend, I need to say something. Warren's not stable. Everyone in town knows it. The obsession with his family history, the resentment. It's been building for years." His jaw tightened slightly. "I treated his neighbor's dog last month, and she mentioned Warren had been getting worse. More isolated, more fixated."

"The sheriff has it under control."

"I'm sure she does. But if you need anything..." He paused, seemed to be choosing his words carefully. "I know Lionel already offered to camp out here. And I don't want to pile on. But my clinic is even closer than his shop. And I have experience dealing with aggressive animals, which isn't that different from dealing with aggressive people."

The joke fell flat, and he winced. "Sorry. Bad attempt at lightening the mood."

"It's okay."

"The offer stands. Not because I think you can't handle yourself. But because nobody should have to handle dangerous situations alone." He picked up his coffee, met my eyes. "Take care of yourself, Alexis. Call if you need anything. Anything at all."

After he left, Lily raised an eyebrow at me. "He's worried about you."

"Everyone's worried."

"No. He's worried about you. There's a difference." She smiled slightly. "The whole town's in love with you, you know. You just don't see it."

My phone rang. Sheriff Iris.

"He's being released," she said without preamble. "Judge granted bail. I argued against it, but Warren's lawyer convinced the judge that stalking charges weren't enough to hold him on murder suspicion alone. He's being processed now. Should be out within the hour."

My stomach dropped. "Okay."

"I'm going to hold him here as long as I legally can with the paperwork. Every form filled out slowly, every signature double-checked. But realistically, he'll be out by one-thirty, maybe quarter to two. I'll head to your location as soon as he's out the door. Ramsey's already across the street, Duchamp is two blocks down. Are you ready?"

"As ready as I'll ever be."

"Remember the signal. Any sign of danger, you say the word and we're there."

After we hung up, I relayed the information to Lily.

"He'll be here soon," she said. "I should get the mixture ready."

She disappeared into the back storage room and returned a moment later with a small vial of dark liquid. It looked almost like vanilla extract or some other common baking ingredient.

"This is it?" I asked quietly.

"The spell is concentrated in liquid form. We add it to his drink, whatever he orders. It has no taste, no smell. He won't notice anything different." She set the vial on the back counter, hidden behind the espresso machine. "Once he drinks it, the compulsion takes about two minutes to build. Then he'll feel an overwhelming need to tell the truth. To confess."

"And if he resists?"

"He can't. Not once he's consumed it. The magic is designed to override resistance." She met my eyes. "This will work, Alexis. We've done everything right."

"What if he doesn't order anything? What if he just wants to talk?"

"Then you offer him coffee. Tell him you just made a fresh pot. He'll drink it. People always accept offered hospitality, especially when they're trying to appear non-threatening."

The lunch rush came and went. Regular customers, tourists, a few people who'd heard about Warren and wanted to check on me. All of them kind, concerned, supportive. All of them unknowingly witnessing the calm before the storm.

At one-forty, my phone buzzed with a text from Iris: "He just left. In position now. Ready."

I showed it to Lily. She nodded, her expression determined.

"The café is almost empty," she observed. "Just Felix in the corner and that couple by the window."

"Should I ask them to leave?"

"No. Witnesses are good. As long as they're not in danger."

At one-forty-five, Felix packed up his sketchbook and left with a wave. The couple finished their coffee and headed out five minutes later.

The door chimed again almost immediately. Two tourists wandered in, a man and woman in hiking gear, and settled at a corner table with a trail map spread between them. They ordered coffee and seemed completely absorbed in planning their route.

Good. Witnesses who wouldn't interfere.

The cats watched from their various perches. Sage had finally stopped playing and sat very still on the counter, her gray and white fur slightly puffed.

"Something feels funny," she said quietly. "The air tastes different."

"She's right," Poppy said from the window. "He's coming. I can feel it."

"How do you know?" I asked.

"The same way I know when storms are coming. The air changes. Gets heavier." Poppy's tail twitched. "Even the kitten can sense it."

Sage pressed closer to me, suddenly very small and very young. "I don't like it."

"Stay close to me," I told her. "All of you, stay where you are. Don't approach him."

At one fifty-eight, I saw movement outside. A figure approaching from down the street, walking with deliberate purpose.

Warren Jacobs.

He reached the door, paused for just a moment, then pushed it open.

The bell chimed cheerfully, completely at odds with the tension that flooded the room.

Warren stepped inside and let the door close behind him. His eyes found mine immediately, and he smiled.

It was the same smile he'd given me Saturday night through the glass. Cold. Calculating. Threatening.

"Alexis," he said pleasantly. "We need to talk."

Chapter Seventeen

Warren stood in the center of my café, hands loose at his sides, his expression pleasant but his eyes cold. Behind the counter, I felt Lily go still. In the viewing room, the cats had stopped moving, watching.

Two tourists sat at a corner table, oblivious, studying a trail map between sips of coffee.

"We need to talk," Warren repeated, his voice conversational. Almost friendly.

"About what?" I kept my tone neutral, professional.

"About how involved you've gotten in things that don't concern you." He took a step closer. "The sheriff's investigation. The questions you've been asking. The way you keep inserting yourself into matters you don't understand."

"I run a café. People talk. I listen. That's not inserting myself into anything."

"Don't play innocent with me, Alexis." His smile didn't reach his eyes. "I know you know more than you let on. I saw it at the party. The way you looked at me. The way you've been watching."

My heart hammered against my ribs, but I forced myself to stay calm. "Can I get you your usual?"

The sudden shift caught him off guard. He blinked, reassessing.

"What?"

"Your usual. Black coffee." I moved behind the counter, putting the solid wood between us. "You look like you could use some."

He stared at me for a long moment, trying to read my intentions. Then, slowly, he nodded.

"Yes. Black coffee."

Lily moved smoothly to the coffee station, her hands steady as she poured from the fresh pot. I watched her palm the small vial, add three drops to the cup. The liquid disappeared into the dark coffee without a trace.

She set the cup on the counter between Warren and me.

He didn't move to take it immediately. Instead, he continued watching me with those calculating eyes.

"You think you're clever," he said quietly. "Running this little café, befriending everyone, making yourself indispensable to the community. But I see through it. You're an outsider. You always will be."

"The coffee's getting cold," I said.

He picked up the cup, still holding my gaze, and took a long drink.

"You need to understand something," he continued, setting the cup down. "This town has a history. A legacy. And not everyone gets to be part of that legacy, no matter how much they pretend to belong."

"Is that what this is about? Legacy?"

"It's about recognition. About truth. About families who built this town being erased from history while others take all the credit." His voice was rising slightly, passion bleeding through the controlled facade. "Do you know what it's like to watch your family's contributions be forgotten? To see statues and street names honoring people who did no more than your own ancestors, but somehow they get remembered and you get nothing?"

He took another drink of coffee, a longer one this time.

"The Hendrys act like they founded this town alone. Like the Jacobs family contributed nothing. Like we weren't there from the beginning, working just as hard, sacrificing just as much." His jaw tightened. "My great-great-grandfather Elias built half the buildings on Main Street. But does anyone remember that? No. They remember Henry Hendry. They put up a statue of Henry Hendry. They named the main square after Henry Hendry."

"That must be frustrating," I said carefully.

"Frustrating?" He laughed, bitter and sharp. "It's infuriating. It's wrong. And I tried to fix it. I spent years researching, documenting, proving that the Jacobs family deserved recognition. But no one cared. The historical society dismissed me. The town council ignored my petitions. Even Flo—" He stopped abruptly, pressing his lips together.

But his hand was trembling slightly. He noticed, frowned, took another sip of coffee as if to steady himself.

"Even Flo what?" I prompted.

"Even Flo acted like I was being unreasonable. Like wanting my family's story told was somehow offensive to her family's legacy." The words came faster now, tumbling out. "She has everything. The diner, the house, the recognition, the necklace. Six generations of Hendry women wore that necklace. Six generations of being celebrated and honored while my family gets nothing."

He drained the rest of his coffee in one gulp, then gripped the edge of the counter.

"I shouldn't be telling you this." His voice had changed, becoming confused. "Why am I telling you this?"

"Maybe you need to tell someone," Lily said softly from behind me.

"No. No, I don't need—" He shook his head sharply. "I cheated on my taxes last year. Why did I just say that? I cheated on my taxes. Took deductions I wasn't entitled to. And the year before. And—"

He clapped a hand over his mouth, eyes wide.

The tourists glanced over, curious but not alarmed. Just a man having an odd conversation.

"What's happening?" Warren's voice was muffled behind his hand. He lowered it slowly. "I lied to my wife. About where I was last Tuesday. I told her I was at the library but I was actually at a bar in Silverpine. I do that sometimes. Lie to her. About small things. About big things. I—"

He stumbled back from the counter, breathing hard.

"Stop. I need to stop talking. I need to—" His face contorted with effort. "I stole office supplies from my job. For years. Pens, paper, staplers. Things they wouldn't miss. But I took them anyway because I could. Because they don't pay me enough. Because—"

"Mr. Jacobs," I said gently. "Maybe you should sit down."

"No. No, I need to leave. I need to—" But his feet didn't move. Instead, more words poured out. "I took the necklace. I went to Flo's house during the party. I knew where she kept it. Second floor, master bedroom, in the display case by the window. I waited until everyone was downstairs, until the house tour had moved to the first floor. I went up the back stairs, the servants' stairs that no one uses anymore. I had gloves. I had a plan."

His face had gone pale, sweat beading on his forehead.

"I shouldn't be saying this. Why can't I stop saying this?" He gripped his head with both hands. "The case wasn't locked. She never locked it. Too trusting. Too sure that nothing bad would happen in her perfect house with her perfect life. I opened it. I took the necklace. I put it in my jacket pocket. I walked back down the servants' stairs. No one saw me. No one suspected."

"Where is it now?" I asked quietly.

"Hidden. In my garage. Behind the false panel I installed in the wall. My wife doesn't know about the panel. No one knows about the panel. I was going to sell it. Not here. Somewhere far away. Somewhere they couldn't trace it back to—" He made a choking sound, trying to stop the words. "I researched pawn shops. Anonymous sales. How to remove identifying marks from jewelry. I planned it for months. Months of watching, waiting, planning every detail."

The tourists had stopped pretending not to listen. They sat frozen, staring.

"And Theo," Warren continued, the words ripping out of him now like he was being torn apart. "Theo figured it out. He confronted me. Thursday afternoon at the library. He said he had proof. He said he found documents that showed I'd researched the necklace, that I'd been asking questions about how to sell stolen goods. He said he was going to the sheriff."

"So you killed him," I said.

"No. No, I didn't mean to—" But the spell wouldn't let him lie. "Yes. Yes, I killed him. I told him to meet me Friday night. Near Aspen Falls. I said I'd explain everything, that he'd misunderstood. He came. He believed me. He always was too trusting, too eager to see the best in people even when—"

Warren's whole body was shaking now, fighting the compulsion with everything he had. But the magic was stronger.

"I hit him. With a rock from the trail. He fell. There was blood. So much blood. I didn't think— I didn't plan— But then he was on the ground and he wasn't moving and I realized what I'd done. So I dragged him. Closer to the falls. Made it look like an accident. Like he'd slipped and hit his head. I arranged the body. I wiped the rock clean. I threw it in the water. I went home and burned my clothes."

He collapsed against the counter, gasping for breath.

"Please. Please make it stop. I'll do anything. Just make it stop."

"You can't stop it," Lily said. "The truth always comes out."

"What did you do to me?" Warren's eyes were wild, darting between us. "What was in that coffee? You drugged me. You did something—"

"We didn't drug you," I said truthfully. "You're just finally telling the truth."

"I need to leave. I need to get out of here." He pushed away from the counter, stumbling toward the door.

But before he could reach it, the door opened.

Sheriff Iris stood in the doorway, Deputies Duchamp and Ramsey flanking her. Behind them, I could see Lionel and Jasper on the sidewalk, drawn by the commotion.

"Warren Jacobs," Iris said, her voice hard as stone. "You're under arrest for the murder of Theo Vincent and the theft of the Hendry family necklace."

Warren stared at her, then at the deputies, then back at me. The realization of what had just happened, of what he'd just confessed, crashed over his face like a wave.

"You set me up." His voice was hoarse. "You made me…? How did you …? What did you …?"

"Turn around," Duchamp ordered. "Hands behind your back."

Warren didn't move. For a moment, I thought he might try to fight, to run. But then the fight drained out of him all at once. His shoulders slumped. His face crumpled.

"I just wanted them to remember," he whispered. "I just wanted my family to matter."

Duchamp cuffed him, reading him his rights in a flat, professional tone. Warren didn't resist. Didn't speak. Just stood there until they led him out, past the shocked tourists, past Lionel and Jasper, into the waiting patrol car.

Iris remained in the doorway, watching until the car pulled away. Then she turned to me.

"Well," she said. "That was even more effective than last time. I don't suppose you're going to tell me how you did it?"

"Probably not."

"Didn't think so." She pulled out her notebook. "But I heard everything. Every word. So did Duchamp and Ramsey through the equipment. And we have two witnesses." She nodded at the tourists, who looked like they were reconsidering their vacation destination. "That's enough for a conviction. More than enough."

"The necklace is in his garage," I said. "Behind a false panel."

"We'll get a search warrant. Have it back to Flo by tonight, hopefully." Iris studied me for a long moment. "You did good work here, Alexis. Dangerous work, but good. Thank you."

After she left, the café fell into stunned silence. The tourists finished their coffee and hurried out, whispering to each other. Lionel started to come in but I shook my head. Not yet. I needed a moment.

Lily moved around the counter and pulled me into a hug.

"It's over," she said. "It's finally over."

I hugged her back, feeling the tension drain from my body all at once. My knees went weak. My hands started shaking, all the fear I'd been suppressing crashing over me now that the danger had passed.

"You did it," Poppy said from her perch. "You caught him."

"We all did it," I said.

"True," Rocky agreed. "But mostly you."

Sage jumped down from the viewing room and wound around my ankles, pressing close. "You were very brave. Even though you were scared. I could feel it."

"Being brave means doing the right thing even when you're scared," I told her, picking her up. She was trembling slightly. "You were brave too, staying quiet and watching."

She purred against my chest, finally relaxing.

Through the window, I could see people gathering on the sidewalk. Word was spreading fast. Warren had been arrested. He'd confessed. To murder. To theft. To everything.

By tomorrow, the whole town would know.

"Are you okay?" Lily asked softly.

I thought about it. About Warren's face as the truth poured out of him. About Theo, who'd died trying to expose the truth. About Flo, who would finally get her necklace back.

"I am," I said, still holding Sage close. "I really am."

And for the first time in a week, I meant it.

Chapter Eighteen

Two weeks later, Larkspur Valley looked like a Christmas card come to life. Snow blanketed the streets and rooftops, transforming the town into something magical. Every building on Main Street was draped in lights, twinkling against the early December darkness. Wreaths hung on doors, garlands wrapped around lampposts, and the town square's massive tree glowed with hundreds of colored bulbs.

Inside The Cozy Purrch, I'd decorated with slightly more restraint. A small tree stood in the corner by the window, decorated with cat-themed ornaments that the regulars had been bringing in all week. Garland wrapped around the counter, and fairy lights outlined the viewing room where the cats lounged among scattered bits of tinsel.

"Stop eating that," I told Rocky for the third time that morning.

"But it's shiny and crinkly."

"It's also not food. Spit it out."

He did, grudgingly, then went back to batting at a felt mouse ornament hanging from the tree's lowest branch.

The café was busy despite the cold. People were in good spirits, holiday shopping and stopping for warm drinks. The shadow that had hung over the town since the theft had finally lifted. Warren was in jail awaiting trial. The necklace had been returned to Flo. Theo's family had closure, however painful.

Life was returning to normal. Or as normal as it ever got in a town built on convergence points that attracted magical beings like moths to flame.

The door chimed, bringing in a blast of cold air along with Sheriff Iris. She stomped snow off her boots and headed straight for the counter.

"Large black coffee to-go," she said. "And maybe one of those gingerbread cookies if you have any left."

"Fresh batch from Flo this morning." I poured her coffee into a to-go cup and bagged a cookie. "How are things at the station?"

"Quiet, thankfully. Warren's lawyer is trying every angle to get the confession thrown out, but with two civilian witnesses and three law enforcement officers all hearing the same thing, it's not going anywhere." She took a sip of coffee, then studied me over the rim of the cup. "We did drug test him, since he and his lawyer insisted. No drugs found in his system. Nothing that would explain why he suddenly decided to confess everything, including crimes we didn't even know about."

Lily, wiping down the espresso machine, smiled slightly. "Sometimes guilty people just can't hold it in any longer. The weight of what they've done becomes too much. They need to tell someone, to get it off their chest."

Iris's gaze shifted to Lily, then back to me. She studied us both for a long moment, her expression thoughtful.

"Maybe so," she said finally. "Maybe so."

She finished her coffee, declined a refill, and headed back out into the snow. Through the window, I watched her pause on the sidewalk, looking back at the café with that same contemplative expression. Then she shook her head and walked toward the station.

"She's getting suspicious," Lily murmured.

"She's always been suspicious. But she can't prove anything, and more importantly, she doesn't want to. As long as we're helping, she's willing to not look too closely at the how."

"That's a dangerous game."

"Living in this town is a dangerous game." I started restocking the pastry case. "But it's worth it."

Lily smiled. "It really is, isn't it? I forgot what this felt like. Having a community. Being part of something."

"Me too."

The rest of the day passed in the comfortable rhythm I'd come to love. Customers came and went. The cats charmed visitors. Mabel held court at her usual table, holding forth on her opinions about Warren's trial. Felix sketched the Christmas tree.

Maeve came by mid-afternoon, ostensibly to return a book she'd borrowed, but really to check on us. She'd become more present in our lives since helping with the truth spell preparation.

"The town feels lighter," she observed, accepting a cup of chamomile tea. "The darkness has lifted."

"For now," Lily said quietly.

"For now," Maeve agreed. "But you both did well. You protected this place. Protected people who needed protecting."

Her eyes held mine for a moment, acknowledging what we'd done together. The spell. The risk. The choice to act.

"We're building something good here," I said. "Something that matters."

"We are," Maeve confirmed. "And when the darkness comes again, and it will, we won't face it alone."

It was a promise. A commitment. We were forming something real, the three of us. A coven of our own choosing, built on protection rather than power.

Flo stopped by around four, carrying her usual pastry boxes but also something else. She set everything on the counter and pulled out a small velvet box.

"I wanted you to see this," she said, opening it.

The necklace lay inside, gleaming under the café lights. The sapphires caught the glow from the Christmas tree, throwing tiny blue sparkles across the counter.

"It's beautiful," Lily breathed.

"It is." Flo's fingers traced the delicate metalwork. "I can't believe we got it back. I can't believe..." Her voice caught. "Warren could have sold it. Destroyed it. But he just kept it hidden, like some trophy."

"He wanted what it represented more than its value," I said gently. "Recognition. Acknowledgment."

"I know." Flo closed the box carefully. "And that's partly my fault. Not the stealing, obviously. But the fact that the Jacobs and Hargraves families have been overlooked for so long. That's on the Hendrys. On my family."

"It's not your fault that history was recorded the way it was," Lily said.

"Maybe not. But I can do something about it now." Flo set down the box and pulled out a folder from her bag. "After we got the necklace back, I went through my father's papers. Old family documents, receipts, correspondence. I wanted to understand its history completely."

She opened the folder, showing us aged papers protected in plastic sleeves.

"Grayson St. Martin was right that his great-great-grandfather Silas designed and created the necklace. That part is true. But here's the commission agreement." She pointed to an elegant script on yellowed paper. "Henry Hendry commissioned it as an anniversary gift for his wife Margaret in 1875. Paid in full, with a generous bonus for the exceptional craftsmanship. It was always meant for the Hendry family."

"So the St. Martins didn't have rightful ownership," I said.

"No. The lawsuit in the 1880s was based on a misunderstanding that got passed down through generations." Flo's expression was sad. "Silas St. Martin's grandson believed his family had been cheated because they'd had to sue to get paid for other commissions. He conflated those disputes with the necklace, and the family has believed it ever since."

"That must have been hard to discover," Lily said.

"It was. But it also gave me an opportunity." Flo pulled out her phone. "I called Grayson yesterday. Explained what I'd found. Showed him the documentation."

"How did he take it?"

"Better than I expected. I think part of him suspected the family story might not be accurate." She smiled slightly. "I told him I'm having high-quality photographs taken of the necklace from every angle. Detailed close-ups of Silas's craftsmanship, the silverwork, the stone settings. Everything. And I'm giving him copies for his sister's book, along with copies of the commission papers showing his great-great-grandfather's exceptional work."

"That's generous," I said.

"It's fair. Silas St. Martin was a master craftsman. He deserves recognition for creating something so beautiful. The necklace belongs to my family, but the credit for its creation belongs to his." Flo tucked the folder back in her bag. "Grayson cried when I told him. Said his sister would be so happy to include it in the family history."

My throat tightened. "How is his sister?"

"Not well. Weeks, maybe days now." Flo's voice softened. "But she'll get to see the photographs before... before the end. That matters to him."

We sat in silence for a moment, honoring that grief.

"Which brings me to my other reason for coming," Flo said, her tone shifting to something more determined. "That historical display you mentioned. The one you were using as a cover to investigate."

I felt heat creep up my neck. "Flo, I'm sorry about that. I shouldn't have—"

"Don't apologize." She held up her hand. "You solved the theft. Found who killed Theo. You did what you had to do." She paused. "But I've been thinking about that display. And I want to actually do it."

"You do?"

"Not right away. The town needs time to heal first. Spring, maybe. Early next year." Her expression was determined. "But I want to work with you on it. A proper exhibit honoring all three founding families equally. Hendry, Jacobs, and Hargraves. Their real contributions, their real stories."

"All three families," I repeated.

"Henry Hendry didn't build this town alone. He had partners. Equals. And it's time we acknowledged that publicly." Flo's voice strengthened. "Maybe something good can come from all this tragedy. Maybe we can finally give the Jacobs and Hargraves families the recognition they've always deserved."

"That's a beautiful idea," Lily said.

"Warren will be in prison," Flo continued. "But his family is still here. His cousins, his extended family. Same with the Hargraves. They shouldn't have to carry the weight of resentment anymore. We can change the narrative. Show that all three families matter."

"I think that would mean a lot to people," I said. "To Zeke especially. He's been trying to preserve his family's legacy through his architectural book."

"Then we'll help him. We'll feature his great-great-grandfather's buildings, Silas St. Martin's craftsmanship, the Jacobs family's contributions. Everyone." Flo pulled me into a hug. "Thank you, Alexis. For everything you did. For caring enough to investigate. For bringing my necklace home."

"I'm just glad you have it back."

"Piper's presentation ceremony is scheduled for Christmas Eve now. At the town tree lighting." Flo's eyes glistened with tears. "My daughter gets her moment after all. And then, in the new year, we'll work on that display. Make sure everyone's story gets told."

After she left, Lily turned to me with a smile. "See? Something good from something terrible."

"Maybe that's all we can hope for," I said. "Taking the broken pieces and building something better."

"That's all any of us can do."

At six o'clock, I locked the door and flipped the sign to closed. Lily and I cleaned up together, falling into the easy partnership we'd developed over the past few weeks.

"Are you coming to the tree lighting ceremony tomorrow?" she asked as she wiped down the last table.

"Wouldn't miss it. You?"

"Absolutely. Cordelia's closing the yarn shop early so we can all go together." She hung up the towel. "I'm heading home. See you in the morning?"

"See you then."

Just as Lily opened the back door to leave, a knock came at the front. Through the glass, I could see Lionel holding a takeout bag from Flo's diner.

I unlocked the door. "We're closed."

"I know. I saw you flipping the sign and thought you might not have eaten yet." He held up the bag. "Flo's beef stew and fresh bread. Figured after a long day, you might want something you didn't have to cook yourself."

"That's very thoughtful." I felt something warm unfurl in my chest at the gesture.

"And there's enough to share." He looked at me hopefully, then quickly added, "You know, if Lily is hungry too."

Lily, still standing by the back door, smiled knowingly. "I already ate, actually. But thank you, Lionel. Very kind of you." She gave me a look that clearly said *don't be an idiot* and slipped out into the night.

I stood there, holding the door, suddenly very aware that I was alone with him. That he'd brought me dinner. That he was looking at me with those patient, gentle eyes.

"Would you like to come up?" I asked. "To my apartment? The café's closed but the food smells amazing and I haven't eaten since breakfast."

His face lit up. "I'd like that very much."

We headed upstairs, the cats immediately abandoning their various perches to investigate the newcomer. Rocky wound around Lionel's ankles while Sage sniffed at his shoes with intense interest.

"Your apartment is nice," Lionel said, looking around at the cozy space. "Very you."

"Meaning cluttered with cat toys and plants?"

"Meaning warm. Comfortable. Like you actually live here instead of just existing."

I wasn't sure what to say to that, so I busied myself getting plates and silverware. He unpacked the food, and soon we were sitting at my small dining table, steam rising from bowls of rich, hearty stew.

"So," he said, tearing off a piece of bread. "That was quite the two weeks. Warren confessing like that. Pretty dramatic."

"It was necessary." I took a bite of stew, savoring Flo's cooking. "He needed to tell the truth."

"The whole town's been talking about it. How he just started confessing to everything. Even things nobody knew about." Lionel studied me over his spoon. "It was almost like he couldn't help himself."

"Guilt does that sometimes," I said carefully. "Makes people need to unburden themselves."

"Mm." He didn't push, just smiled that knowing smile. "Well, whatever happened, I'm glad it's over. Glad you're safe."

We ate in comfortable silence for a moment. Rocky jumped onto the empty chair beside us, watching hopefully for dropped food.

"No begging," I told him.

"But it smells so good," Rocky protested.

"Do you always talk to them like that?" Lionel asked, amused.

"Yes, they understand me," I said truthfully.

He smiled. "I like that. Most people just ignore their pets. You treat them like they're part of the conversation."

"They are," I said, which was more honest than he knew.

"Finally, someone who appreciates my contributions to this household," Gus rumbled from under the table.

"How's the comic shop?" I asked Lionel. "Holiday rush keeping you busy?"

"Crazy busy. Everyone wants graphic novels for Christmas. Had a kid come in yesterday looking for something specific about cats solving mysteries." He grinned. "I thought of you immediately."

"Did you sell him one?"

"Her. And yes. Recommended three different series." He paused. "I've been thinking about hosting a comic book club in the new year. Maybe partner with you for coffee and snacks?"

"At the café?"

"If you'd be interested. Once a month, maybe Saturday afternoons. Bring in a different crowd, good for both our businesses."

"I like that idea," I said, surprised by how much I meant it. "Lily and I were actually talking about doing poetry readings or open mic nights. A comic book club would fit perfectly with that vision."

"See? This is why we work well together." His eyes held mine. "We make a good team."

The words hung in the air between us, meaning more than just business partnerships.

"Lionel," I started.

"I know," he said gently. "You're not ready. I'm not asking you to be. I just wanted you to know that I'm here. As a friend. As a business partner. As whatever you need." He took another bite of stew. "And when you are ready, if you ever are, I'll still be here. Three shops down."

"That's very patient of you."

"I can be patient." He smiled. "Besides, you're worth waiting for."

My throat tightened. "I don't know if I'll ever be ready. My past is complicated."

"Everyone's past is complicated. It's what makes us interesting." He reached across the table, his hand hovering near mine but not quite touching. "You don't owe me anything, Alexis. Not explanations, not promises, nothing. I just wanted to share a meal with someone I care about. That's all this has to be."

I looked at his hand, so close to mine. It would be easy to close that distance. To take what he was offering.

But not yet. Not quite yet.

"Thank you for dinner," I said softly. "And for understanding."

"Anytime." He pulled his hand back, no hurt in his expression, just that same patient warmth. "So, tell me about Sage's war with the ornaments. Did she win?"

I laughed, grateful for the shift back to safer ground. "She knocked three off the tree this morning. Rocky's encouraging her bad behavior."

"Naturally."

We finished our meal talking about cats and Christmas decorations and the upcoming tree lighting ceremony. Easy conversation, comfortable silences, the kind of evening that felt like coming home.

When he left, after helping me wash the dishes, after saying goodnight at my door with that same patient smile, I watched from my window as he walked back to his shop through the falling snow.

Maybe someday I'd be ready for more.

But for now, this was enough. Friendship. Community. Safety.

It was more than I'd had in years.

After he left, the apartment felt quiet. I made myself tea and settled on the couch with the cats, Poppy in my lap, Gus at my feet, Rocky and Sage curled together on the cushion beside me, and Millie tucked against my side.

"This was a good day," Poppy said contentedly.

"It was."

"You're happy here. Really happy."

I thought about it. About the café, the community, the friends I'd made. About Lily living just two blocks away. About Lionel's patient kindness and even Colton's well-meaning concern. About Flo treating me like family and Ella's emerging gifts that I could help nurture.

"I am," I said. "For the first time in a long time, I'm really happy."

"Good," Gus rumbled. "You deserve to be happy."

Outside, snow continued to fall, covering the town in fresh white. Christmas lights twinkled in windows up and down the street. Somewhere, carolers were singing. The world felt peaceful. Safe.

But over a thousand miles away, in a city Alexis had left behind, a woman with sharp eyes and sharper magic stood in a circle of power, holding something that pulsed with familiar energy.

A strand of hair. Brown, slightly wavy. Left behind in an apartment abandoned in haste over a year ago.

Margot smiled, her expression cold and satisfied. The tracking spell had finally worked. After months of searching, of casting and recasting, of following dead ends and false trails, she'd found her.

"Larkspur Valley, Colorado," she said to the other figures standing in the circle with her. "Our lost sister has been hiding in Larkspur Valley."

She let out a bitter laugh. "Of course that's where she would go. That's where they all go. I never thought I would have to go back there."

"So we are going to retrieve her?" one of them asked.

"Not yet. Let her think she's safe for a while longer. Let her build her little life, make her connections, grow comfortable." Margot's smile widened. "And then we'll remind her that no one leaves the coven. Not really. Not ever."

She closed her fist around the hair, and the spell extinguished with a whisper of smoke.

The game had changed.

And Alexis had no idea.

THE END

Before you go: If you loved Catastrophic Brew, be sure to visit my website to sign up for my newsletter (if you haven't already) and to stay up to date on new releases and other bookish things.

When signing up, you will receive **either a prequel from my Medium with a Heart series or a recipe that goes along with my Alphabet Soup Series. Your choice!**

Also, check out my other books! You can find links on my website.

www.ejwheltonwrites.com

Author note:

Well? What did you think? Fun, right? A little hook at the end to set up the next book too.

Lily and Alexis are the perfect friends. Everyone should have a Lily in their life. And then sweet little Ella and Cleo, I have big plans for them in future books.

Not much else to say about this one at the moment. I was just so happy with how it turned out. I'm looking forward to book 3 (yet to be named) and hope you will follow along for all the quirky fun to come.

www.ejwheltonwrites.com

9 781956 069501